ELECHI AMADI, an Ekwerri, was born in Aluu near Port Harcourt in Eastern Nigeria and educated at Government College, Umuahia. He graduated with a degree in mathematics and physics from University College, Ibadan. He was employed for a time as a land surveyor and later as a teacher in the Nigerian army at the Military School in Zaria, where he attained the rank of captain. In 1965 he left the army to teach at the Anglican Grammar School, Igrito, Port Harcourt.

Amadi's first novel, *The Concubine* (1966), was greeted as an 'outstanding work of pure fiction'. It was followed by *The Great Ponds* and then *Sunset in Biafra*, a chronicle of Amadi's experiences during the civil war. During the seventies Amadi wrote several plays – *Isiburu*, *The Road to Ibadan* and *Peppersoup* among them – and in 1978 published another novel, *The Slave*. His most recent novel, *Estrangement*, was published in 1986.

ELECHI AMADI

ESTRANGEMENT

HEINEMANN

Heinemann Educational Books Ltd.
22 Bedford Square, London WC1B 3HH

Heinemann Educational Books (Nigeria) Ltd.
PMB 5205, Ibadan
Heinemann Educational Books (Kenya) Ltd.
Kijabe Street, PO Box 45314, Nairobi
Heinemann Educational Books Inc.
70 Court Street, Portsmouth, New Hampshire, 03801, USA
Heinemann Educational Books (Caribbean) Ltd.
175 Mountain View Avenue, Kingston 6, Jamaica

EDINBURGH MELBOURNE AUCKLAND HONG KONG
SINGAPORE KUALA LUMPUR NEW DELHI

British Library Cataloguing in Publication Data

Amadi, Elechi
    Estrangement. —— (African writers series)
    I. Title   II. Series
    823 [F]   PR9387.9.A48

ISBN 0-435-90564-3

Typeset by Activity Ltd., Salisbury, Wilts.
Printed in Great Britain by Richard Clay (The Chaucer Press) Ltd, Bungay,
Suffolk.

Chapter I

Major Sule Dansuku passed his left hand across Alekiri's smooth shoulders. She turned towards him and frowned a smile. It was a trick of hers, this smile overlaid with a faint frown and pout. In it anxiety and pleasure were curiously mingled. It charmed him. He cuddled her on the settee and for a moment they sat still. Then his right hand began to wander over her body. She arrested the caressing hand, tightening her grip when he tried to free it. He relaxed and studied her face. The smile was gone. The frown and anxiety remained.

'What is it?'

She sighed and worked her lips, blurring the firm lines of her lipstick.

'Sule, listen,' she said seriously.

'What?'

'My husband is back from Biafra.'

Dansuku paused.

'Allah?'

'Yes.'

'*Kai!*'

He heaved a sigh and released her. His luxuriant moustache met his nose as he worked his face in thought.

'Let's eat first, and discuss later.'

Bukar the batman laid on a meal. As usual he was in battledress but without the sacks and pouches. This was a carry-over from the hectic days when the Biafrans recaptured Owerri and threatened Port Harcourt, and all soldiers were put on twenty-four-hour alert. Alekiri had found the soldier-cook in battledress strange and sometimes did the cooking

1

herself. Dansuku did not always allow her. He preferred to have her by him whenever they were together, which was not half as often as he wished. In this, she understood his feelings. Officers did not always come back from the war front and she found it hard to grudge Dansuku his momentary snatches of pleasure. She knew of another major who took the matter a little too far by acquiring four girlfriends at a time. One would caress his legs, another his head and shoulders; a third would spoon-feed him while a fourth would operate the music set. It was quite disgusting, some civilians said. When a few weeks later the officer was killed at the front, disgust turned to deep sympathy. Some said he knew he was going to die and had made the best of his short life.

Bukar's mixture of crudely cut vegetables and tomato pureé, which passed for soup, did not go down well with Alekiri. She called it war-front soup. Often she visited Dansuku with ready-made soup tucked away in her shopping bag.

Dansuku ate quietly, morosely.

'Bukar!'

'Sir.'

'Fetch a bottle of beer.'

'Yessir!'

'Alee, what will you have?'

'That red wine.'

'You seem to like it.'

'Yes. It is bitter and yet sweet.'

'You can take two bottles when you leave tomorrow.'

'Tomorrow?'

'Yes.'

'I can't stay the night,' she said.

'Why not?'

'He may come to Port Harcourt looking for me.'

'When did he come back?'

'I don't know, but I learnt of his arrival only this morning.'

'It does not matter. You will stay the night.'

Bukar served the drinks, which they sipped in silence.

Outside the *harmattan* blew, reminding Dansuku of his home in Kano where the dry dusty wind was at that moment blowing with suffocating intensity. He listened to the rustling of palm trees. This was what he liked best about his quarters in Forces Avenue, the trees and the shrubs.

'By the way, Bukar!'

'Sir.'

'What of that man who said he would tap the palm tree behind the house?'

'He brought some palmwine this morning, sir.'

'Bloody hell! Why didn't you tell me, idiot?'

'I thought ...'

'Shurrup! Pour away this thing or drink it yourself. Fetch the palm wine.'

Alekiri also abandoned her red wine as Bukar served them with bubbling palm wine. Dansuku smacked his lips as he savoured it. It was the oil-palm variety.

They went early to bed.

'Alee, why won't you marry me?'

'I have told you, I am married.'

'Divorce him.'

'I have no reason to do so.'

'You love someone and that is a reason.'

'For my people, that is no reason.'

'To hell with your people.'

'Already they think I am wayward for joining the Commando Girls and wearing khaki trousers. I don't want to worsen my bad name.'

'You were helping your country win a war.'

'Those people in the village do not reason that way. Any woman in trousers is a harlot as far as they are concerned.'

'You care too much about what people say. They should not live your life for you, damn it!'

'True, but that is the way we live. I cannot run away from my people and so I cannot marry you without their consent. How could I visit the village after that?'

'You don't have to.'

3

'Mm?' Her eyes widened in the semi-darkness. 'I don't have to visit my people?'

'I mean if we are married, we are married and we stay together.'

'And I won't see my people?'

'If they are hostile, why should you?'

'Mm-mm, that would be too much.'

'Your relations could visit us.'

'Not if they disapprove of the marriage. In any case my father could never travel to Kano.'

The half-light provided by a weak blue bulb blurred their troubled faces. The crunch crunch of the boots of a soldier on guard outside punctuated the silence of the night.

'Alee'.

'Mm?'

'Do you love me?'

'Now, yes, but not at first.'

'Do you love him?'

'Yes … he is my husband.'

'Suppose he rejects you?'

'Let's wait till he does.'

'Answer me. Suppose he rejects you?'

'If he rejects me, I shall not reject myself,' she said sadly in a whisper enforced somehow by the darkness.

'Would you then marry me?'

She was silent.

'Would you?'

'I don't know.'

'That is no answer. Would you?'

'No.'

Alekiri could not lie easily and Dansuku found this quality endearing. It led him to boast to his colleagues that he had found an 'unspoilt' village beauty. As for beauty, Alekiri had it. She was of average height, dark and delicately buxom. Dansuku's favourite description of her was 'portable' and it never failed to amuse her. He said although he did not like fat women, he liked to embrace someone rounded and soft.

'Why not, if, as you say, you love me?'

'I can't speak Hausa.'

'Are we speaking Hausa now?'

'But I would have to speak to your people.'

'That is no reason and you know it. Surely you can learn Hausa in a matter of months?'

'I am sure my people would not approve.'

'But some girls from here are married to people from the north.'

'That is true.'

'So what are you talking about?'

'There are other problems.'

'Which now?'

'I hear, up north, you keep your wives in purdah and they are not permitted to move about.'

'True, devout Moslems of the older generation keep their wives in purdah; but that is changing. Anyway I certainly will not put my wife in purdah. A soldier has no time for all that complicated business.'

'There is no complication; you simply lock up the woman.' They laughed.

'You make it sound like Kirikiri prison.'

'Isn't it?'

'Actually the women are quite happy. They are very well looked after.'

'Sule, only the women can say whether they are happy or not.'

'Maybe so. Anyway, purdah is not for me. If that is your fear, dismiss it.'

'And being a Moslem you will marry four wives, won't you?' Dansuku laughed.

'I don't seem to show any signs of that, do I? I am over thirty and still single. Men in my age group, including soldiers like me, have children already in school. The fact is I am not very keen on marriage.'

'But you keep talking about it.'

'That's because I like you so much. You are so far the one

5

woman who makes me feel like marrying.'

She was pleased but did not want to show it.

'Sule, reserve that flattery for younger women. What about your fiancée in college?'

'My father is arranging all that business. He was getting worried I was staying single for too long. I don't know much about Habiba except that she is young, pretty and clever at school; but she doesn't attract me. The last time we met she was talking of going to university and all that.'

'Isn't that good?'

'I suppose it is. In fact, I encouraged her to work hard.'

'That's good of you.'

'Not at all. I am hoping that by the time she graduates she will fall in love with one bald-headed professor. I think she will make a good wife for a professor.'

'Is she not in love with you?'

'I say, we scarcely know each other.'

'She may prefer a brigadier to a professor, you can't say.'

'Not her type.'

'But tell me, what will you do if she comes to you after schooling?'

'It depends …'

'On what?'

'On whether I am still single by then.'

'Let's say you are married by then.'

'In that case she won't have me, I am sure.'

'Let's say she still wants you.'

'Alee you are an interrogator!'

They laughed.

'Listen, Alee, if we get married all these problems won't arise.'

Alekiri was not so sure. She thought she could see the problems far more clearly than Dansuku could. Anyway, she was determined not to leave her husband unless he did not want her. Ibekwe was not a bad husband, but his pride was something else. His friends would tease him about his wife flirting with soldiers and having a child by them. He would

6

find that hard to take. He would throw her out.

'Alee,' Dansuku broke her train of thought, 'what do you say?'

'Let's wait and see how my husband feels about the child.'

That sounded more hopeful and Dansuku was soothed somewhat.

'Do you know what you should do?'

'What?'

'When he talks about the child, don't apologize. Defy him and accuse him of fathering twenty babies while in Biafra. He would then throw you out.'

'Sule, you are wicked,' she said, laughing and throwing a leg across his thigh in the process. Her waist beads rattled. These beads had convinced Dansuku that his lover was indeed an unspoilt village beauty. He had never before had a girl who wore waist beads. This detail he had revealed only to his intimate childhood friend Captain Olaitan. In ecstasy he had said: 'Ola, that girl will kill me!' Alekiri's leg and the rattling beads provoked a chain reaction and they began a long mutual caress.

Later, spent and happy, they lay apart. Dansuku, though relaxed, could not fall asleep. His mind focussed on the beautiful woman by his side. She was already asleep, judging by the whispering of her regular breathing. He would have to give her up of course. Their thirty-month flirtation would have to come to an end, he told himself over and over. He reminded himself of his resolution never again to lose his sense of direction because of women. Twice in his life, he had come to grief because of them. The incidents were documented in his diary: Dansuku was a good diarist. The first time had been in Britain while he was undergoing military training. Along with other cadets he had been granted a free long weekend in which to rest before a rigorous physical endurance test the following Monday. He travelled to the countryside with Eva and had a marvellous time. She was a beautiful fun-loving girl and her parents were very kind and understanding. She persuaded him to spend Sunday night with her against his training instructions. Eva was sure she could drive him back to camp early on Monday morning within an hour. Her sports car had plenty of power. Dansuku was friendly with the soldiers on guard duty and he was sure they would let him in. Everything worked according to plan. But on Monday morning when he got into battledress with full packs, boots and rifle, he found he had overestimated his endurance. He felt groggy from loss of sleep. The endurance test included clambering over an eight-foot wall and jumping across a ten-foot ditch filled with broken bottles and barbed wire. He cleared the wall but was unable to develop enough speed to clear the ditch. His boots protected him from broken bottles but barbed wire gashed his neck and chin badly. He failed the test and had to repeat it the following week. What annoyed him was not the stitches he had to endure, nor the extra training time he had to spend, but his friends' teasing. They said it was one thing to hug Eva but quite another to hug barbed wire and broken bottles. Much of their teasing was out of envy. Eva the red-head in the red sports car had everybody's eyes popping. The second incident had occurred after he had been commissioned and posted to a unit. During a sick spell at the hospital he had become infatuated with a female nursing officer. She was a captain and he a subaltern at the time. It thrilled him to have for a lover a superior officer. The fact that the nurse was his commanding officer's girlfriend made the affair even more exciting. His friends had advised him to lay off. He had not. He had accused them of jealousy, and he was partly right. One night when his CO was supposed to be attending a conference outside the station, he had called on the nurse and come face to face with the colonel. He snapped to attention and offered a greeting. The colonel smiled and asked him to relax. He did not know whether to sit down or double right back. Then what he thought was a brilliant idea occurred to him. He had come, he told the nurse, to collect some anti-malaria medicine.

'Have you an attack?' the nurse had asked in her confusion.

'Yes, I think so.'

'Do you stock medicine in your house?' the colonel had asked, the threat of military discipline in his voice.

'Of course not,' the nurse replied quickly. The colonel turned to Dansuku.

'Surely, officer, you know where to go for treatment if you are ill.'

'Yes, sir, but I thought I could collect a few tablets quickly'.

'Well the shortest routes are not always the quickest'.

'That's true, sir.'

'Nor the safest!' the colonel added chuckling.

'Quite so, sir. Goodnight, sir.'

Dansuku was dropped at the next promotion. The colonel's report read: 'He has been rather sickly and so his efficiency has not been what it should be.'

As was usual in the army, Dansuku was given a chance to read the report on him in order to correct his shortcomings. At a subsequent interview the colonel wished him better luck next time and hoped his health would improve.

After these incidents Dansuku concluded that he had to be wary of women if he was to make something of his career. His other problem might have been gambling, but army regulations which barred officers from gambling houses saved him from that. He had no problem with drink. He got tipsy once in a while, but he never lost control.

He switched on the main light and looked at his companion. She was snoring gently now. Her face looked innocent and serene. Her breasts, perfectly conical as she lay supine, were bare, but by an instinct which did not fail even in sleep, she held a corner of her wrapper over her pubic hair. Exposed parts of her beads gleamed. Dansuku switched off the light, cuddled up to her, and slept.

Chapter II

When Alekiri woke next morning, she was alone in bed. She opened the bedroom door a chink and saw Dansuku already at breakfast. She felt a little wobbly but she hurried through her toilet, which was simple because she used no make-up except a dash of lipstick – and even that was at Dansuku's encouragement. The reddish-brown lipstick against her dark face and gleaming white teeth was dramatic, driving her lover to kiss her often. He had taught her how to kiss. Her initial reaction had been one of disgust. The only person she had ever kissed was her toothless baby. That was a spontaneous motherly reaction far different from kissing an adult, and a man at that. But she was a fast learner. At first she tolerated, then liked, and finally desired Dansuku's kisses.

Dansuku looked at her with admiration when she joined him at the breakfast table. Her 'up-and-down' print dress became her so well. Her charm over him seemed permanent, and it was increasing. The urge to kiss her was powerful. It was as if he had not slept with her. He restrained himself; after all, he was already in uniform. During his military training the mystique of the uniform had been drummed into him. No well trained officer fooled around in uniform.

'*Ina kwana?*'

'*Lafiya,*' came the reply half lost in giggles.

'*Ina gajiya?*'

'*Ba gajiya.*'

'You see, your Hausa is perfect.'

'Hm. I have a very long way to go, I am sure.'

'If you show more interest I can teach you the language in

10

three months.'

'Hey, Sule, you seem to think that learning a language is like army work which is always done in a hurry.'

'Army methods work, I tell you.'

'I am not a soldier.'

'You were until a month ago.'

'Wearing khaki shirts and trousers does not make one a soldier.'

'You had some training. You can march and salute.'

'Sule, I am not a soldier, leave me alone!'

'Okay, okay,' he chuckled. This subject had become increasingly annoying to her in the past few weeks. He studied his watch.

'I can't wait for you. The driver will come to take you back by 9 o'clock. Okay?'

'I shan't need the driver.'

'Why?'

'Well, my husband may be waiting at my place.'

'I see. Please yourself,' Dansuku said rather snappily. He got up and walked to the mirror. He adjusted his belt and hat and rapped his left palm with his ivory-tipped cane. His uniform set off his athletic figure very well. The small wrinkles on his brow, his moustache and bearded square jaw made him ruggedly handsome, especially when he wore his red-and-white commando belt and his hat half hid his piercing eyes.

'When do I see you again?'

'I can't say until I reach home and meet my husband. But I shall send you a message the day after tomorrow if I am unable to come.'

There was a clap at the door. Dansuku frowned. He hated callers who came just when he was setting out for work. It was Mama Iyabo. 'Major, I salute,' she said and executed a mock salute which set them all laughing. Tall, fat and affable, Bisi always seemed to exude good humour. She was Alekiri's neighbour in Ohaeto Street. She had a pretty vivacious seven-year old daughter, Iyabo, to whom she had virtually lost her name. Her husband was a food contractor to the army. He had come soon after the capture of Port Harcourt, sporting a battered five-year old motor cycle. By the end of the war he had acquired several trucks and a Mercedes saloon in which he and his family rode to a spiritual church hard by every Sunday. Mama Iyabo herself provided an accurate index of her husband's rapid rise in affluence. She had arrived in Port Harcourt a tall slim pretty woman, but her girth and the price of the lace blouses she wore had increased in direct proportion to her husband's wealth.

'Mama Iyabo, you are just in time to give Alee a ride back to her house.'

'E-eh, I have sent the driver off to the market. But he will be back soon. Alee, you are not in a hurry?'
She embraced her, almost smothering her.

'No, I am not in a hurry. What will you have?'

'Anything.'

'If you haven't had breakfast, then perhaps you may like some pap and fried plantains.'

'Yes, thanks.'

'Some *suya* too?'

'Just bring all you have,' Mama Iyabo said laughing. As they exchanged pleasantries Dansuku left them. While Bukar laid on the meal, Mama Iyabo drew a chair close to Alekiri. There was urgency in the movement.

'Alee, your husband has arrived!'

'I suspected so.'

'And he seems extremely angry.'

'I expected that.'

'When he came, your little sister called me. He introduced himself and asked for you. I explained you are a subcontractor to my husband, and that you went off early to the waterside market to buy some fish urgently needed by the army. So I decided to rush down and brief you on the lie.'

'Well, half of it is true; I am a subcontractor to your husband.'

'Yes, but my dear, you are nowhere near the waterside market now.' They laughed nervously.

'Alee, why did you leave your album lying around?'

'He saw my commando pictures?'

'He did, and *Oluwa*! you had to see his face! I feared he would tear the album and burn down the house. Each time he struck the table with his fist he exclaimed: "*Cha*! Prince Ibekwe has suffered!" Look Alee, you have to plead with that man. He is angry. I shall help you in any way I can.'

Bisi turned to the plates of pap and fried plantains. The spoon looked like a toy in her large hand.

'Mama Iyabo, I don't know what to do.'

'Ask for forgiveness.'

'I can do that, but will he accept?'

'I am sure he will, but it may take some time for his anger to cool down.'

'Ibekwe is a proud man, that is the trouble. He will find it hard to harbour the child.'

'But the child is his, according to custom.'

'That is true. If I were married to an old man in the village, he would thank God for the child and for my safety and take me back without a word. Young men are different.'

'I wish he had not seen those photographs.'

'People will still tell him I was a Commando Girl.'

'But Alee, that was a bit rascally, joining the Commando Girls.'

'My sister, you know, when things want to go wrong, nothing can stop them. When Port Harcourt was liberated there was some confusion and it was difficult to think properly. When Dansuku saved me at the war front I asked him to take me to the village. He was very kind. When we got there, my sister, I could not believe my eyes. It was like the end of the world.'

'E-eh,' Bisi said, momentarily halting a spoon of pap in mid-air, and getting her wrapper soiled with several drops of it.

'The village was completely deserted. Nobody. No animals except wild ones like squirrels and bush rats. The compound was full of weeds. The door to my father's house was broken. Inside, everything was in confusion, I mean those things that they could not steal. Mama Iyabo, I cried.'

'Ee-yaah!'

'Dansuku said nothing. He took me by the hand to the Land-Rover and we drove to Port Harcourt. Even the town was empty with only a few people here and there. I did not see a single person whom I knew. I asked Dansuku's driver to take me to some houses in town where my relations and friends used to live. None of them had come back. Mama Iyabo, it was like the end of the world.'

'Ee-yah! Those of us in the west, ah, we are lucky-o.'

'Mama Iyabo, you are lucky, I tell you. When we reached Dansuku's place he noticed I was crying and felt sorry for me. He did his best to comfort me.'

'All that sorrow was *yeye*. I am sure he was thanking God for capturing a pretty woman.' They laughed.

Bukar overheard the remark and smiled. Mama Iyabo was known among her friends for her outrageous sexy jokes. But she was also known to be a faithful wife, uninterested in flirting outside her marriage.

'Keep your jokes and listen. Mama Iyabo, this a serious matter.'

'True, love is a serious matter *ke*,' she replied in a comical voice.

Alekiri laughed again in spite of herself.

'I shall stop if you won't let me continue.'

'Go on, Alee, don't mind me.'

'When I came back to the house, Dansuku offered me his guest room. It was well furnished and self-contained and I was comfortable. I think the house was captured with everything inside. They said a big government man used to live there. There was a woman staying with Dansuku when I arrived. She was young and pretty but I could see she was the type who used to hang around Hotel Presidential. I could see she did not like my arrival.'

'Of course. She thought you had come to share Dansuku with her.'

'For the first week or so I slept in the guest room while Dansuku and Arit – that was her name – slept in the main house. I was very happy with the arrangement. Every morning

I went to the kitchen to help Bukar with the cooking and cleaning. Whenever Bukar was very busy ironing Dansuku's uniform and cleaning his boots and belt, I served the food myself. Sometimes Arit said thank you, sometimes she just crossed her legs and smoked. Each time Dansuku praised me, she frowned.'

'Ee-yah! Jealousy!'

'She was stupid, because Dansuku was not in my mind at all. I was mourning my little daughter whom I lost at the front. Also I hated soldiers and did not want to be near them. They frightened me. Do you know that until the war broke out I had not seen a soldier within a short distance?'

'Ah, my sister, you know, my husband found it very difficult to persuade me to come to Port Harcourt. We fought and quarrelled for a long time. We heard that Port Harcourt was a war front full of Biafran soldiers, so I told my husband he should take another woman to Port Harcourt. Me, I hate soldiers. They get annoyed for no reason and, next thing, they are fighting and shooting. *Oluwa!*'

'As I had no work to do, I tried to occupy myself. First I cleaned the guest room thoroughly, then the kitchen and dining room. Then the living room. You know I find an untidy place difficult to live in. Bukar had no time for thorough cleaning. Dansuku was pleased and I was glad I was returning his kindness. One day Arit was not present for lunch. He asked me to eat with him. I refused and ate in the kitchen as usual. I could see he was not pleased. I inquired about Arit. He said she had gone to see her people in town. Then he said his bedroom was untidy and that I should clean and rearrange it.'

'Ee-ee! Trouble has come! Satan has started to work overtime.'

'Mama Iyabo, I refused. I told him that in our custom it is the wife who cleans her husband's bedroom, never another woman. He said Arit was not his wife. I said she ought to do it since she slept with him. He did not argue further. That night, after I had gone to bed I heard a knock at my door. I opened and it was Dansuku in his nightdress.'

'Hey! I hear the sound of shelling!'

'Shut your mouth! He came in, closed the door and sat on the bed. I was afraid. He took my hand gently. Mama Iyabo I did not know what to do or say.'

'You should have said: Oga I beg-o.'

They laughed.

'He spoke softly', Alekiri went on.

'Don't mind them. That is their trick.'

'He said he wanted us to be lovers. I said what of Arit? He said he would send her away. I said what of your wife? He said he had no wife. I did not believe him. I said he should stick to Arit. He said Arit was a prostitute; he had just found out. I said it did not matter so long as she had decided to change. He said she can't change. Mama Iyabo I did not know what to do. I could not withdraw my hand from his hand. The man had been so kind. Also I was afraid to say no. He might beat me up or kill me. No one would ask him. No one knew where I was. Mama Iyabo my body began to shake. He asked whether I was feeling cold. I said no. He said, what was my answer. I said I was married. He said it did not matter. I said it did. Then without a knock the door opened. Arit came in. She looked at both of us as if we were shit. Then she walked out and banged the door so hard that the key fell out of the key hole. Dansuku released my hand and followed her. For over an hour I heard them fighting. Then Arit began to cry. After that night I did not see her for a long time. The next day I hardly saw Dansuku. I stayed in my room and read old magazines. I was afraid. If I had a place to go, I should have run away. After two nights he came to my room again. He said he had sent Arit away and wanted me. I said I was married. He said it did not matter. I said it did. He tried to kiss me. I turned my face.

'We struggled a little but he did not try to force me. After that he pulled a long face for some days and I was afraid. One afternoon after lunch he said I should clean his bedroom and rearrange it. Since Arit was no longer there I could not say no. I was afraid. As soon as I entered the bedroom he followed me, locked the door and put the key in his pocket. Mama Iyabo the

16

broom fell out of my hand. I sat on a chair and waited. He came and sat by me, held me gently and began to plead. I said my husband would reject me if I put up with another man in his absence. He said my husband would not find out and that he would fix me up in another house from where I could visit him. I said I would be pregnant. He said no, he would take precautions. I said it was a lie. He said it would be alright. We talked and argued. I was getting tired. Then I asked him to fix me up in another house first. From there I could come to him. I said this to gain time but his face brightened. He said I would get a house soon. He opened the door and went out. Then I sat down and thought and thought. I decided that while he arranged for a house for me I would run away to another village near my own. I was not sure that would work because soldiers were in every village. He could find me out and beat me up or even kill me. Men can be wild. Still I planned to run away as soon as possible. Bukar!'

'Madam.'

'Clear the plates. Mama Iyabo do you want wine? We have some nice red wine. You will like it.'

'Yes, thank you, but continue your story.'

'Bukar, bring the red wine and glasses. Mama Iyabo, soldiers are terrible. Do you know that within a week he repaired, painted and furnished the flat I now live in at Ohaeto Street? He just said, "Alee, let's drive to your house." I thought he was giving me a chance to choose a house which he would then repair. When we reached, I was surprised. Everything was in place. Chairs, blinds, beds, tables, cooker, fridge, everything. He laughed quietly as I looked round in surprise. Then he gave me a surprise kiss. I pushed him off and wiped my lips. He laughed. He said I could move in any time and that he would put a soldier to guard the house.

'The next day I moved into the house. I found the store already filled with food: stockfish, yams, *garri*, oil. In the bedroom I found some beautiful georges, prints and lace blouses carefully placed in the wardrobe. Mama Iyabo, I could not speak.'

'You turned the man's head.'

'No, I think he felt lonely after he sent Arit away.'

'But he sent her away because of you.'

'No, they quarrelled.'

'Because of you, have you forgotten?'

'But they could have patched it up. That was not their first quarrel.'

'That is what I am saying, that Dansuku wanted you; so he drove the girl away.'

'You think so?'

'Ah, you are a baby.'

'Shut up. Anyway, I stayed in the house for two days and Dansuku did not come. I decided to visit him, and thank him. He said I shouldn't mention it. He said he just wanted me to be comfortable. For several days after I packed in, Dansuku did not come. I visited him about three times. He did not mention the love business. I thought of a way to thank him. I invited him for an evening meal. I prepared the meal very well and he liked it. He had brought a lot of drinks, and after the meal we conversed and drank. I told him that I had found some clothes in the wardrobe and that it appeared he had forgotten to remove them. He expressed surprise and asked me to show him. When we entered the bedroom, I opened the wardrobe, but he showed no interest. Instead he took my hand and led me to the bed. Mama Iyabo, tell me, what would you have done in my place?'

'Give the child what it was crying for and rest.'

'No, no, I am serious. What would you have done?'

'Alee, don't blame yourself. No one can escape that kind of trap.'

'As he held me I thought of my husband and cried.'

'Ah, you were adding fuel to the fire.'

'What?'

'The more you cry, the more tightly they hold you!'

'Oh, Mama Iyabo!'

'It is true, men are terrible.'

'You are right. He did not listen.'

There was a clap at the door. It was Mama Iyabo's driver.

'I done come back,' he said.

'Alright, wait for car.'

'Yes madam.'

'Alee, we have stayed so long. Don't you think we should send the driver to find out if your husband is still there?'

'It is a good idea.'

The driver was sent to find out discreetly if Ibekwe was still there.

'You still have not told me about the commando business.'

'That's what I was coming to when I got into this long story of …'

'How Dansuku shelled you.' They laughed.

'I did not like staying idle. Schools had not opened then, so I could not go back to teaching. I told Dansuku I wanted to work with the army. There was no one else to work for at the time. He asked what I could do. I said I could type. People say I am rascally but sometimes it helps. Do you know how I learnt to type?'

'Tell me.'

'When I was at the teacher-training college I was friendly with the principal's typist. She was a kind, open-hearted girl and I used to play with her typewriter. One day she said she could teach me to type if I was interested. I said yes. She gave me some lessons and within a few weeks I could type. Just before I left the college because of an unplanned pregnancy – that is the daughter I lost at the front – I helped her type some office correspondence after school hours. So Dansuku took me to the Commando Office. The chief clerk, one fat army sergeant, tested me and said they could manage me. So I was employed as a typist.'

'Were you in Dansuku's office?'

'At that time he was always going to the war front and had no office at their headquarters. He used to say his office was in the trench. After some time, the GOC came with his *wahala*. He said all the girls working in the headquarters should wear uniform and learn to march and salute. No one could argue.'

'Ah, that man, you argue, he shoots.'

'I discussed it with Dansuku and he said it did not matter. The training would be for only a week or two and would not be serious. And it was like that. Mama Iyabo, you know, I enjoyed it! After that I could march and salute. So I wore khaki shirt and trousers to work. Luckily they had no boots to fit us, so we wore brown canvas shoes. That was all, Mama Iyabo. It is true some of the Commando Girls flirted with officers, but I know only Dansuku. I did not care for anyone else.'

'You don't need to explain. I know you well by now, Alee.'

'But people admired us and we were quite proud. Sometimes we took photographs with officers. We attended war-front parties and dances in uniform and it was a lot of fun. Also the soldiers looked after us very well and protected us. Later some refugees from my village began to arrive in town. Many did not approve of my army uniform. Some even threatened to tell my husband about it. That was when I decided to leave the typing job. You know the rest. Dansuku asked your husband to take me on as a subcontractor and he kindly agreed. Mama Iyabo, what is so bad about this commando business?'

'Nothing. It is just that village people see things in a different way.'

Mama Iyabo sipped some more wine.

'Do you think my husband will take me back?'

'Why not? You are not the only wife who is in this position. Your husband should understand and forgive you. After all, I do not think he kept away from women throughout the time he was away. Men are lucky because they cannot become pregnant.'

'Mama Iyabo, there is one other big problem. You remember I told you that just before I was captured at the war front I was separated from my three-year old daughter and I never saw her again. My husband had gone to the bush to look for food when the attack started. He may say I abandoned my child to save myself. Oh God, I don't know what to do.'

Alekiri broke down and cried. Mama Iyabo fought to control her tears. She failed and sobbed in sympathy.

A knock at the door roused them. They wiped their eyes. Mama Iyabo's driver came in, looked with puzzlement at the weeping women, and moistened his lips to speak.

'Madam, the man done go,' he said. The women looked at each other.

'Let's go,' Mama Iyabo said.

Alekiri found her eight-year old sister Iwai sitting on the doorstep. She was carrying her baby. On seeing her mother, the baby stretched her hands and threatened to leap out of the struggling nanny's grasp. Alekiri took her and nuzzled her.

'Alee! Alee!!'

She paused and turned round.

'Hey! It's Tam Jaja, Alee!'

A young man hurried towards her. They shook hands, but finding the handshake inadequate, they embraced while the baby sandwiched between them kicked.

'Happy survival!'

'Happy survival!!'

'Come in.'

'You live here?'

'Mm. Come in. I am so glad to see you. I don't think we've met since I left the training college.'

'No, we haven't. And how's the baby that stopped your training.'

'She died during the war.'

'I am sorry.'

'Thank you. That's past now.'

They went into the house; and Tam Jaja took in the comfortably furnished living room.

'Alee, it seems you were not in Biafra.'

'No.'

'You are so lucky-o. *Chei*! Alee, we suffered. See how miserable I look.'

'Everyone looks miserable after a war.'

'Alee, you look all right. In fact you look more beautiful than before the war.'

'Shut up. What will you drink?'

'Coke. Is this your baby?'

'Mm.'

'How is your husband?'

'He's okay', she said.

'Was he here or in Biafra?'

'In Biafra.'

Alekiri extracted a Coke from the fridge. Jaja's eyes scanned the room continually.

'Alee, how did you manage?'

'I was lucky. I have a neighbour in the house next door, who was supplying the army food. I helped him with minor supplies like vegetables, palm oil, fish, you know, things like that. That's how I lived.'

'So you are a big army contractor!' Tam teased.

'Not at all. In fact now that the war is over I supply very little. I am not interested in contracts. I want to continue my studies. You know I had only a year to go before I became pregnant.'

'I think that's a good idea. I like teaching even though there is no money in it.'

'You finished your course successfully?'

'Oh yes. I passed out the year after you left. I taught for just over two years before the civil war.'

'Will you go back to teaching?'

'Definitely.'

'Tam, let me prepare you some food.'

'Don't worry,' he said weakly, but she saw at once that he needed a meal.

'It won't take long. I have soup. I can boil hot water for the *garri* over the gas in a few minutes.'

'All right.'

She went into the kitchen, filled a kettle with water and set it over the gas.

During their days together at the teacher-training college,

Alekiri had been quite fond of Tam Jaja. He was a brilliant student and was usually first or second in college examinations. She had often taken her mathematical problems to him and he had helped her willingly. He would put aside his own work and attend to her each time she came. What endeared him to her was that he did not seize that chance to make passes at her. So their relationship had been smooth and did not have the turbulence and conflicts always inherent in a love affair.

'You shouldn't have any difficulty getting back to teacher training,' Tam said when Alekiri emerged from the kitchen.

'I think so, too.'

'Unless your husband objects.'

'If I still have a husband,' she muttered, but it was loud enough for him to hear.

'He's back from Biafra, you said?'

'Yes.'

'So what do you mean?'

'Tam, that is a long story. Let it wait till next time.'

Tam Jaja looked at her, then at the baby and his quick mind began to draw conclusions. But he did not press her. And this was another quality of Jaja's which Alekiri liked. He was very sensitive to people's feelings and did not nose around.

The kettle whistled and Alekiri rushed back to the kitchen. Tam Jaja felt at home as he listened to familiar kitchen sounds. They assured him he really had escaped from the hunger and privations of Biafra.

He heard the gurgling sound of water pouring from the kettle into a plate, the sound of *garri* being scooped up in a cup and poured into the hot water, the sound of Alekiri's spoon as it kneaded the *garri* into shape and of the containing plate as it scraped against the table surface in the process. Finally came the mouth-watering aroma of overnight *agbono* soup as it warmed over the fire.

'Tam, come and eat.'

Tam Jaja rose and moved to the dining section of the living room. Alekiri held up the plate as he washed his hands.

'You don't have to hold it up. Put it on the table.'

'Go on Tam.'

As Tam Jaja worked his way through the generous round of *garri* and the rich soup, he was thinking it was the first solid meal he had had since he came back from Biafra.

'Alee, your soup is fantabulous.'

'Thank you,' she said, laughing.

'You have put in so much fish.'

'Make sure you eat everything.'

'I won't disappoint you.'

After Tam Jaja had gorged himself, he belched contentedly, washed his hands and rebuttoned his trousers. Alekiri offered him another Coke.

'Wash down the food with this.'

'Alee, you have played the big mama.' They laughed as she saw him off.

When she came back to the house, her mind flashed back to Ibekwe. She called Iwai.

'Did anybody come here?'

'Ibekwe came here', Iwai said.

'Did he leave a message?'

'No.'

'Did he say anything?'

'He asked for you. I said I did not know where you went. Then I called Mama Iyabo and she said you went to buy fish.'

'Then what did he say?'

'He asked, when will you come back, Mama Iyabo said, in the afternoon.'

'Then he said what?'

'Nothing.'

'Nothing at all?'

'He looked round the room. He looked at the photos. Then he struck the table and his chest. I think he was annoyed.'

'Why?'

'I think the photos annoyed him.'

'And what did he say?'

'He said you are a harlot.'

'Then?'

'He went into the bedroom.'

'Did he?'

'Yes.'

Alekiri dashed into the bedroom. The wardrobe was slightly ajar. She pulled out a drawer. All her money was gone.

'Why did you allow him into my bedroom?'

'I did not.'

'You ought to have locked it. Oh, you idiot.'

She sat on the bed, clutching her baby, and began to weep. Iwai looked on in fear. Iwai had been picked up from the war front some three months after Dansuku had rescued Alekiri.

'Aki, did he steal your clothes?'

'Ssh. Call Mama Iyabo quickly.'

Mama Iyabo came rushing in.

'Ee-yah! Alee, what's matter?'

'All my money is gone,' she sobbed, pointing at the wardrobe.

'Did you not lock it?'

'I did, but the lock is weak and the door opens if it is pulled hard.'

'Ee-yah. Did he take much?'

'He took everything. All my trading money. All the money I now have is in this handbag,' she said, holding up a black handbag Dansuku had given her.

'Alee, he has no right to take your money. Let's call the police.'

Alekiri shook her head as she continued to weep.

'I am not blaming you, but you should have banked your money.'

'There is only one bank, far away in Ikwerre Road. It is more or less a soldiers' bank and I just could not go there. Also it is easier to have the money ready to hand for buying fish and vegetables for the army. You know how it is.'

'I know, my sister, I know. Ee-yah!'

'I know why he took the money.'

'Why?'

'He wants to punish me.'

'He wants to use it.'

'He may use it but that is not his main reason. Mama Iyabo, I know the man. He wants to punish me. You see, before the war, when we lived together, he allowed me to keep my salary. He said I should use it any way I liked. He is a proud man. And he gave me housekeeping money. I helped a little but I saved the bulk of my money for the house we were planning to build. Then the war came and things were difficult. Teachers were not paid and his business dried up. I withdrew all my money and we used it up.'

'What will you do?'

'I shall go to the village and report to my people.'

'When?'

'Tomorrow.'

'My driver can drop you.'

'Thank you.'

'Do you want me to come with you?'

'Let me go alone first.'

'Are you sure? I don't want that man to take your money and then beat you up in addition.'

'I shall manage.'

'Are your people all back now?'

'All except my mother who died in Biafra, and a cousin who they say was a captain in the Biafran army. My father and my other relations are all back.'

'Look, Alee, if I can help in any way, don't think twice to ask me. Let me start by lending you some money. I shall not tell Doyin about it although I am sure he too would be glad to help.'

'Thank you Mama Iyabo.'

Mama Iyabo embraced her and as she left said:

'Don't worry, you will get back your money from Ibekwe.'

Chapter III

When Ibekwe left Ohaeto Street, he was feeling very angry. Alekiri's money, a large sum, was in his handbag but that did not make him feel any better. His wife putting up with a soldier! Worse, getting a baby with him! Women were completely untrustworthy! Who could have imagined such a thing? He wished he had not been so fond and proud of her. He remembered those happy days when she was attending a teacher-training institution. They had just been married. She was beautiful, clean and always simply but attractively dressed. She had brought her knowledge of Home Economics, acquired in her teacher training, to the home. Their two-room apartment in Diobu was well cleaned; his clothes carefully washed and ironed; meals tastefully prepared. Ibekwe's friends said his wife would squander all his money on tea, milk, fruits and salad. But he did not mind. His business in fancy goods was profitable and his shed in Diobu market was one of the richest. He dealt in women's wear and cosmetics. His problem was how to buy goods fast enough to satisfy his crazy female customers. They never seemed to tire of buying. He knew some who visited his stall every week. These were the wives of rich politicians who hardly bothered to haggle over prices. Ibekwe wondered how their husbands could afford it. He found it difficult not to believe that politicians stole a lot of public funds. Under this pressure from his customers he bought a motorcycle. With that he could dash to Aba and Onitsha any time, buy goods quickly, consign them to friendly truck drivers and dash back to Port Harcourt to await delivery. Traders like Ibekwe had an edge over the big supermarkets in that they had a faster turnover and were always the first to get at the latest fashions. Ibekwe always reserved the best dresses for his wife and they became her well. But what fascinated him was that she was not spoilt. She used no lipstick or nail polish. No skin lotions discoloured the rich dark mystery of her skin. And she still wore her waist beads, a fact which only Ibekwe knew except perhaps for one rascally young man who, while pretending to fall in the slippery Diobu market, had caressed her waist for the briefest of moments. Alekiri had been furious but the man had been so apologetic, and his posture during his sham fall so funny, that her frown had turned to laughter.

When, on Sundays, Ibekwe rode through Ohiamini community with his wife beautifully dressed and perching delicately behind him, every young man envied him. He had no eyes for other women. Although she did not know it, he had made up his mind to be monogamous, if only she could give him two or three sons. He had every reason to believe he had picked one of the best girls that Ohiamini could produce. Alekiri was both beautiful and intelligent. She was doing very well at the teacher-training college until the fourth year – only a year to the end – when she became pregnant. As it was a Christian mission college the principal terminated her course. He said he had to protect other girls from any exposure to immorality. Alekiri was married, yet to the missionaries her pregnancy still had a hint of sin.

Ibekwe himself had had two years of secondary education which was terminated at his uncle's death. He was not particularly bright, but his neatness and hard work had made him a favourite of the teachers. His uniform was always bright and ironed, his nails trimmed, and his hair frequently cut and parted. His written work, while not always brilliant, was invariably neatly done. But unlike many dandies, he was not lazy and overbearing. He was obedient to his teachers and got on well with his schoolmates, though he chose for his friends only those who were tidy and hardworking. He was chosen as the monitor for his class and he justified the choice. He ensured that the classroom was clean. He concocted a varnish

28

from palm-kernel oil and kerosene and polished the teacher's old table until it shone. When his uncle's death terminated his studies, his teachers grieved, but Ibekwe, only sixteen then, was undaunted. During his primary school days he had lived with Nwena, a relative who was a trader in Port Harcourt. Sometimes after school he had assisted at the market stall. So when his uncle died he opted for trade. His mother could give him no money, because her brother's second burial ceremony had cleaned her out. It was Nwena who came to the resuce. He started by hawking cheap prints along the road leading to the market. His handsome and clean appearance seemed to have paid off. Women customers in particular found him irresistible. He was not talkative, nor did he smile unnecessarily. But he was very attentive to his customers. He would relieve a woman of her bicycle, park it conveniently, then dash back to sell. His prices were modest. Altogether his customers got the impression of an honest and courteous young hawker.

Within half a year he found he needed a stall. Once again Nwena helped him out. As a hawker he had found women customers easier to deal with, so he concentrated on women's wear and cosmetics. His stall was well arranged and festooned with Christmas decorations. One of them said 'Merry Xmas'. When his customers commented on this, he told them every day was Christmas in his shed. Some of them began to call him Christmas. He hung a large mirror in front of his stall so that women could admire themselves while trying on new blouses and necklaces. The mirror itself proved a useful bait, for quite often women passing by would stop to adjust their dresses. Ibekwe would then invite them to see the 'latest'. He always had the 'latest'.

One of Ibekwe's ambitions was to ensure that his friends who were more educated than he did not have an edge over him except perhaps in education itself. Even there, he toyed with the idea of going to a night school and writing the GCE examination, but he could not find the time. Buying and selling was a very exacting business. No matter, he was determined to achieve all that his better educated friends would achieve. He would marry an educated woman, build a modern house, buy a car and send his children to universities abroad if necessary. Then the war came. At the end of it, it was as if he had never owned a penny.

Ibekwe did not know his father. He took his uncle for his father until one day a quarrel arose between him and Olulu's two younger sons over a piece of meat. They had shared out the meat into three portions on a cocoyam leaf. Ibekwe being the oldest proceeded to pick first, but the other two boys objected. The older of them explained that their mother had told them that Ibekwe was "a child of a child" of the compound and so could not take precedence over any of them. Ibekwe had picked first anyway, and there had been a fight. When Olulu heard the din he rushed out of the house to make peace. Ibekwe was surprised that he did not side with him firmly.

'Dede, should they pick before me?' he asked. Olulu paused, scratched his chin and took a deep breath.

'Am I not the oldest?' the boy pressed on.

'You are, my son.'

'And should I not pick first?'

'You are all brothers; you should share things without fighting,' the man said evasively. Baffled and disappointed, Ibekwe ran off to seek further explanation from his mother. Erinwo saw no way out, she had to tell him the truth.

'Olulu is my brother, not your father,' she said softly.

'Who is my father?'

'He is called Jemisi.'

'Where is he?'

'He is not here. He comes from a place called Ohaji.'

Ibekwe was only ten then, and he was quite baffled.

'Why are we not living with him?'

'He did not marry me.'

'But he is my father.'

'Yes. You see, Jemisi and I were just friends when you were born.'

'Why did he not marry you?'

'He wanted to, but I refused.'

'Why?'

'Because I did not want to live at Ohaji.'

'Why?'

'It is too far. But before I met Jemisi I was married to someone in Ohiamini.'

'Who?'

'Never mind. He is dead now.'

'But you say Jemisi is my father.'

'Yes. When I lived with my husband I did not have any child.'

'Why?'

Erinwo laughed shortly.

'God decides when children will be born.'

'Why did you leave your husband?'

'We quarrelled and he beat me up badly, so I ran back to my father. They tried to settle the quarrel, but I refused to go back. Then I met Jemisi. We became friends and you were born.'

'Why does he not come to see me?'

'He used to when you were very young.'

'Why does he not come now?'

'I don't know.'

'I want to see him.'

'One day you will, when you grow up.'

'Can we not travel to his place?'

'No, we can't. It is too far.'

Ibekwe was not satisfied. The idea of not being with his father hurt him.

'Why did you quarrel with your husband?'

'Ibekwe, must you know everything?'

'Tell me.'

'He annoyed me.'

'How?'

Erinwo thought rapidly. She could not tell him how while she was in bed with her husband one night there had been a knock at the door; how he opened the door and admitted a strange woman; how he asked her to leave the bed and spread a mat on the floor; how she sprang at the other woman and

31

beat her up thoroughly, and how she herself had in turn been thoroughly beaten up by her husband.

'He beat me up, so we quarrelled,' she said at last.

From that day Ibekwe's relationship with his cousins took a turn. He avoided them as much as possible and refused to share anything with them. Occasionally they would call him a bastard and they would fight. Sometimes he hated his mother for running away from her husband. She it was who brought all that humiliation on him. He resolved never to quarrel with his wife when he grew up. At least he would not give her a cause to run away.

Over the years Ibekwe had heard his mother recounting to her friends her experiences with her former husband and so learnt why she had quarrelled with him. He would not bring another woman into the house when he got married. He and his wife would be faithful to each other. Their children would stay with them and would not have to ask about their father. No one would call them bastards.

When Ibekwe became a trader and began to travel to Aba and other places to buy goods, he had toyed with the idea of seeking out his father James, but anger and pride restrained him. A father who did not show the least interest in his child was not worth bothering about. Moreover, James might have got other children about his age. He did not see how he could interact with them without a feeling of humiliation.

During the war Olulu's two wives and four of their children died in a bomb blast. The two young sons who survived the war could not live with Erinwo, so they sought refuge at their grandfather's place. Ibekwe found himself alone with his mother in his uncle's compound. But he knew that one day, those two boys would return to claim the compound and their father's farmlands. They would have the full backing of tradition and he would not have a leg to stand on. The thing to do was to make money, establish himself and not depend on his uncle's property and land. He would build a house in a compound of his own as soon as he had the money. If only the war had not deprived him of his wife. Well, he would have to start all over again.

He walked on disconsolately from Ohaeto Street to Ikwerre Road and towards his former house in Mile Three. He could see refugees returning from Biafra. Most of them looked haggard and wretched. They carried dirty bundles containing worn out clothes and mouldy food. Only three days ago he himself had been one of them. The refugees were glad to be back. Greetings of "happy survival!" filled the air. Here and there groups of returnees, as they sometimes called themselves, blocked the street in a mass embrace. Fortunately vehicles were still rare. Near his former house, Deko, a grizzly-bearded former neighbour who used to work as a labourer for the railways, saw him, shouted his name and hobbled towards him for an embrace. Ibekwe's dress, though poor, was clean and the imminent encounter promised a possible transfer of grease and lice. He did not care for that sort of thing. Just at the critical moment, he bent low to adjust his shoes. The man stopped short. Ibekwe straightened up, apologized and offered a handshake and a backslap. The man's confidence, momentarily lost, was quickly restored.

'Happy survival!' the man shouted. Ibekwe was pained to discover that his neighbour had lost three teeth and had sores at the corners of his mouth.

'Happy survival!' Ibekwe replied.

'Brother, when did you come back?'

'Three days ago.'

'Where were you?'

'Atta, in the last days anyway.'

'Ah, I was at Ohaji. You know we were cut off at Ozuaha by federal troops. I doubled back, then took a bush track to Elele. I had to catch up with my wife and children who had been separated from me. Before I got to Elele I fell into the hands of Biafran soldiers. They said I was a federal spy and knocked out three of my teeth. They held me for a week until a friend pleaded on my behalf and they released me. By this time I had no idea where my wife was. Some said she had gone to Ubumini, others that she ...'

33

'Sorry, there is a relation waiting for me. We shall discuss some other time.'

'I shall not go into details,' the man insisted, 'but do you know I have not seen my wife and two children ever since?' Ibekwe's interest returned.

'What happened to her?'

'I can't say exactly, but yesterday a friend told me she was living at Elele with a soldier. Ibekwe, can you imagine that?'

'What will you do?'

'I shall get her back, what else? Who will give me money with which to marry another wife? But I have to go gently. These soldiers are dangerous, they say.'

'I wish you luck.'

'Thank you. How is your wife?'

'She is well.'

'And the child – a daughter if I remember.'

'Very well.' Ibekwe was losing patience again.

'Greet her for me.'

'I will.'

Ibekwe walked away slowly. So he was not alone in his tragedy. His neighbour was a practical man and he wished he could emulate him. But then there were wives and wives, he thought. His neighbour's wife was not educated and did not know her left from right. For her and her like survival meant everything. As for his neighbour, well he was just a grass-cutter working for the railways. They did not belong to the same class. People said he was proud, so what? He did not get into anybody's way and he had a right to live the way he wanted. He styled himself Prince Ibekwe and no one could take that title from him. No, people were different, that was all. He was not like his neighbour. His wife was not like his neighbour's. Alekiri, wife of Prince Ibekwe, had no business living with a soldier and bearing a child for him. He stopped in the street, bit his lips and clenched his fist.

People stared at him. If he had gesticulated much longer they would have passed him off as one of the many shell-shocked soldiers whose sanity had not returned immediately with the end of the war. Actually there were not as many of them as some imagined. The confusion lay in distinguishing between sane but ragged refugees who were soliloquizing over their misfortunes and insane people dressed up in that pathetic gaudiness which only the deranged mind can conjure.

When he reached his former abode, he found the doors and windows broken and all his property looted. He had expected that, but what annoyed him was the human excrement all over the floor. The house had been converted into a lavatory. He walked out in disgust.

He realized he was hungry. He had not eaten all day. He had left the village early to catch the only bus going to town. On his way to his old house he had seen an eating shack labelled 'Hotel de Aburi'. He was amused. The war had encroached even on names. Hotels and inns and guest houses were named after towns and villages immortalized by the war. Obolo-Eke, Obolo-Afo, Gakem, Opi, all boasted of eating places named after them. A palm-wine shed close to Hotel de Aburi was labelled 'Ojukwu's Bunker'. It was quite popular, drawing its customers from former Biafran soldiers, some of them amputees. Their language drew heavily from the war. Every search or investigation was a 'recce', every enterprise an 'operation'; they did not make love to women, they 'shelled' them.

Inside Hotel de Aburi there were some customers arguing and swopping stories of the war. Ibekwe ordered a plate of *garri* and sat down on the bench on one side of the rough long table covered with a dirty blue plastic table cloth. Flies hovered incessantly. Yet there was a cosiness about the place in spite of the squalor, and a comforting comradeship among the customers that defied their grim poverty. Suddenly there was a burst of laughter. Ibekwe looked up.

A tall bearded man in a dirty badly sown white gown with a red sash was holding forth. His listeners called him professor.

'In Biafra, I was called father, not professor,' he said, 'and I will tell you how it happened. Every other day Biafran soldiers came on recruitment drives. Each time I ran away or hid in the ceiling under the bed or even under a heap of cassava.' The audience laughed. 'So I was, in fact, a prisoner. Sometimes I said, why not join and end this hide-and-seek business? My wife said no, they would kill me. So one day a friend gave me an idea. I collected all the money I had and made this long gown you see here and borrowed my wife's rosary and bible. My wife nearly died of laughter when she saw me in my priest's dress.' The audience roared 'Father! Father!' The professor made the sign of the cross. There was more laughter. 'The next day the recruitment team came. I came out boldly – but brother, my heart was beating – I said: "*Pax vobiscum*" and made the sign of the cross. The Biafran soldiers greeted me as Father, and asked for a blessing. Wonders will never end!' Another roar of laughter. 'They knelt down and I prayed for them, for Ojukwu, for Nzeogwu, for anyone I could think of. After that I joined the welfare people, but my eyes were on the food distribution centres. In the end I was asked to work in one of them. I made sure I did not come within a mile of any real Catholic priest. Brothers, I did not lack food after that. That is how I survived.'

Ibekwe ate quietly and quickly. The driver of the only bus to Ohiamini had told him that his last departure was usually at about 5 p.m.

'What is your time?' he inquired from the man sitting next to him.

'Half past three.'

The bus station was hard by, just five minutes walk. He had plenty of time.

The man who ran the eating shack came out to greet his customers. He was brimming with sweat, having just finished pounding a huge mortar of *garri*. He wore a pair of khaki shorts but his torso was bare. With a handkerchief black with dirt, he tried in vain to stem the rivulets of sweat.

'Manager! Manager!' some customers called out. The man smiled a greeting then walked to the door and blew his nose, emitting a two-tone trumpet-like sound. He came back, cleaning mucus off his moustache.

'Ona de talk of Biafra. Make I tell ona my own tory.'

'Manager! Manager!'

'Okay. Make ona quiet. You know say I de for Owerri for war time. One day Biafra soldiers come capture me. Dem say make I join army. I tell dem say I be old man. They no 'gree. I talk all the grammar wey I sabi, still they no 'gree. So I say, oya make we go. Wetin! Man no die man no rotin. When we reach dem headquarter the OC say I too old for go army. 'E say make I cook. Na him I begin cook. One day wahala burst. Dem say make I carry food go war front. I hala. Dem say make I shut up. Brother I no lie, I piss for my troza. Na him I begin load food inside one yeye gwongworo. They gi' me only two small Biafra soldier with one catapult rifle. The bullet way they give them no reach three sef. I say, O God I done die today. Na him we begin go. When we reach war front we no see our men. Biafra soldier no dey again. I ask driver if him sure say na di place. 'E say make I no make noise. But I see say the man done confuse. 'E say our men done move to front. As 'e wan' kick the moto' again I hear, kakaka kakakakaka. Bullet begin scatter for the gwongworo, katakatakataka. My brother 'e remain small I shit for my troza. Na him I take cover inside gwongworo. Small time I no hear nothing again. I opin my eye small. I see two vandals wey de point gun for my head. Dem surrender me and say make I come down follow dem. When I commot for the gwongworo I see say dem done kill the driver and the two Biafra soldier. Before we move dem burn the gwongworo. They take me come Port Harcourt. After, dem come know say I be ordinary bloody civilian from Rivers State. Na him dem lef me.'

'Manager, your wife nko?' Ibekwe asked.

''E return with my pickin dem last week. Ah, I tank God-o.'

As Ibekwe walked towards the bus station, more refugees and 'returnees' greeted him. He was in no mood to listen to any more tales of Biafra. His mind was in a tumult. He had much to sort out. There was a feeling of emptiness he could not overcome.

'Isn't that Christmas?' a woman's voice said behind him. He turned round and saw Ibia, one of his faithful pre-war customers. Her face lit up in a smile. Ibekwe spread his arms in a spontaneous movement and she embraced him warmly. It was a time for embraces.

'Christmas, happy survival!'

'Happy survival!'

'When did you come back?'

'Three days ago. And you?'

'About a week now. How is Alekiri?'

'I ... er ... I don't know.'

'What do you mean?'

'I mean I haven't seen her yet.'

'But she is okay?'

'So they say.'

'Thank God. But aren't you both in the village?'

'No, she is in Port Harcourt here.'

'Oh ...', she stopped, seeing some strain on his face.

'Christmas, they must have looted your shed.'

'I have not bothered to check. I left very little there any-way.'

'That was lucky.'

'You know before the war started, goods became very scarce and traders sold off nearly everything they had.'

'That's true.'

It was good chatting with Ibia. The heaviness in his mind lifted a little, momentarily. Before the war Ibia was a typist with a private company. Light-skinned and pleasant-faced, she laughed easily. Like most people she had lost weight, and suffering had lent a certain sharpness to her face; but only those who knew her well before the war could tell that.

'Are you going to the village?'

'Yes. And you?'

'I live near here. Come, let me show you.'

They walked a short distance and came to a street just before the bus station.

'You see that house hit by a bomb?'

38

'Yes.'

'And the white one – well it used to be white – by its side?'

'Yes.'

'That's where I live with my sister. I am still looking for a place of my own. There are many houses, but no money to repair and furnish them.'

'Are you back to your old job?'

'I have no problem there. I went to the company office yesterday to report my return. I am sure to start work whenever the company takes off again. Bianco told me so.'

'Who is Bianco?'

'An engineer in our company. He is a white man who has just arrived. And what about your trading?'

'Well, you know how it is. Traders take a long time to take off. There is no money to buy goods and it is not easy to get credit.'

'Don't worry, you'll make it.'

'I hope so.'

'I can afford a soft drink.'

'No, no. Don't worry. I am about to catch the only bus to the village.'

'Christmas! it is nice to see you again.'

She put out her hand. As they shook hands, she swung Ibekwe's hand to and fro, smiling affectionately.

'Christmas, you must start your stall again.'

In the bus, Ibekwe greeted his fellow villagers who made up the majority of passengers. He chose a window seat and sat wrapped in thought. He was deaf to the war stories being swapped all around. He stared at the road, now so overgrown that it had room for only one vehicle. To pass by each other, vehicles had first to stop dead and cautiously mow down the tall grass on either side. Often there was nothing but grass. Occasionally there were obstacles which vehicles could not negotiate. Passengers by the window collected a lot of grass seeds and leaves in their clothes and hair. Now and then one yelled as grass blades lashed an eye or grazed a nose.

When Ibekwe arrived, Erinwo, his mother, was waiting

anxiously. She was alone. Ibekwe's two sisters, one older, the other younger than he, were married, and Wibari, his five-year-old daughter had gone to bed.

'Did you see her?'

'No.'

'You could not trace her house?'

'I found her house alright, but she was nowhere to be seen. Her neighbour said she had gone to buy fish for the army but I could see she was lying.'

'Where do you think she went?'

'I am sure she went to visit her new husband.'

'God forbid! Here is a woman who has not seen her husband for two years. If she had any sense she should be in the village waiting and praying for your return. Instead she runs around with soldiers. God forbid!'

'Mother I think this marriage is ended.'

'No, don't say that, although I don't blame you. Let's see her first and hear what she has to say. She should bring the marriage to an end if she wants to, not you.'

Erinwo was being supremely tactful. She hated Alekiri with a hatred that was very carefully concealed. She thought Alekiri was an expensive woman who squandered her son's money on clothes and white man's food. She never helped at the farm although she readily consumed the products so laboriously extracted from it. True, Alekiri gave her old clothes and little sums of money from time to time, but she considered these far from sufficient. Alekiri had been aware of her mother-in-law's resentments but there was very little she could do about them. She had to put on clothes and cook the type of food her husband liked. Because she had attended primary school in Port Harcourt, she was not used to farm work and could not help her mother-in-law. In compensation, Ibekwe always gave his mother enough money to hire labourers to do much of the work. Still, Erinwo pined for the companionship which other women enjoyed with their daughters-in-law. She had urged her son to marry an illiterate second wife who would live with her in the village, but Ibekwe had said it was too early. In order not to frustrate her, he had not refused outright.

'No mother, I can't live with that woman again.'

'Let's see her first.'

After his meal at Hotel de Aburi, Ibekwe had no appetite for supper; but Erinwo moaned and he ate a little. Then he entered his room and bolted the door. He lit a hurricane lamp and studied three photographs he had extracted from Alekiri's album. In the first one she was sitting at a table covered with assorted drinks. Two army officers flanked her. She was holding a glass of wine and smiling broadly, probably laughing. The officers were laughing too and one of them was looking at her with unmistakable admiration and affection. In the second picture Alekiri was dancing wildly with Major Dansuku. It was obviously a highlife for her knees were acutely flexed and her buttocks stuck out in her commando trousers. Dansuku towered above her, laughing, and admiring her. In the third photograph Alekiri was in normal dress and dancing, this time cheek-to-cheek with Dansuku. The camera had caught her face and Dansuku's broad back. She appeared to hold him tight and her dreamy eyes were half closed. Ibekwe bit his lips until he felt a sharp pain. For a moment he felt giddy and the room spun round. He closed his eyes. God! Was this his Alee, this woman clutching this strange man passionately, this woman dancing and drinking while he languished in Biafra trying to fend for their only daughter? So, she could forget him so easily. So, she could live with and keep house for another man, lie with him, make love to him and perhaps moan in her characteristic manner, and above all have a baby with him. No, that was the limit, the very limit. Marriage was no longer possible. He would die of resentment and rage if he tried to live with her. He would probably kill her. She deserved to die anyway. He began to sweat. His heart beat wildly and his eyes were bloodshot and brimmed with unshed tears. He got up, put on his clothes and walked the half mile to the next village where his father-in-law lived.

41

A light was burning in Kinika's sitting room, which was open. He could see his father-in-law passing his snuff-box to an elderly neighbour. With them was a young woman whom he could not identify until he came to the door. She turned out to be Ada, Kinika's first daughter, better known as Christiana, a name which the church agent had insisted on using at her baptism. Christie was rarely seen in the village. She had left home at an early age to live with a married but childless aunt in Lagos. Kinika had been reluctant to let her go but his sister's tearful plea had proved irresistible. Neighbours had added their prayers to hers. As she was childless, they said, the least her brother could do was to let her live with one of his many children. So to Lagos Christie went and had been there ever since, except for occasional visits to the village, usually at Christmas.

Ibekwe knocked and was admitted.

'Ibekwe!'

'My in-law.'

'Thank God, you are back.'

'Same for you. When did you return?'

'Three days…? four days…?'

He turned to his neighbour for assistance.

'Azunda, when was it?'

'I remember you came back on a market day, because I left my yams to greet you as you passed. That was *nkwo*. Today is *nkwo*, so you came back four days ago.'

'Thank God,' Ibekwe said.

Azunda passed the snuff back to Kinika. He offered it to Ibekwe who touched it but declined to take any.

'Christie.'

'Ibekwe.'

They shook hands.

'Christie came back yesterday,' explained Kinika, 'and just in time too.' He brought out cola nut and some beer.

'You have Christie to thank for these,' he said.

'Christie, you have done well,' Ibekwe said.

'Oh, it's nothing,' she said, waving her hand and rattling

42

the expensive gold bangles she wore. Well groomed and impeccably dressed she looked totally out of place in her father's dusty, unpainted, cobweb-ridden ruin of a living room. Kinika offered cola.

Ibekwe wanted neither cola nor drink but he could hardly refuse. It would be the height of ill-breeding, in fact an insult big enough to make Kinika withdraw his daughter. Ibekwe toyed with the idea of refusing. It would make his mission easier. For a long painful moment Kinika's outstretched hand hung in mid air. Custom could be powerful. In the end Ibekwe touched the cola but refused to accept it.'

'What?' Kinika and his neighbour shouted at once and in a loud voice.

'What?' Kinika shouted again, his eyes popping. Ibekwe was unnerved.

'Let me have it then,' he said. But Kinika had withdrawn his hand.

'I am sorry, let me have it. You see I was not myself. I came with a lot of anger in my mind. I meant no insult to you.'

Azunda pleaded on his behalf and Kinika offered the cola nut once again. Ibekwe took it then passed it to Azunda who returned it to Kinika who then asked Ibekwe, who was the youngest, to break and share it.

Christie did not join in the cola and beer. She just sat still and watched Ibekwe. The anger and contempt in her face were embarrassingly apparent.

When at last Kinika and his son-in-law were alone, he asked in a voice that contained traces of his anger over the cola: 'What is it you are so angry about?'

'It is about your daughter, Alekiri.'

'What about her?'

'I want to terminate the marriage.'

'*What?*'

'I have indeed terminated the marriage and you may keep the bride price if you like.'

Kinika stared at the young man for a while, then heaved a sigh of patience and understanding. He smiled sadly and said:

43

'I would have been angry with you if you had been an older man. But you are young and inexperienced. Besides, your uncle was my great friend. And so let me answer thus: if your wife has annoyed you, come with members of your family and complain formally. We shall look into the matter and settle it.'

'I don't want a settlement,' Ibekwe said doggedly.

Kinika smiled sadly again: 'My son, I have heard you. May the day break.'

With that he rose to barricade a window with an old ceiling board.

'May the day break,' Ibekwe said and disappeared into the night.

Chapter IV

The next morning Alekiri prepared to visit the village. Mama Iyabo fulfilled her promise to make her pick-up van and driver available; more, she loaded the van with yams, *garri* and dried fish. Alekiri was overwhelmed.

'Mama Iyabo, you don't have to go into all this expense,' she said hugging her.

'It is from my husband.'

Adedoyin was a few steps behind his wife.

'Yes, Alee, it is a little thing from me,' he said. 'You have been so helpful, dashing up and down under rain and sun to buy fish, vegetables and whatnot. But for you, the army boys might have shot me by now.' He laughed and adjusted his robe.

'Doyin, thank you. Mama Iyabo, please help me thank your husband. This is really too much.'

'Ah, it is nothing. By the way, will you come back today?'

'I am not sure.'

'If you will come back today then you may keep the vehicle and ride back in it. If not let the driver come back after dropping you.'

'Thank you, Doyin.'

'Driver, do you hear?'

'Yes, *Oga*.'

The ride to the village was fast in spite of the bad road. The pick-up was almost new and rode the pot-holes with hardly a squeak. The twenty-mile journey was over before she could collect her thoughts. It was best, she thought, to visit her father first, although it would be awkward because she would have to pass through her husband's village. But there was no

45

better course to take. Her meeting with her husband could take any turn and she wanted to see her father first before that ordeal. She need not have worried. She passed through the village without being recognized, thanks to the speed of the van and her head-tie and large dark sun-glasses.

First her father hugged her, then Christie came running from the house. Their embrace was so forceful that they were both thrown against the bonnet of the van. They recovered, giggling and clinging to each other. Soon Christie was wiping tears of joy with the corners of her wrapper.

'Alee, I am glad you are looking so well. We heard such awful news about Port Harcourt that we thought everyone here was dead. Alee, hey!'

They began another round of hugging.

'Give me a chance, Christie,' Alekiri's stepmother said.

'Okay, your turn now.'

Alekiri embraced Wiche, her stepmother, then her father's third wife, and all the many children still clad in the rags and dirt of war. A crowd of neighbours soon formed. Alekiri was looking so well; how they wished they had remained behind. And was the van hers? And who was the driver who could not understand what they were saying?

First Alekiri unloaded loaves of bread and distributed them to the children, who gradually dispersed. Then she brought out a large bottle of snuff for her father. Azunda's eyes opened wide with envy.

'That's a year's supply!' he said.

'Never mind, we shall share it,' Kinika said warmly.

'Don't worry Nana, I have some more for papa Azunda.' She rummaged in a carton and fished out a round snuff-box and gave it to Azunda. He opened it, spilling some snuff for it was packed. He danced comically for joy. Kinika and his wives laughed.

Alekiri spent the next hour or two distributing food and clothes to his father, his wives, and their more intimate neighbours. Soon the van was empty. Alekiri reckoned it would take a whole wagon of supplies to meet the yawning needs of his family and neighbours. However it was some comfort to think that there was food, at least for the next few days.

After the tumultous greetings, embraces and tears, Alekiri had decided to send the driver back to Port Harcourt and spend the night with her family. The driver could not leave immediately because Alekiri's stepmother insisted that he should eat first. 'We are not so poor that we cannot spare a meal for a visitor,' she said. But while the food was being prepared, Alekiri made a tour of the compound and changed her mind. Most of the doors and windows were broken and had to be covered with old planks, cardboard and other debris. There were only two iron beds in the whole compound and not a single mattress. Christie explained she had been sleeping on a mat on the floor, but that she did not mind. She was so glad to see their father. But Alekiri could see she was suffering considerable discomfort.

'Christie, let's spend the night in Port Harcourt. Tomorrow we can come back with mattresses, mats and anything else we can bring.'

Christie hesitated a moment. It was a reasonable suggestion.

'A good idea, but will they let you go?'

'Why not? Port Harcourt is only twenty miles away.'

Kinika did not argue. In fact he welcomed the idea. It pained him that Christie was sleeping on the dusty floor. He cursed his war-induced poverty.

'Yes, you can ride back to town this evening and come back tomorrow.'

'Thank you Nana. I feared you would not let us, after missing us for so long.'

'No, my daughters. I should not let you suffer unnecessarily. Tomorrow is here already. By the way, do you intend to visit your husband before you go?'

'Yes, Nana.'

'Have a word with me after your meal.'

Later, Kinika summoned his daughter to the living room. Christie joined them.

'Alee, your husband came here late last night.'

'Did he?'

'Yes. And he behaved in a very bad manner, but I ignored his insolence because he is young and inexperienced and his uncle was a good friend of mine. I feel I should help and advise him whenever I can. I thought of all this last night and my anger went away. Ibekwe is very angry with you, why?'

Alekiri was mute for a while. How could she explain all the intricacies of the war-time situation to her father? No, it was not possible.

'Nana, I cannot hide anything from you. I had a baby by another man during the war.'

'I see,' the old man said after a long pause.

'I see,' he muttered a second time. 'Now I understand Ibekwe's anger. Most young men would feel that way. Where is the baby?'

'In Port Harcourt.'

'Hm.'

'Also he may be angry with me for losing our baby at the time I was captured at the war front.'

'Is Wibari dead?'

'Yes, Nana.'

'How did it happen?'

'I left her to look for water when the attack came. As thousands of refugees fled, there was great confusion and I never saw her again.'

Kinika knit his brows as he pondered.

'Ibekwe cannot blame you really. Even adults were trampled to death at the front.'

'He may say I ought to have carried the baby on my back all the time. Sometimes I think so too.' Alekiri began to cry.

'I am sure you have cried enough in the last two and a half years. Stop now. Wipe your tears.'

With a corner of her wrapper Alekiri wiped her face.

Kinika studied the floor for some time. Without looking up, he asked:

'What do you intend to do?'

'I shall ask him to forgive me.'

'Good. That's exactly what I was about to advise. But don't imagine he will forgive you immediately.'

'I know that.'

'Don't go to him alone.'

'You think he will beat her up?' Christie asked.

'But Ada, you saw him last night.'

'Yes, Nana. You are right.'

'I shall go with Christie,' Alekiri said.

'And your stepmother,' her father said.

'And Mama Iyabo.'

'Who is Mama Iyabo?'

'My neighbour in Port Harcourt, who owns this pick-up.'

'Does she understand our language?'

'No, but she can talk to Ibekwe in English.'

'That's a good idea,' Christie said.

'Which means you can't go there today, since Mama-what-do-you-call-her is not here.'

Alekiri and Christie exchanged glances.

'Christie, what do you think?' her sister asked, staring intently at her as if trying to extract the answer from her face.

'I think there will be a lot of *wahala* when you meet your husband. So we should be prepared. Also the presence of a stranger may stop him from being violent. You know I am not good at wrestling.' They laughed.

Back at Port Harcourt, Alekiri went to Mama Iyabo to thank her again and to introduce Christie.

'Mama Iyabo, this is Christie my senior sister. You know, the one in Lagos I talked to you about. Christie, this is my neighbour, Mama Iyabo. Her name is Bisi but we all call her Mama Iyabo – after Iyabo her beautiful daughter.'

'Christie, *e kabo*.'

'O-o,' Christie replied. '*Omode nko*?'

'E-eh, Alee, your sister is a real Eko woman. She speaks our language perfectly.'

'Why not? I have been there for years,' Christie said.

Mama Iyabo embraced Christie and took to her immediately. She offered them fried meat and beer.

49

'Alee, your sister is a very beautiful woman and looks younger than you.'

'That's not true,' Christie said mildly. 'I look much older than Alee.'

'Thank God you were not here during the war. Soldiers would have captured you as soon as they set eyes on you.'

'Did they capture every woman in Port Harcourt?'

'E-eh, you don't know these soldiers. They finished all the women in this town.'

Mama Iyabo chuckled but the sisters did not join in the laughter. She quickly realized it was an awkward joke, considering the dilemma Alekiri was in. She tried to make amends.

'And it was not the fault of the women. In most cases the soldiers forced them. And they have spoilt many marriages. Look at the trouble Alee now has.'

'That is one reason we are here,' Christie said, deciding that the woman was good-natured.

'Can I help?'

'Yes. As you know, Alee's husband is very angry. I suppose he has good reasons to be angry and Alee has decided to ask for his forgiveness. But if she goes alone he may beat her up. We wonder …'

'If I can go with her?'

'Yes.'

'*Oluwa*! You don't have to ask. I have already offered to plead on her behalf. Alee, is that not so?'

'That's true.'

Doyin emerged from one of the rooms.

'Christie, this is Doyin my husband. Doyin this is Christie, Alee's sister who lives in Lagos.'

Doyin and Christie exchanged greetings and shook hands.

'I shall see you again,' Doyin said. 'I hope you will stay in Port Harcourt for a while. Please feel at home. Bisi, I am off to the army headquarters for discussions with some army officers.' He said goodbye and swept out of the room in his *agbada* made from an expensive lace material. As the door closed on the women, Mama Iyabo muttered:

'Don't mind him, he is going to visit one skinny girl with half-past-four eyes.'

There was sustained laughter.

'You may be wrong,' Christie said.

'I am right. I know the girl and I know how Doyin walks when he is about to visit a woman. He walks like a smuggler trying to get past a customs official. But she is not the first. He will soon tire of her.'

'That's the right spirit,' Alekiri put in, chuckling. 'I shall never put up with that kind of thing,' Christie said.

'That's what I said before I got married.'

'Then I think I shall remain single.'

'God forbid!' Alekiri said.

'Alee I mean it. Any man who thinks I can stay in the house while he roams about chasing every *asawo* is mistaken,' Christie replied with some heat.

'As for me,' Mama Iyabo said, 'I don't bother about that kind of thing, so long as he does not do it here in the house. One day he will be too old to engage in that dance without music.'

Christie laughed and began to cough as a bit of meat went the wrong way.

'Christie, you must beware of Mama Iyabo,' Alekiri said. 'She can break your sides if you are not careful.'

'Christie, I am sorry,' Mama Iyabo said. 'Sip a little beer. Don't mind your sister. I do nothing but speak the truth.'

'You tell the truth in a funny way,' Christie said between coughs. 'But tell me, will he not be jealous if he finds you flirting with other men?'

'Ah! *Oluwa*! He will cut off my head!'

'You see!'

'Fortunately, Mama Iyabo has no time for other men. She only talks,' Alekiri said. Mama Iyabo stretched her big body against the back of the low well-padded chair and laughed.

'The thing is, men are childish. They bore me. Except when they are doing business, they think of nothing else except how

51

to go between your legs. Sometimes I wonder if they are well.'

They all laughed.

'You know, after I left secondary school, men poured into my father's house like flies. I used to look good in those days; never mind, I am now old and fat.'

'Mama Iyabo, you are a pretty woman,' Christie said.

'Anyway in those days I was pretty. My father was an easy-going man and that encouraged the men. My mother died two years before I left school and as I was the first daughter I had no senior sister to advise me. Each time my father was away on business, insurance business, the men besieged the house with their cars. I went out with some of them to the cinema, nightclubs and so on. They all behaved in the same way. They promised marriage, this and that, but in the end they asked for the same thing.

'But I never gave in. I was very stubborn. I remember one night after a film show, the man I went with tried to drive me to his place by force. We struggled over the steering wheel. In the end he was fed-up. He stopped the car and pushed me out. My blouse caught in the door-handle and was torn. It was a beautiful blouse and I cried. I never saw the man again. After that I refused to go out with any man.'

'But Doyin caught you after all,' Alekiri put in.

'It was a football match that did it. It was a tough match and it was hard to get into Liberty Stadium. People pushed, pulled and squeezed. I found myself between two men who were almost squeezing me to death. I cried out. Then one of them smiled and made way for me. When at last I gained a seat, I found that same man by my side. I thanked him. At half time he offered me a can of soft drink. I said to myself, that's how they start. I refused. He said, "Don't worry, I won't chase you. My girlfriend is here," and pointed to a girl on his right. The girl looked at him in surprise, then laughed. "Don't mind him, I don't know him." We all laughed. He offered the drink again and I took it. After the match he followed me and asked me where I lived. I refused to tell him. I said if he did not stop following me, I will shout. He stopped and I went home in

peace. Next day when I went out in the evening to buy
something from a shop near our house, I heard a man greet me
"Good evening". I looked, it was the same man. *Oluwa*! I was
surprised. I did not talk to him. But he kept coming.

'E-eh ... it is a long story. To cut it short we got married
in the end.'

That night Alekiri and her sister hardly slept as Alekiri
retold the story of her commando days and of her involvement
with Major Dansuku.

'There is one thing I want to know,' Christie said.

'Yes?'

'Did you desert Ibekwe at the war front or was it an
accidental separation?'

'How could I desert him? Look Christie, I love that man
very much. Right now my greatest desire is to patch up this
quarrel, if it can be patched up.'

'How did the separation occur? I want to prepare what to
say to him if he accuses you of desertion.'

'Oh, he can't. I was not the only one cut off at Omademe.
After a narrow escape from Ozuaha during which I lost
everything I had, Ibekwe and I found ourselves among a huge
crowd at Omademe school compound. It was a terrible sight.
There were people in all conditions. We had nothing to eat.
Christie, can you imagine? Nothing at all. After three days
we were hopelessly hungry. My daughter Wibari was about
three years old. She was dying before my eyes. Ibekwe carried
her and dragged me to the house of a friend who was his
former classmate. The man could hardly greet us. I saw that
he was afraid we would ask for some favours. On looking back
now I cannot blame him. His house was filled with relatives,
friends and people who said they knew him. His food supply
was finished. He told Ibekwe he could not help us. He was
bitter. He said refugees had stolen not only food but his
property – pots, mortars, mats, knives, baskets, clothes,
anything they could find. His house of four rooms had nearly
fifty people in it. He could not drive them away. It was all

53

because of his kindness, he said. His neighbours who were not so kind did not have so much trouble.

'Ibekwe and I went back to the school compound. Wibari was dying. Hardly knowing what he was doing, Ibekwe plunged into the nearest bush and just before night, came back with a yam. He confessed he stole it from a farm. We cooked a bit of it quickly and fed Wibari. The next day we were as hungry as ever. You know Ibekwe had a beautiful gold chain with a cross pendant. He used to wear it to market and he said it brought him luck. And he looked handsome when it dangled over his hairy chest. You know he exchanged that chain for food which lasted only two days. When the food was finished, he went into the bush again. Not up to an hour after that, the Nigerians began to shell Omademe. As soon as the first shell landed, hey, Christie, there was confusion. People ran here and there shouting. I had gone to fetch water and as soon as the confusion started I thought of Wibari and tried to reach her. It was impossible. The crowd pushed me along the direction in which they ran.

'A few children were trampled to death and I screamed in fear. I was mad. I made another effort to get to Wibari. This time the crowd pushed me to the ground. Several others fell on me. I escaped being trampled to death by a miracle. Then the Nigerian soldiers appeared. I managed to get up and ran blindly in the opposite direction along a farm path. Suddenly people began to run back from the path. They said Nigerian soldiers had blocked that way too. Christie, my heart jumped. I turned to the right and jumped into the bush. Before I could move from here to there someone said, stop or I fire, in a deep voice. I stopped and trembled.'

Christie sobbed.

'Christie it was terrible. Don't cry. Should I stop?'

'No, go on.'

'When I looked up I did not see anybody. I was very afraid. I tried to move again and the same voice said stop. Then I saw a hand waving to me. I looked and saw a soldier carefully hidden among the trees. He had leaves and branches all over his body. As I moved to him I found that the whole bush was full of soldiers but it was very difficult to see them because of the leaves they stuck to their bodies. I stayed with the soldiers until the shelling and shooting stopped. Then the soldier who captured me took me back to the village now filled with Nigerian soldiers and other refugees who had been cut off. Then I met a woman who said she had seen my husband calling me as I ran along the farm path, and that when I could not stop he had turned back and ran along another path. Christie, you could not hear even if twenty people called your name at the same time because of the noise of the shelling and the shooting. You cannot imagine it.

'All this time the soldier who captured me was holding me firmly. He hushed the woman who was talking to me and began to drag me to an empty house. I shouted and fell on the ground. He slapped me and dragged me along like a log of wood. I thought he was going to kill me and shouted very loud.'

'Oh God! oh my God!' Christie sobbed again.

'In the end the soldier dragged me to an empty room and asked me to remove my clothes. I shouted, No! He pointed his gun at me and began to count. He said he would shoot me after ten. As in a dream I heard, three, four, five ... My sister, let me tell you in secret: I urinated in my wrapper. When he counted nine, I shouted like a mad woman. The soldier released many bullets at the roof and made a hole in it. As he was firing I ran out of the house. He pursued me. My legs were weak and he quickly caught me. I shouted as we struggled. Then suddenly I saw a Land Rover coming towards us. When it stopped near us the soldier let me go. An officer came out. The soldier saluted him. The officer looked at both of us and ordered the soldier to move forward. By this time I was sitting on the ground crying. He asked me to climb into the Land Rover. I was so weak I could not move. He said I should not be afraid. Then I got up and one of the soldiers with him helped me into the Land Rover.'

'Who was the officer who saved you?'

'It was Major Dansuku.'

The two sisters were quiet for a while except for Christie's sighs.

'Have you seen Ibekwe since he came back?'

'Mm-mm.'

'Has he tried to look for you?'

'Yes. And that is another story. He came here, looked at my album and got angry over some pictures he saw. I agree I was foolish to have exposed those pictures.'

'And what did he do?'

'Nothing, except take my money from the wardrobe.'

'Your money?'

'Mm.'

'Why?'

'I don't know, perhaps because of his anger.'

'That is stealing.'

'Well, I try not to think of it as such.'

'How much?'

Alee told her.

'What? That's a large sum. You should demand it from him.'

'I believe he will give it back to me. But if he uses it to start his business again, I won't mind. Christie, I am just tired of the whole thing. If that money will bring peace, let him take it.'

'Alee, what will you do if your marriage breaks down?'

'I have not thought of that seriously.'

'You should.'

'I feel he will take me back after a while. He is a young man and I understand his anger, but I believe he will cool down and take me back.'

'How long do you think that will take?'

'Three months … six months … perhaps a year.'

'You are prepared to wait for as long as a year?'

'Mm.'

Christie sighed and paused.

'Alee, don't let that man spoil your life.'

'I hope not.'

'Listen, if he tries to form a mess, come with me to Lagos. I shall look after you well and in a short time you will be driving your own car.'

'Lagos is far. I don't want to go too far from home.'

'If your husband breaks the marriage, what will keep you here? In fact, to forget the whole thing, it would be better for you to leave home for some time.'

'Christie, Lagos is a rough place. I don't think I can live there.'   *ausi*

'I am your sister and I live there, why can't you? After all, we are the same.'

'True, but you went to Lagos when you were very young. So you are used to the place. I shall find it very difficult.'

'This is what people say in the village until they get to Lagos, then they regret they didn't go there sooner. Look at me. I live in Lagos and I am doing well.'

'By the way, Christie, you have not told me how you are getting on in Lagos. My troubles seem to have covered every other thing. Looking at you, I can see you are enjoying Lagos. How do you live? What do you do? How are you getting on? The last letter I got from you was just before the war. I remember you said you had got a job in a firm as a receptionist or typist. Is that where you are still?'

Christie laughed shortly.

'No, no.'

'Tell me.'

'After I left secondary school I joined thousands of young boys and girls looking for work. As you know, our aunt's husband is a poor government worker. He did very well to send me to secondary school and I shall never forget him. However after leaving school, things became more and more difficult. His children from his second wife were growing up and his house became very congested. I had to share a room with a kind school mate who lived across the street. Her father is very rich. Every day I walked around attending useless interviews. One day I was waiting at a bus stop, feeling very

57

tired and disappointed, when a handsome young man in a flashy car stopped and offered me a lift. At first I refused but he smiled and assured me he had no ulterior motives. I didn't believe him but I was too tired to argue much longer. As soon as we drove off, he began the usual you-know. Where do you live? Where do you work? What is your name? And so on. I was used to all this and I had a complete set of false answers. I gave them without a single slip of tongue.'

Alekiri laughed.

'I said my name was Aduke – luckily I speak Yoruba very well. I said I was a clerk in the Ministry of Mines and Power, and so on.'

Alekiri laughed again.

'But the young man was very clever. When I had finished, he laughed and said: "Well done, radio announcer, now tell me your real name." I said I was telling the truth. He snatched my diary and tried to open it to see my real name. I snatched it back. As he was driving he could not do anything. I asked him to stop several houses before our own. He stopped. I thanked him and got out, and he drove off. Three days later, as I left the house to attend one more interview, the same man stopped by me. He smiled and said "Christie, where are you going? Come in." Alee, I was shocked. I said I was not Christie. He laughed the more. "Christiana Kinika, come in." He laughed again and told me where I lived. I stood by the pavement and refused to ride with him. He came out of the car and stood by me. I asked him, "Why are you so interested in me? What do you want? Who are you?" He said he was from Bendel State; his father was a rich contractor; he liked me so much, this and that, you know. Alee, Lagos boys can talk your pants off, believe me.'

Alekiri laughed. 'Don't tell me you entered the car.'

'That is exactly what I did. Within a week I was spending nights with him in motels and places like that. He never took me to where he lived, which he said was somewhere in Ikeja. As I was supposed to be sleeping with my classmate across the street, our aunt and her husband did not know what was

happening. This man Joe, he said his name was Joe, [...]
small presents, dresses, shoes, things like that, you [...]
promised to find me a job. When I asked him [...]
worked, he said he was a private businessman enga[...]
er ... what was it? ... er ... yes, clearing and forwarding. I
didn't know what that meant but I didn't bother. He was very
nice to me and I think I was beginning to like him very much,
or as they say, to fall in love. Mind you I don't believe in falling
in love. It is all rubbish. Anyway, after two months I became
pregnant. I told Joe. He laughed it off, and said he would
arrange an abortion. I had heard of too many sad abortion
stories and I was afraid.

'Soon after that, Joe disappeared and I never saw him
again. I cried and cried. In my third month of pregnancy our
aunt called me and questioned me. I admitted I was pregnant.
To my surprise she was happy. You know she has no child.
She said she would look after the child when it was born and
not to worry. Unluckily for her, I miscarried in the fourth
month. My aunt cried for days. A month later my aunt's
husband managed to get me a job in an engineering firm as a
receptionist. He had helped the expatriate director of the firm
to secure a contract with the Ministry of Defence. Actually all
he did was to show him the advertisement and tell him the
people he should meet in the Ministry.

'I was happy in my new job. The place was near, only about
twenty minutes by bus. The firm was a big one and many
people came to them for smaller contracts like supplying sand,
gravel, cement, furniture, and so on. After some time I knew
many of these contractors. One day a woman contractor came
into the office. She was very attractive and well dressed. She
was young too. I don't think she was more than thirty years
old. We liked each other at once. She said I resembled her
younger sister who died in a car crash two years before. I made
her some coffee. You know, as a receptionist you have to be an
expert coffee- and tea-maker. By the time she finished with the
boss, it was closing time and she offered me a lift. As her driver
drove us off she kept saying she liked me very much. Almost as

a man talks to a woman. She said, you are a pretty girl and you are wasting your time doing a receptionist job. "Did you pass secondary school?" I said, yes. She said, "Come and work for me". I did not understand. She said again, "Come and work for me; I am a contractor; I have my own company." She said, "How much do they pay you?" I told her. She said, "I shall pay you one and half times that. You will be my outdoor secretary. I have an indoor secretary, but I need someone to travel about with me. Men are useless. I tried a young man once. He was no good. As soon as I allowed him sleep with me he thought he was God. He started telling me what to do." Alee, I was surprised at her frankness. She spoke as if I was her daughter or as if we had been friends for long. She invited me to have lunch with her. I could not refuse.

'Alee, are you sleeping?'

'No, go on, Christie. I am wide awake.'

'She had a bungalow all to herself, with boys' quarters and so on. The rooms were well furnished. And the food we ate was wonderful. Alee, she treated me like her daughter. We ate from the same table. After the meal she asked me to work for her again. Still I had doubts. I asked her exactly what kind of job I would do. She said, "You will be my companion as I drive around like a mad woman looking for contracts. You will take care of my files and papers. When I go for interviews you will come along. Sometimes you will sign contracts as a witness. If a big man who will offer us a big contract wants to sleep with you, I shall expect you to do so. Sometimes I do so myself. Men are very stupid and I do not allow their stupidity to stand in my way. When you sleep with a man you will have double pay. But you must not fall in love with any man. When that happens then you become the stupid one. You will not be pregnant because I shall give you contraceptives. You will have my guest room which is in this house and you will eat with me. In short I shall treat you like a daughter if you behave well. Go and think about it. If you like my offer, give me a ring and you can start any time you like. I shall give you money to pay your employers a month's salary in lieu of notice". Then she opened her wallet and gave me ten pounds. She said, "That is a small present from me. My driver will take you home".

'Alee, as her driver took me home I thought I was dreaming. After three days I decided to join her. I told my aunt and her husband and they said I was mad and warned me against Lagos tricksters. I decided to go ahead without their approval. I gave my employers a month's notice and joined the madam. She did all that she said. She put me up in her guest room which was well furnished and I ate with her. All I did was drive about with her in her big air-conditioned car.'

'What was this woman's name?'

'Bimpe Adekurun. Sorry, I left that out.'

'Go on.'

'One of the first contracts was to furnish some government guest houses for over a hundred thousand pounds. Bimpe made all the contacts and signed the agreement. But the officer who was to give us the list of furniture became difficult. Bimpe sent me to him and the man said he wanted me or else nothing doing. I slept with him and left his house the next morning with the papers. As I handed over the papers to Bimpe she noticed I was sad. In fact I had been weeping. She smiled and said: "You are feeling like a prostitute, not so?" I nodded. She said: "Christie, my daughter, forget it. You are not a prostitute. The real prostitutes are the highly placed men in government who demand sex to do the jobs for which they are paid. What should we do? Starve because of stupid men? If we do, it means we too are stupid. They are the people to be ashamed, not us. Anyway, it will not happen often, but when it does don't let it worry you. Things will change. One day we shall have men in government who will do their job without first unzipping their trousers." At the end of the month Bimpe paid me double salary as she promised. She also took me to a boutique and bought me very expensive clothes. She said it was necessary for me to be very well dressed all the time. We went on like this for over a year. As the war was still

61

on we got a lot of contracts, especially food and uniform contracts. You know army business, always in a hurry. I was smart and madam liked me very much. She increased my salary and helped me to open a savings account. I was able to give my aunt money and presents from time to time. They noticed the difference in my clothes and general appearance and I had to tell them I had changed my job. It was too late for them to argue. Still they warned me to be very careful.

'Alee, are you awake?'

'Wide awake. Go on.'

'Madam and I became so intimate that she hid very little from me. She told me about her three marriages. She left her first husband because he drank too much and had too many lovers. Her second husband was a very rich and kind man. He did not bother her much. He was always occupied with his business. Unfortunately, he died of diabetes after two years of their marriage. In his will he left Bimpe a considerable amount. As members of the family were bothering her, she left them and set up as a contractor. Later she married for the third time. He was a young man, younger than madam. She said the man did no work. He spent her money and beat her up. So she drove him out and, according to her, she put full stop to marriage.'

'I don't blame her,' Alee said.

'Alee, that woman loved me. You know, after a while she allowed me to do small contracts in her name. She said she did not expect me to stay with her for ever and that I should now learn to handle contracts. Alee, she was wonderful. My bank account grew rapidly.

'Alee, believe me some people are making more money and much faster than before the war. There are many millionaires in Lagos and other large cities. But the opposite is happening in the villages. The people are poorer. Look at our father sleeping on the floor and eating with broken plates.'

'It is what the Bible says,' Alekiri replied, 'unto him that hath more shall ...'"

'No, no. I don't think it is like that. Some of the new

millionaires were poor workers like us before the war. They just happen to be where the money is and so they are taking it without thinking of the rest of us.'

'I am sure you are right,' Alekiri said, and added with a chuckle, 'and I hope you are getting near where the money is.'

They laughed.

'Alee, what people like me get is what in Lagos they call chickenfeed. In Lagos when you talk of money you mean millions of pounds.'

'Hm. But go on with Bimpe's story.'

'Well, a very sad thing happened. You know Bimpe had a bodyguard who always sat with the driver in front. He was a tall tough man and always carried two pistols. He tried to start an affair with me. I refused and told madam about it. She praised me for being open with her and said I should have nothing to do with the man because that would spoil her business. However, that is by the way.'

'You said a sad thing happened,' Alee said.

'Yes. You see, I don't know what happened but Bimpe quarrelled with the bodyguard and sacked him. The following Sunday while we were driving to the Bar Beach two armed men waylaid us. They shot the driver and when Bimpe refused to leave the car they shot her too. I opened the door and ran out shouting while the robbers drove away. Alee, I cried more for that woman than for our mother.'

'I cannot understand this kind of killing. When was this?'

'Less than a year ago. By this time I was so used to the contract business that I could not think of doing anything else. I had a good sum in the bank and I knew a lot of people. So I rented a small flat and bought a 'Beetle'. I could have bought a bigger car, but I was afraid of armed robbers. They were increasing in numbers. Also I did not think I could work alone, so I got one civil engineer as a partner. I get the contracts and he does more of the supervising. I supervise too, but not so much.'

'Do you sleep with him?'

'Yes, occasionally. Alee, I found that was the only way to

get along with him since he kept worrying me.'

'Is he married?'

'Luckily he is married and that helps a bit. But he is careless and his wife has known about the affair and is making trouble. I have no time for that kind of thing. I shall have to separate from the man as soon as we finish the contract we have now.'

'Christie, you have done very well.'

'I have not done badly. Now look Alee, come with me and let's work together. Forget this idiot who is bothering you here. All these men in the provinces have very narrow minds. They don't know what the world is doing. All they think about is their wife's arse. If you come with me you will be a completely different person within six months. You will ride a car and live a better life. Later you can think of marriage.'

'Christie, I don't think I can live in Lagos. It is too hot and fast for me. Also one of us should stay at home and look after our father. You know he is getting old.'

'So what do you want to do? To stay and wait for that idiot to forgive you?'

'I want to complete my teacher training. You know I was in the fourth year when I became pregnant.'

'After that?'

'I shall teach.'

'Teaching is a poor job. You are already in the contract business, why don't you continue?'

'The war has ended and much of the contract has stopped.'

'But soldiers still have to eat and put on clothes.'

'You see, Christie, I was not a contractor in the real sense. Doyin got the contracts and he allowed me to buy a few things like fish, yams and oil for him.'

'Why not become a full contractor yourself? You know some of the officers here. At least you know Major Dansuku,' Christie laughed.

'Sule is not interested in that kind of thing. He is interested in fighting, that's all. His fellow officers have made a lot of money in this war but Sule has nothing except his salary which he does not even save properly.'

'Okay, do what you like. If you need money, let me know.'

Christie looked at her watch. The luminous dials read 5 a.m. Outside in the street, a self-styled prophet of a spiritual church was ringing a bell and talking of the fall of Babylon and King Nebuchadnezzar.

Chapter V

'Get Arit back.'

'No, Ola.'

'Well then, get another girl, that's easy.'

'I suppose so,' Dansuku said rather absent-mindedly.

'I mean you have no choice now that Alee's husband is back.'

'I know, I know.' There was some irritation in Dansuku's voice.

Captain Olaitan shrugged and drained his glass of beer.

'I refuse to get attached to any girl. It creates problems in a war front.'

'I said the same thing until I met Alee. One day you too will get attached, believe me.'

Captain Olaitan shrugged again and picked up his beret. He turned it round and round carefully to ensure that the Octopus, the commando emblem, was at the correct spot, then put it on. He patted it gently to produce the usual rakish overhang to the right. He looked up at his friend who was studying his glass of beer. Though lower in rank, he was older than Major Dansuku. Six months before they were both captains, but Dansuku's posting to the front had earned him a rapid promotion. Captain Olaitan was at the rear. He preferred working out strategies to actual fighting. He was shorter and stouter than his friend, and his long, balding brow lent him an intellectual air, which was not entirely misleading. He had studied history and philosophy at the University before enlisting in the Nigerian Army Education Corps on a short-service commission. When the war broke out he had converted to combatant status under the 3rd Marine

Commandos. On joining the army his reading interests switched to politics and war histories, and he impressed senior officers with his knowledge of the various strategies used by the Allied Forces in the Second World War. He picked up his cane, then asked:

'What do you intend to do?'

'I am hoping Alee's husband will reject her.'

'Are you planning to marry her?'

'If possible, yes.'

'Have you asked her?'

'Mm.'

'And did she agree?'

'Mm-mm.' Dansuku shook his head, turning his glass of beer round and round on the table. Olaitan rose.

'Then what are you talking about?'

'You know, some women need persuading. No can turn to yes quite easily.'

Captain Olaitan sat down again.

'Look, Sule, let me give you some advice. I think you should let Alee go. You don't want to abduct another man's wife, do you? There is no need at all for all that complication. We may be here for quite some time and you don't want to be the target of hatred of Alee's husband and his relations, and possibly his clan.'

'That's rubbish, Ola. If Alee's husband rejects her and she agrees to marry me, I don't see what is wrong with that. Anyway, I am the cause of her troubles. I should not abandon her if she is thrown out.'

'It is not so simple. Put yourself in her husband's place. You find your wife with someone's baby, would you not be angry?'

Dansuku did not answer. He stared at his friend.

'You would, of course, and you are likely to tell the woman to pack and go to hell the first time you meet. Later you may cool off and take her back. What I am saying is that you should not snatch up Alee as soon as her husband tells her to go because it may take them a year or two to settle the quarrel.'

As Olaitan spoke, Dansuku's face fell. Ola was right as

usual. Damn him and his cold reasoning. But he had always been a good and dependable friend right from their childhood days when they played in the streets of Port Harcourt.

'Ola, go to hell!'

'Yessir!'

Captain Olaitan gave a mock salute and moved towards the door. As he turned the door knob he said: 'Just remember to put on your thinking cap, sir!'

Then he drove off.

Dansuku gulped another glass of beer and hissed through his teeth. Women again. First the English girl with her tiny waist and alluring crown of red hair, and then the Edo nurse with her stunning bottom, and now Alee with her ... with her ... now, what was her real attraction? He could not pinpoint it. She was just beautiful. No, it was not just her beauty. There were more beautiful girls around. She was simply his type of girl. That was it. His type of girl. They got on very well together. And the baby. Oh God. He refilled his glass, drained it and asked Bukar to bring him another bottle. Halfway through that he said:

'Bukar!'

'Sir.'

'Go with the driver and fetch Arit. Move!'

'Yessir!'

He heard the Land-Rover take off and leaned back in his chair. As the beer eroded his sadness and loneliness, he wondered how Arit would react. Would she feign anger and refuse to come or would she put on her nearest evening dress and jump into the truck? She was always in evening dress, that girl; always garishly groomed with green nail polish, blue mascara and high-heeled shoes. He had often wondered how she obtained these things during a war. The screech of brakes of the Land Rover broke his train of thought. Bukar came in and saluted.

'*Oga*, Arit say she cannot come.'

'Why?'

'There is another man in her house.'

By this time Dansuku was half drunk.

'Take four more soldiers and bring Arit and the man here.'

'*Oga*, I think the man is officer.'

'How do you know?'

'He has army Land Rover.'

'Okay, get out!'

'Yessir!'

Dansuku swallowed another mouthful of beer and tried to imagine Arit in her inevitable evening gown smoking and blowing smoke coquettishly at her new officer lover.

When Dansuku first met her, Arit was a modestly dressed young woman cowering with fright in a back room in Dansuku's father's house in Bende Street. Dansuku had gone to check whether his father's only house in Port Harcourt had been shelled. That was barely a week after the Biafran soldiers had been driven out of the city. The house was intact, but appeared deserted. He knocked at the door, half convinced there would be no answer. He turned the knob. The door was locked. He lifted his rifle butt to break it open but changed his mind. He walked towards the back of the house and tried a side entrance. That too was bolted inside. This door, now rickety with age, led into the open courtyard between the main house and the kitchens and conveniences behind. Dansuku nodded at the soldiers with him and they booted it open. Almost immediately a door was heard to slam in the main house. A rat jumped out of a dustbin and scurried towards the lavatory. At the noise of the slamming door Dansuku and his men cocked their rifles and approached the main building very cautiously. They knew there were Biafran soldiers still lurking around and they did not want to take chances. Dansuku entered one of the two corridors in the house, closely followed by his men. They paused and listened intently. The sound of a metal container crashing to the cement floor broke the silence. The soldiers looked at one another. Dansuku identified the room from which the sound came and pointed to the door leading to it. Two soldiers kicked it simultaneously and the old door broke open. Immediately they took cover on either side. Dansuku nodded again and the soldiers charged into the room, guns at the ready. The room appeared empty,

69

but the clothes hanging on the wall, the rumpled bedsheets on the bed, and a dressing table redolent with the smell of assorted powders and lotions indicated that the room was in use. A soldier opened the back window and as light flooded the room, a rustle and a whimper were heard under the bed.

'Come out!' Dansuku yelled.

'Please, please,' answered a voice, clearly feminine.

'After four, I fire. One, two …'

A young woman scrambled out, shaking with fright. The knot of her wrapper had loosened and as she tried to stand, it began to slide down her thighs. Quickly, she arrested the erring wrapper and nervously retied the knot.

'How many of you live in this house?'

'Four.'

'Where are they?'

'They have all gone out.'

'Show us their rooms.'

'Yes sir.'

'Move fast!'

'Yes sir!'

The girl pointed to two rooms on the other side of the corridor. The doors were forced, but the rooms yielded nothing of interest.

'Where are the men from?' Dansuku asked.

'Calabar.'

'What about you?'

'Same place.'

'What's your name?'

'Arit.'

'So you all planned to take over my father's house.'

'No sir,' Arit said quickly, alarmed.

'Never mind. Come with us.'

'Sir?'

'I say come with us. I have to ask you some more questions.'

'*Oga*, I swear I am not a Biafran at all. I swear I come from …'

'Shut up. Move!'

70

'Can I put on another dress?'

'Go on. One minute.'

As they emerged into the backyard, another rat jumped out of the dustbin and escaped along the same route to the latrine. Disgusted, Dansuku kicked the dustbin. It fell on its side spilling its murky contents. An empty milk can rolled off, grogrogroing along the concrete floor.

Back at his house in Forces Avenue, Major Dansuku had allocated a room to Arit, much to her surprise. He had asked her to bathe and help herself to any clothes she fancied in the wardrobe. The room obviously belonged to a woman and she must have left in a very great hurry. Half of the clothes were left behind. There was also a trunk full of georges, laces and other expensive clothes which Dansuku had carried to his own bedroom for safety. After bathing, Arit helped hersef to the cosmetics on the dressing table. Some jars of pomade and bottles of nail polish were strewn about the floor, evidence of a hurried departure. Arit surveyed her naked body in the tall mirror. She was in her late twenties. She did not look bad. Her face was alright, she thought, although she wished her nose was not quite so broad. She considered her hair her greatest asset. It was black and luxuriant. Hairdressers complained of its length when they had to plait it. Arit took full advantage of her hair. She dressed it in many styles and her face changed accordingly. She could look dark and alluring, open and friendly; now an innocent village girl, then a sophisticated Lagos-bound undergraduate in a hurry. Arit's long hair was now particularly useful in covering a small scar high on her right temple. She got that scar in a recent scuffle with another girl over her new officer lover. Her legs were her other asset. They were well formed. She would have liked a little more bottom, but, not to worry, she had enough to wiggle. She smiled at her reflection in the mirror. Ah, she really had to smoke less, for in spite of the smokers' toothpaste which she used, her teeth were losing their lustre. There was a knock at the door and she rushed for her wrapper on the bed. How foolish not to have bolted the door. She turned her back to

Dansuku and struggled to wrap the tangled cloth around her. He caught her arm and pushed her gently to the bed without a word. Confused, speechless and a little frightened, she did not resist.

'Thank you, Arit.'

'Yes, "thank you", after taking me by force. Let me go,' she said in mock anger.

'You know, I have not touched a woman for many weeks.'

'Why?'

'I have been busy fighting. Do you think we just walked into Port Harcourt?'

Arit stayed with Major Dansuku for a couple of weeks. The 3rd Marine Commandos were consolidating their hold on Port Harcourt and were in no hurry to push forward. Some said the commando unit was tied down by loot and women. Major Dansuku and the other officers did not listen. The capture of Port Harcourt was a major achievement and they thought they deserved a rest.

Dansuku soon discovered that Arit smoked and had many lovers. He was too busy to bother about all that. It was enough that he had her when he wanted her. He would treat her as a war-front diversion and no more.

Dansuku finished his beer and drunkenly staggered to his bedroom. He slept until late the next morning. Without bothering to shave and bathe, he ate breakfast and staggered back to bed. It was Sunday morning and he was not on duty. He felt lonely and thought of sending for Arit again but pride restrained him. That woman was cheeky. She was taunting him and right in his father's house too. Perhaps he should eject her from the house. Yes, and all the other tenants as well while he was at it. He would then renovate the house and rent it out properly. It should provide a sizeable income.

The house in Bende Street had a prominent place in Dansuku's childhood memories. He had spent many a holiday there. He would roam the streets and spend the pennies his father gave him in 'egg-knocking'. This was a favourite pastime of his during the guinea-fowl egg season. He would carefully select a hard-boiled egg from an egg-hawker's basket and a friend would do the same. They would then knock the eggs together. Usually one egg would break and its owner would lose it to the winner, who would either eat it or sell it at half price to the many urchins who usually formed the noisy audience at an egg-knock. Dansuku became an expert in the game. He could judge the shell strength of an egg by the colour and size of the egg. As an additional test he would knock the egg against his strong teeth. From the sound he made up his mind finally. He would then hold up the pointed end of the egg, exposing as little a surface area as possible. His opponent would protest and a long argument would ensue. The only fight he had with Ola arose from this. Ola was to do the knocking. He tried the end of his egg against Dansuku's gently. 'Show your egg,' he said, 'my egg can't even make contact.' Dansuku made further adjustments. Ola noticed that his friend wore a ring on the index finger that encircled the exposed portion of the egg.

'Sule, remove your ring. It will crack my egg.'

Several urchins joined in the protest.

'It is unfair,' said one.

'Sule is playing *ojoro*,' said another.

Sule said the ring was too tight to be removed.

'Were you born with it?'

'Will you die with it?'

Urchins who sided with Ola were indignant. In the end Sule removed the ring. Then came the moment. All the boys held their breath. Ola tried the exposed surface gently. He made contact. He gave a gentle blow. It fell on Sule's encircling index finger.

'Sule, you have covered the egg again.'

Sule relaxed his finger.

Crack!

The two boys looked at their eggs. It was Ola's that was broken. Sule stretched out his other hand to receive Ola's broken egg.

'You didn't display your egg well, that's why.'

Ola refused to hand over the egg and a scuffle followed. Sule and Ola took comical boxing stances they had observed in boxing films like *Gentleman Jim* and the other boys urged them on. There were many straight-lefts and upper-cuts but most of them merely fanned the air. Those that landed were feeble and inaccurate. In the end they were separated. Ola had to hand over his broken egg. The laws of egg-knocking were rigid and could not be broken.

In the innocent manner of children, they made up their quarrel soon afterwards and went off on a game of 'throw-throw'. For this each had a handful of rubber seeds which they had picked from Government Reservation Area where rubber trees provided shady comfort for British administrators and traders and a few Nigerians in the Senior Service. Ola selected the most spherical seed he had and threw it along the street. Sule rolled one of his in an attempt to hit Ola's. It missed and rolled beyond. Ola picked up his where it lay and without moving from that point aimed at Sule's. He missed. When they came to Sule's seed, Sule tried and missed. In this way they moved along the street which happily had very few cars in those days. Still, now and then cyclists cursed as the boys, playing with intense concentration, bumped into them. At the fifth attempt Ola hit Sule's seed, and according to the rules of the game, Sule paid him a seed. By the time hunger and fatigue brought the game to an end, they had covered a good half mile. Ola was clearly the winner: his pockets were bulging with seeds while Sule had just a few left. But hunger had to wait for there were more urgent considerations. The boys dashed off to a tailor in Niger Street to find out what progress he had made on their Accra Dance suits. The Accra Dance for the Easter season was to be staged in three days time. In spite of its name no one knew where the dance had originated from, or how it had come to Port Harcourt. For the past week or so the air had been alive with the deep vibrations of heavy bass drums and the shrill sound of many flutes. Sule had already got his mask made of wire gauze and painted with gay colours.

His father had *koboko* whips, so that should present no problem. He was too young to be a 'cowboy', so he had no need to hire a children's bicycle which would have served for a horse.

Yes, the tailor was as fast as he had promised. On arrival Sule saw his suit finished and on display. He felt very proud. He had chosen a light cotton material with a very bright floral pattern. The tailor had done a good job. The long-sleeved shirt and the trousers fitted him well. As he turned this way and that to admire himself in a mirror, the breeze fluttered the many frills worked into the dress. These frills gave the Accra Dance suit its distinctive character. Ola was equally jubilant. He stood side by side with his friend making comparisons. At last, with the dresses folded and tucked under their arms, the boys dashed to their homes.

The morning of the dance refused to break, but, no matter, the drums had begun to throb long before the muezzin in the mosque in Victoria Street called the faithful to prayer. By the time the rays of the sun had acquired some sting, Aggrey Road had become a restless rainbow sea of hundreds of boys in very colourful dresses. At the head of the procession were the 'cowboys'. This year the dance was spectacular because the head of the 'cowboys' was actually riding a horse. Adults jammed their doorways to watch. The other 'cowboys' rode bicycles in lieu of horses. Their *koboko* whips crackled and whistled menacingly as they cracked them repeatedly. But the heart of the dance was in the flutes and the huge bass drums. As the flutes shrilled, the seething crowd sang the comic choruses and Aggrey Road reverberated:

> *Ori-garri di n'Aba*
> *Dodokido!*
> *Ori-garri di n'Aba*
> *Dodokido!*

Sometimes the drums took over, and as they boomed, the dancers replied in thunderous unison:

> *Bumgudu bumgudu bum*
> *Ose!*

Bum bum bum bum bum
Ose!

Sule danced tirelessy and unabashedly thanks to his mask. When eventually the dancers moved to Bende Street, he did a special dance in front of his father's house and Mallam Dansuku threw him a shilling. Even when the main body of dancers had gone far towards the Borikiri end of the street, stragglers and admiring girls still thronged the street, generating a great deal of noise and dust and heat. Mallam Dansuku, a tall black burly man sweated in the steamy heat. He was always sweating and fanning himself with whatever came readily to hand – a piece of cardboard, a hat or a clammy singlet just pulled off his greasy body. Today he had a proper leather fan and he worked it absent-mindedly as he gazed at the retreating crowd of joyous youthful dancers. He remembered similar carnival dances he had participated in, back home in Kano decades ago and his eyes grew misty. As he watched, the head of the comet-like procession turned right and made for Niger Street.

'*Kai*!' he muttered, as he broke out of his reverie.

It was good to feel that his son was in that joyous crowd. Sule should grow into a strong healthy man. He was doing the best he could for him.

Sule's mother had died when he was four and his father had sent him back to Kano to live with his younger brother who was a stricter parent. Mallam Dansuku hoped young Sule would thereby have a disciplined upbringing and also acquire a good knowledge of the Koran from his brother, who taught in a Koranic school. A knowledge of the Koran Sule seemed to have in plenty, but his father had doubts on the matter of discipline. Still, he was sure the boy could have fared worse under him. At the time Sule's mother died he was living at Egbelu, a rural community some forty miles from Port Harcourt. He was the head of a Hausa community of six or so families. He was then a butcher, getting his cows from Port Harcourt after they had trekked for months from the north. When later he branched out into the trade in cola nuts, onions and beans, the need to stay in Port Harcourt arose, for these goods sold much faster in Ogwumabiri, the great central market of Port Harcourt. A retired senior civil servant from Sierra Leone was going home for good and had put his house on sale. Mallam Dansuku bought the house in Bende Street and made an outright payment without much trouble. When he moved into Port Harcourt he prospered considerably and was soon able to build a house back in Kano.

Mallam Dansuku liked Port Harcourt very much. In the forties it was a clean little town, cleaner by far than giant Kano. The six famous streets of which Bende was one were long, straight and clean. The gutters were regularly cleaned and the ever vigilant sanitary inspectors and the police arrested anyone caught pissing or dropping litter in the streets. Indeed the sanitary inspectors were so thorough that they inspected private water pots to check for mosquito larvae. When Dansuku first moved into his house he thought the pot inspection was a joke. When to his surprise he was charged in court and fined, he learnt a hard lesson.

Chapter VI

Christie and Alekiri were ready, Mama Iyabo was not. Each time Alekiri poked her head into the house and called, Mama Iyabo answered in a muffled voice from the bedroom. When Alekiri went for the third time Mama Iyabo was desperate.

'Alee, come, come, come!'

'What is it?' Alekiri went into the living room.

'Come into the bedroom.'

Alekiri found Mama Iyabo struggling with a headtie. The large shiny and slippery scarf defied all her attempts to coax it into the then popular 'commando style.' Alekiri came to the rescue. What made the operation more difficult was Mama Iyabo's wig. Each time they thought success had been achieved the wig came off and with it the headtie.

'Mama Iyabo, take off the wig. You have a lot of hair,' Alekiri advised.

'But it is rumpled and unplaited. I don't want to look like a mad woman when I remove my headtie in the village.'

So the wig had to stay. Later Christie joined them and after much tying and untying, joking and giggling, the commando style was finally achieved.

'Don't touch it!' Alekiri warned.

'God forbid!' Mama Iyabo said.

The effort was certainly not wasted. When Mama Iyabo finally emerged from the house she looked resplendent in her expensive up-and-down lace outfit. She wore a heavy gold necklace and its pendant, shaped like a tiger's tooth, rested between her big breasts. Massive spider-and-web earrings and thick bangles coiled like snakes all in solid gold made up the outfit. The woman had not chosen these gold ornaments herself. Once when she complained that she lacked these things, Doyin had simply gone to a rich goldsmith at Ibadan and bought up nearly all that the man had in stock. Tall and big, Mama Iyabo's presence might have been overpowering but for her frequent smiles and laughter. The innocence and friendliness in her laughter were charming and infectious. Christie's dress was more controlled. Her white lace blouse was a perfect fit and must have been made by an expensive seamstress. Her george wrapper though expensive was not loud. She too wore a gold necklace but it was a thin chain. Her earrings were tiny gold butterflies. Her white handbag and black-and-white shoes blended with her clothes. The overall effect was one of pleasant colour harmony. Her make-up was simple but sophisticated. Her eyebrows, eyelashes and lips had received a lot of attention but they looked natural. Indeed it was easy to see that Christie did not belong to the war-torn city of Port Harcourt. Alekiri was in one of her working dresses: an up-and-down print suit, set off by a simple headtie and a necklace of beads. She wore no make-up and this appeared to emphasize her youthfulness and freshness.

When they arrived at Ohiamini, Kinika and his wife Wiche were waiting for them. His sitting room had been cleaned and furnished with comfortable chairs. There was even a low centre table and two side stools. Christie had arranged for all these. War or no war she did not want her father to appear too wretched in front of strangers.

'Nana, this is my friend. Mama Iyabo this is my father.'
'Ee-yah!' Mama Iyabo exclaimed.
Kinika put out his hand to shake Mama Iyabo but to his surprise she drew near and hugged him. When presently Kinika recovered from his surprise he tried to return the gesture but as his two hands barely managed to go half-way round Mama Iyabo's body, he could not achieve a real hug. Anyway this encounter pleased him very much and he liked Mama Iyabo instantly. Mama Iyabo went on to embrace Wiche and the children. Azunda, Kinika's neighbour had just

come back from tapping palm wine when he heard the arrival of the vehicle in Kinika's compound. He decided to investigate and was just in time to see Kinika in Mama Iyabo's embrace. Azunda's head reeled. How on earth did Kinika find himself in the arms of this fantastic woman? When he found Mama Iyabo embracing Wiche and the children he thought he stood a chance for a hug. He was clad in a tattered shirt and khaki shorts and smelled heavily of palm wine. When he came forward and Alekiri introduced him, his two arms began to travel out for a hug. Unfortunately as Mama Iyabo was busy retying her wrapper she could only manage a handshake with her right hand, while the left finished off the retying process. But Azunda's two hands had travelled too far out to return empty with dignity. He ignored Mama Iyabo's hand and moved closer to embrace her. The woman laughed and hugged him with one hand. The onlookers laughed and Kinika ended coughing.

'Azunda, you are a rascal,' Kinika said between coughs.

'Thanks. I suppose you think pretty women are meant for you alone.'

There was more laughter. Azunda hobbled back to his compound and brought the keg of palm wine he had just tapped. It was fresh and delicious.

'This is for our visitors,' he said, 'and especially for my wife.'

'Who is your wife?' Kinika asked.

'This one,' he said, pointing at Mama Iyabo.

'My friend, you will find yourself in prison sooner than you think.'

'That is to say she is married?'

'Yes, you rogue.'

'*Chei*, I am too late,' Azunda said comically.

When Kinika interpreted the conversation to Mama Iyabo, she said to Azunda:

'Papa, don't worry, you will be my second husband,' and drew laughter.

As Azunda moved away Wiche remarked quietly to her husband in their language:

'It is rare to see the rich embrace poor people like us in this way. Wealth always separates people.'

'That is true, but we are not that poor. After all, Christie has a car too.'

'Has she?'

'Yes. Has she not told you?'

'No. Why did she not bring it home?'

'Lagos is far. It is not Port Harcourt, you know.'

Later, over palm wine and beer, Kinika said:

'Yesterday I sent a messenger to Ibekwe to inform him of your visit. He said he had arranged to go to Port Harcourt to see to his business and would not be back until evening.'

'Ah, but we cannot detain Mama Iyabo here until night,' Alekiri said.

But Mama Iyabo raised no objections. She would wait. Kinika was impressed and expressed his appreciation. Turning to Alekiri, he said:

'Alee.'

'Yes, Nana.'

'It appears Wibari is alive.'

Alekiri dropped the glass she had in hand and stared at her father.

'Yes, the messenger I sent to Ibekwe came back to tell us that he saw her.'

Alekiri got up and jumped up and down a couple of times. Hysterically, she hugged Christie, Mama Iyabo, and Kinika in turns upsetting the keg of palm wine. She bent low and danced to imaginary music and straightened up again, her eyes streaming with tears. Then she disappeared into the bedroom. Christie ran after her.

'Take your time. Don't hurt yourself.'

'No, I won't, I won't, I won't, I won't …' and turned the words into a song. Hastily she packed some biscuits and clothes into a handbag and reappeared in the sitting room.

'Where are you going?' Kinika asked.

'To see Wibari.'

'Let's all go in the van,' Christie suggested.

'No, I shall go alone with the driver.'

'Is it safe?'

'Ibekwe is away, so there should be no problems.'

Alekiri rushed out and pulled the driver to the van. The driver looked at Mama Iyabo for instructions. She nodded at him. He rose and entered the car wondering what Alekiri's excitement was all about. In a few minutes they had covered the mile or so to Ibekwe's place. Most adults had gone to the farm; the women to harvest cassava two and a half years old and overgrown with bush, the men to clear the bush for farming. As the car approached, children playing around ran towards it. Soon, the cry of 'Mama Wibari, Mama Wibari' rent the air. When the vehicle stopped the children crowded round it. Alekiri studied them urgently searching for that one face. It was not there. Presently another group of children came to join the others. As they ran, one of them was dragging another by the hand and saying:

'Wibari, your Mama has come.'

Alekiri turned towards the approaching children. Oh, yes, she could never mistake her even after ten years. She ran forward, embraced, and carried her dancing round and round. The child clung to her. The other children looked on, jumping up and down, infected with Alekiri's intense excitement. She hugged the child tightly and wept. When Ibekwe's mother, Erinwo, came out to investigate, Alekiri went to greet her.

'Mama.'

'Alekiri, so you are here at last.'

'Mama ... I am so glad, so very glad Wibari is alive. Thank God, thank God.'

She nuzzled the child, went back to the van, retrieved some biscuits, and gave her some. She wondered what to do about the many children whose eyes devoured the biscuits. In her hurry she had not reckoned with the usual welcoming crowd. But there was no escape. She set Wibari down for a moment and doled out the remaining biscuits to the children, each receiving little more than a crumb. Then they dispersed.

Erinwo had disappeared into the house to avoid any unpleasant conversation with her daughter-in-law. Alekiri sat on a chair in the reception hut and studied her long-lost child. She had grown rapidly. Although rather thin, she did not look too bad. At least she was not ill, thank God. She set her on her knees and rocked her.

'Wibari.'

'Mm.'

'You remember your mama, not so?'

The child nodded.

'Have you eaten?'

The child nodded again.

'You will go with me, not so?'

'Mm.'

'You are taking her nowhere,' Erinwo said, coming out of the room. 'You should come back and stay with your husband. If you can't, then leave the child alone. She is used to doing without you.'

Alekiri was speechless, not knowing what to say. Then Ibekwe walked into the compound.

'So, this harlot is here at last,' he spat out. 'You had better let go that child whom you abandoned, if you value your life.'

Ibekwe tossed his handbag carelessly into the verandah and strode menacingly towards her.

'I say, leave that child, you harlot.'

In that moment Alekiri felt a loneliness she had never experienced before. The man coming towards her was not her husband. This was a mad man in the image of her husband. Ibekwe's face was contorted with rage and his eyes were bloodshot. What would she do? She knew she could not fight him. She had neither the strength nor the inclination to do so. She could not run to Erinwo; she would lock the door against her. Ibekwe was close now. She did not want Wibari to be hurt, so she put her down and said with fright:

'Go, go and tell your grandmother that Ibekwe wants to kill me.'

She barely finished the sentence when Ibekwe grabbed her.

'Driver, driver, come-o-o,' she screamed.

The driver came but Ibekwe gave him such a threatening look that he stood rooted to the spot. During this momentary distraction Alekiri struggled free. Ibekwe gave chase, caught her and as she screamed, struck her hard repeatedly on the face. Soon she was bleeding from the mouth and nose, and her left eye became bloodshot. Erinwo came out and looked on passively. When she saw Alekiri's bleeding face she was a little uncomfortable.

'Don't use your fist. Use a cane if you must beat her. You don't want a corpse on your hands.'

Ibekwe proceeded to drag Alekiri to a bush which promised to yield some canes. But the going was hard as she was struggling frantically. Up till now she had not attempted to return a blow. Perhaps she had no chance to try, perhaps she felt guilty, perhaps both. But as they came close to the bush, her teeth closed on Ibekwe's left hand. He gave her a vicious slap which sent her sprawling on the ground. As she wailed and thrashed about, Ibekwe procured a thick stick.

'*Oga*, I beg you, I beg you,' the driver pleaded, placing himself between husband and wife. Grabbing the driver by his shirt, Ibekwe tossed him to one side.

'Get out or you will die for what you don't know,' he roared.

His shirt torn, the driver ran into the vehicle and drove off, the tires screeching as he accelerated madly. By this time Alekiri had managed to get up. Ibekwe rushed at her again and brought the stick crashing on her head. The wood snapped in two. As he cast around for another stick, Alekiri let out a harrowing scream. But Ibekwe had gone berserk. Picking up another stick, he made for her again. This time, Alekiri rushed at him and held him round the waist, making it difficult for him to flog her. He tugged at her hands madly, loosened her hold and pushed her violently. She fell and rolled on the ground. In the struggle he had dropped the stick and a neighbour who had run to the scene had picked it up and hurled it far into the bush. Ibekwe was undeterred. Before the neighbours could close on him he sat on Alekiri's belly and gave her more blows. Faint and weak Alekiri thought she was about to die. Ibekwe's figure became a blur, a vague black mountain of death. A blow landed on her breast and the stinging pain brought a momentary surge of strength. Like an animal at bay she struggled frantically, scratched his face with her nails and tore his shirt. A deep scratch in the nose made him wince. He let her go and tried to rise. Alekiri, convinced he was going to look for another stick, grabbed his penis. Alarmed, Ibekwe struck her even harder but that only tightened her grip.

'Let me go!' he cried. 'Let me go!'

'No. Kill me, kill me, and let me rest. There is nothing left. I am a useless mother, a harlot, an evil woman. Let me die!'

Now hysterical, she pulled harder and Ibekwe screamed. By this time more neighbours had moved in and were trying to separate them. Ibekwe held up his hands in the air.

'You can see, I have left her. Tell her to let me go.'

Alekiri pulled again. Ibekwe yelled and the whites of his eyes began to stare. Large beads of sweat hung on his face.

'Woman, you are killing your husband. Let him go,' a neighbour said.

With her eyes swollen and closed, Alekiri appeared unaware of the noise of the rapidly increasing crowd. Ibekwe's shorts where a mess. Nearly half of it was in Alekiri's hands. As she squeezed the shorts and its content, Ibekwe had an erection which improved her hold. His pain worsened. He slumped from his squatting position to the ground and lay facing his wife. A classic love position had turned into one of bitterness and agony. Desperate now, two men held Alekiri's wrists and began to twist them cruelly.

'Leave me and I shall let him go.'

When she let go, Ibekwe got up, staggered to his room and banged the door. By this time Christie and Mama Iyabo had arrived in the van. They were just in time to see Alekiri release her husband, and raise herself to a sitting position. Her nose and mouth were caked with blood and dust and her left eye was swollen and completely closed. Her blouse was in tatters and the right shoulder strap of her bra was cut.

Speechless and shaking with rage, Christie picked up her sister and with Mama Iyabo's help put her in the car. Some neighbours who had not seen Christie for years offered feeble greetings. They knew it was useless. Christie did not utter a word. Tears trickled down her face.

When Kinika saw his daughter, he was enraged but he restrained his anger. There were traditional channels for dealing with such matters and he would use them. He let Christie and Mama Iyabo take Alekiri back to Port Harcourt. The next day, at the hospital the doctor examined her and said that although her wounds were severe they were all superficial and no internal organs had been damaged. He was not too sure about the eye and advised them to consult the eye specialist two doors away. He then prescribed painkillers and mild sedatives. Christie insisted on a medical report and got it. The eye-specialist said Alekiri's left eye had slight lacerations but was intact. He prescribed an eye lotion.

That night, as Alekiri lay on her bed in Ohaeto Street, the events of the previous day kept flashing through her mind. As she relived the fight, she tossed this way and that, parrying imaginary blows. Everything came alive in mercilessly vivid pictures. There was Erinwo, an old thin woman with the hatred of years lurking in her breast; Wibari, staring at her new-found mother and raging father; the houses, gloomy and still, suffering from a thirty-month neglect; the neighbours and their cacophony and confused movement; the driver, small and frail, making futile motions; Christie, weeping and shaking with a deep love and anger; Mama Iyabo, distressed. Superimposed on all this was Ibekwe's face, fiendish with rage; the face of a stranger, a mad man. It was as if they had never looked at each other lovingly, never spoken in whispers and planned secret meeting places where they cuddled and moaned in ecstasy, never offered each other drinks in the presence of the elders to affirm their love, never enjoyed together that exciting first meal as man and wife, never made love with bewildering passion to the accompaniment of tropical rainstorms beating wildly on the tin roof. Ibekwe had never before beaten her or even quarrelled violently with her. Only profound bitterness and anger could have led him to beat and hurt her the way he had done. So, was her offence heinous and unpardonable? A wave of anguish swept over her and she sobbed. But then there were other women in her position. Were they receiving the same rough treatment from their husbands? And what of the men themselves? Did they not have lady friends during the war? A pity that men could not get pregnant!

What was she to do? Clearly Ibekwe felt very hurt and that brutal fight was the manifestation of a deep estrangement. What bothered her, in fact annoyed her, was that she still loved the man. Beyond the temporarily insane man, beyond the blind rage and the sting of blows, she could still imagine a loving, caring husband. This love was now like the ghost that was said to escape from the body at death, leaving behind a stinking corpse. Her marriage was a stinking mess, bereft of its powerful love and beauty. Ibekwe's contorted face formed again and again in the darkness. She studied it. It was grim and set; all the old smile-creases were transformed into creases of intense hatred. She heaved a sigh. Ghosts never reinhabit corpses; the smiles would never never return.

Thirty months ago she was a young smiling woman revelling in what seemed a perpetual honeymoon. Today Alekiri thought of herself as an old unhappy woman with a bruised and swollen face, unloved and discarded. For a moment she contemplated suicide. Jump into a well? Lie across a train track? Poison? *What?*

'Alee,' came Christie's voice in the darkness.

'Mm.'

'Come to Lagos with me and rest for a while. You can come back whenever you want.'

'I want to … to … to complete my teacher training.'

'A month in Lagos will not stop you from doing your

teacher training.'

'I want to start now to make inquiries.'

'You are afraid of Lagos,' Christie said with some resentment. She felt very sorry for her sister and had an overwhelming desire to comfort her and protect her from what she could only see as a disastrous future.

'And perhaps after all these years in Lagos, I feel strange to you.'

Alekiri hugged her sister.

'Don't talk like that Christie, don't.'

'It seems I have been sold off to Lagos. No one seems to bother much about what happens to me.'

Suddenly it was Alekiri's turn to comfort and reassure her sister.

'I shall come with you then. I shall bring my baby along.'

'You don't have to if you don't want to.'

'Christie, I shan't lie to you. I am afraid of Lagos. But I know you will look after me. And our aunt is there too. Christie, I shall come with you, I shall come. But I have to recover first. You don't want your friends to see your sister for the first time with a swollen eye, do you?' They laughed.

'You should be much better two weeks from now.'

'Yes.'

'Then we can travel?'

'Mm.'

'That's good,' Christie said, hugging her sister.

'A month in Lagos will help you forget your horrible husband and your sufferings during the war.'

'Still, some things are unforgettable. I can't forget my rescue at the front by Sule and I can't forget Ibekwe's beating.'

'That's true, but time makes a difference.'

'Yes, a long long time can make a difference in how we remember events, but the events themselves become a part of us, like the scar from a wound.'

As they conversed the thought of suicide receded slowly in Alekiri's mind. She seemed to have been talking herself out of it.

Chapter VII

Many people in Kenke village of Ohiamini community agreed that the fight between Ibekwe and his wife had been unusually brutal. Only a few young men thought Alekiri deserved the beating she got. Although Erinwo did not like Alekiri, the fight disturbed her, if only because it exposed her to adverse criticism. Women in her age group thought it was callous, indeed wicked, to have looked on while her son pumelled her daughter-in-law, another woman's daughter. How would she like her own daughter to be beaten up in the same way? they asked. As criticism mounted she became increasingly uncomfortable. The women of the village were not inhibited in matters like this. They spoke out, not caring who was annoyed, so long as they thought they were in the right.

'Erinwo has a dry heart,' said one. 'She is abominable,' said another. The most outspoken was Tia the leader of Omirinya which comprised all women born in Kenke, married or not, and wherever they may be. The day after the fight, Tia went straight to Erinwo and confronted her.

'You were there when your son was beating up Alekiri and you did nothing. Why?'

'What could I do? I have no strength to struggle with young people.'

'You could have shouted for help.'

'I was tired and besides I had a headache.'

'How would you feel if your daughter were treated like that?'

'You talk as if I beat her up myself.'

'Well you did. You and your son are one.'

'Tia are you insulting me in my house?'

'Yes, I am. I think you are wicked. Summon me before the elders if you think I have abused you.'

As leader of Omirinya, Erinwo knew that Tia had much influence and that she was expected to stand for the rights of the women in Kenke village.

'The matter will be settled, don't worry,' Erinwo said appeasingly. A tall, thin and rather languid woman, she hated heated verbal exchanges.

'Pray that Alekiri does not fall ill. If that happens you will answer for it.'

That evening, Erinwo paid Kinika a visit. He and Wiche received her politely but coldly. As they had not met since the war ended they exchanged good wishes and thanked the gods for preserving their lives. Then Erinwo came to the matter in her mind.

'Kinika I have come to talk about Alekiri and her husband.'

'Go on,' Kinika said coolly, but his wife Wiche could not restrain herself.

'Erinwo, can't you first find out the state of Alekiri's health? Can your son marry a corpse?'

'God forbid!' Erinwo said.

'Then behave properly like one who sucked a mother's breast.'

'Kinika, restrain your wife. I did not come here to be insulted. In fact I am here to talk to you not to her.'

But Erinwo did not reckon with Wiche's fury.

'I shall insult you twenty times over,' Wiche said, pointing at Erinwo with fingers only a few inches from her face. 'You allowed your son to beat up my daughter almost to the point of death, and you talk of insult? God will punish you and your son.'

Wiche's voice was so loud that neighbours began to gather and Erinwo grew very uncomfortable.

'I don't want to see your face here. GET OUT! If Ibekwe rejects our daughter, we shall not reject her. What did she do? Hm? What did she do? Did she commit murder? Get out I say.'

Wiche moved menacingly towards Erinwo but neighbours

held her. All this time, Kinika sat rigidly in his chair in the reception hall, grinding his teeth. Azunda said:

'Kinika, do something and stop these quarrelling women.'

'Azunda, my friend, what do you want me to do?' Kinika gave a short, mirthless laugh. 'What will I not see as a result of this war? A young man comes right into my compound to insult me because I allowed him marry my daughter. Then he beats her up almost to the point of death and his mother comes babbling like a fool. Hmm! *Cha*! What have I not seen in this war?'

Erinwo was no fool. She knew when to retrace her steps. She said:

'Kinika, my in-law, I understand your anger. Anyone whose child is flogged will be angry. I have come to …'

'Flogged!'

'Please listen …'

'Flogged! If I flogged you like that you would go straight to the spirit world.'

'Ibekwe will make amends when a settlement …'

'Listen, old woman. Your son came here and told me his marriage with Alekiri was ended. That insult is enough to …'

'Ibekwe is a child. Don't judge him too harshly.'

'I didn't know he was a child. Now that you have told me, he will have nothing to do with my daughter.'

'Kinika, don't talk like that. We shall settle. This is not the first time a husband and wife …'

'Until he comes here and wipes his mouth of that insult, no settlement is possible. In any case you are wasting your time if your son is not interested. Go, go away Erinwo.'

Erinwo went back knowing that matters were more complicated than she had thought. In his bid to punish his wife, Ibekwe appeared to have aroused a lot of sympathy for her. At first Erinwo thought the entire Ohiamini community would side with her son and heap blame on his wife. Now she was not quite so sure.

She spoke to other members of the family. They blamed her for not consulting with them before going to Kinika to talk

91

nonsense. They said the trouble with her was that she assumed that she could deal exclusively with matters concerning Ibekwe simply because he was her son. See what a mess she and her son had made. Ibekwe was called in and ordered to appease Kinika before attempting any settlement.

'I am not a child,' Ibekwe said vehemently, 'I know my own mind. I have said the marriage is over and that is the end of the matter. Anyone not satisfied with that can marry Alekiri himself.'

Ibekwe could not be persuaded. More than that, he threatened to fight anyone who suggested a settlement. But this kind of threat had no effect whatsoever on Omirinya who heard of Erinwo's abortive visit to Kinika almost before she left Kinika's compound. The village is an open book in which all may read the day-to-day and hour-to-hour happenings. At the next meeting of the women, Tia raised the issue.

'We are about to lose a married woman in Kenke village and we cannot look on and let that happen. What shall we do?'

The response was enthusiastic and the decision unanimous. They would summon Ibekwe and his wife to a hearing and effect a settlement. This kind of peacemaking was usual and was in fact an important function of Omirinya.

When Ibekwe received the message he told his mother bluntly he was not interested in any settlement.

'Ibekwe, you cannot defy Omirinya. You should know that.'

'I don't care,' Ibekwe said in English.

'My son, this is not *adonkia* business. You must attend the peace meeting. If you don't, no one would ever side with you. Omirinya have to be handled delicately like an earthenware pot. Can you alone bury me when I die?'

And herein lay Omirinya's trump card. They were at the centre of many of the important rituals without which no corpse in Kenke or any other village in Erekwi clan could be buried. And it did not matter whether the dead person was a Christian and willed to be buried as such. Christian burial alone was not considered enough to send the dead properly to the spirit world. Erinwo knew all this only too well. She herself was a member of the Omirinya of her village.

Ibekwe paused in thought. His mother was right of course. Very well, he would go through the motions to avoid the anger of Omirinya, but on no account would he accept their recommendations, which were easily predictable. The peace meeting was to be held in Wotai's compound. Wotai was the elder of Kenke village. Ibekwe was a distant cousin of his. He had not intervened so far in Ibekwe's quarrel with his wife because he himself was immersed in his share of war-inflicted sorrows. He had lost a wife, and his first two sons, both in their twenties. The back wall of his house had fallen and he was yet to find money to rebuild it. Meanwhile he occupied his dead wife's house. His other wife was still recovering from kwashiorkor. Her feet were less swollen now but she was still too weak for active farming.

When Tia brought Wotai the news, he was relieved.

'I am glad Omirinya are going to look into this matter. I have not been able to intervene.'

'Dede your troubles are many. In fact Ibekwe should be looking after you,' Tia said with sympathy.

'The fact is, I have not seen Alekiri since the war ended. When I asked Erinwo about her, all she told me was that she was living with a soldier in Port Harcourt. I said to myself I shall wait till she comes back, because I don't want to have anything to do with soldiers for the rest of my life. Biafran soldiers, Nigerian soldiers, they are all hard-hearted.'

'I don't think Alekiri is living with any soldier, but we shall soon find out.'

'Fortunately my reception hut is standing and in good condition. All it needs is a broom. You may use it whenever you want.'

Tia decided to contact Alekiri herself and if possible get her story beforehand. When Kinika informed her Alekiri was in Port Harcourt she decided to see her there. When she told her husband she was going to Port Harcourt to see Alekiri he had no objections. In fact he gave her active encouragement. He was proud of her role in the village and hardly ever put any difficulty in her way. What made it easier for him to adopt this attitude was his firm belief that Tia was faithful to him. She was unlike some members of Omirinya who, under the pretext of attending meetings, would disappear briefly into their lovers' embrace.

Tia had some difficulty in tracing Alekiri's house in Ohaeto Street. Alekiri embraced her warmly. The presence of this tall, strong, plain-faced woman was reassuring. How she wished Tia had come before the fight with Ibekwe.

'I cannot say no to Omirinya,' Alekiri said. 'I shall come whenever you ask me.'

'Next Sunday?'

'All right.'

Tia studied Alekiri with sympathy.

'And how are you feeling?'

'Better, after a lot of treatment.'

Alekiri's baby stirred, then cried on the sofa where she was sleeping. She moved over and patted her gently to sleep again.

'A bad dream,' Tia observed.

'Yes.'

'What really happened to you during the war?'

Very briefly Alekiri narrated her experiences and added:

'I don't think Omirinya can resolve my quarrel with Ibekwe. The recent fight has worsened everything. I am not sure I want to go back to him.'

'Shut up! Don't talk like that. Of course you will go back to him. You are not married to this soldier, are you?'

'Mm-mm.'

'Thank God.'

'Why? Is Major Dansuku not a man like Ibekwe?'

'I am sure he is.'

'So why do you say thank God?'

'Marrying a man from so far away sounds a little strange.'

'Many women have done so.'

'That may be so, but please don't be one of them.'

Alekiri laughed shortly.

'You know Ibekwe is still young. Also he is proud. He is very angry now but he will cool down.'

'I don't think so.'

'He will.'

'We shall see.'

'Alee, I shall do my best to talk Ibekwe out of his anger, so don't let me down.'

'How?'

'By refusing to go back to him. Tell me you will go back, go on, tell me.'

'But if the man doesn't want me …'

'Never mind, say yes.'

Alekiri paused and stared at Tia whose face was full of kindness and concern. Alekiri knew her well. Her concern was genuine. It arose partly from her nature and partly from her commitment to the integrity of the village. One woman divorced was one woman lost to Kenke village, one mother lost to many potential children, one voice missing in communal singing and the cheering of wrestlers, one beautiful face lost in the gay Sunday crowd leaving the small quaint church of Ohiamini.

'Yes', Alekiri said at last.

'Thank you. We can't lose a woman like you in Kenke. I am leaving now. Greet Christie and say I want to see her very much. I can't count the years that have gone by since she left for Lagos.'

Next Sunday, the Omirinya of Kenke gathered in Wotai's reception hall. It was large enough to accommodate all of them and with room to spare. The enclosing dwarf wall was tempting, but no woman sat on it. It was considered undignified for a woman to perch precariously on a half-wall. When Ibekwe sat on it, the women objected and gave him a chair.

'What is the difference?' Ibekwe asked.

'When you perch, your words don't sit properly, they perch also,' Tia said, drawing laughter.

Alekiri, Christie, Wiche and two other women from Ekere, Kinika's village, sat opposite Ibekwe and his mother. Wotai entered the hall carrying a bottle of *akaneme*, the local gin. Behind him came a boy carrying a keg of palm wine. He greeted the women and said:

'You cannot assemble here without receiving my greetings. Here are drinks for you. Do your best for Ibekwe and his wife. They are both my children. What you are doing is what I should have done in the first place, but you know how it is.'

'Don't worry, Dede,' Tia said, 'we know how it is. Thank you for the drinks. Sit down and have a sip with us.'

After the ceremonies, Tatai, the women's provost, or Kotima as they called her, blew her whistle and there was dead silence. According to their rules anyone who spoke thereafter without permission would pay a fine of a bottle of local gin – which at the time meant a loss of four shillings. Tia stood, cleared her contralto voice and greeted the gathering.

'*Omirinya mma*!

'*Diali*!

'*Omirinya mma*!

'*Diali*!'

Ibekwe felt overwhelmed by the feminine presence. Elei and another friend he had brought along provided little relief.

'Ibekwe,' Tia began, 'we Omirinya have heard of the quarrel between you and your wife and in particular the recent fight. Personally I did not think that after going through over two years of fighting between Nigeria and Biafra, anyone would fight again so soon. Women did you think so?'

'No, no,' came the chorus.

'We are here to settle your quarrel so that both of you can live peacefully again. Tell us your grievances without anger or shouting. We are listening.'

For a while Ibekwe was silent. He wanted to tell the women straight away that he was not interested in any settlement. A second mind told him that would not do. The women could not be dismissed so easily. He would have to go through the motions. Just then Wotai's son came in and whispered in Ibekwe's ears. Ibekwe rose, obtained permission from the women and went to Wotai.

'Ibekwe,' the old man said, 'you must not disgrace your wife.'

'Dede, she has disgraced herself already.'

'Then don't disgrace her further. Remember you will both live together again.'

'Not me. God forbid!'

'You will, so don't talk in a way that will shame her before her fellow women. That would only deepen the quarrel.'

'Don't worry, Dede. I shall speak as little as possible. All I want is to get rid of the woman.'

Wotai studied his young cousin's face and shook his head slowly. There was a hardness in it which he did not like.

Back to the women Ibekwe began:

'I have two complaints against Alekiri, both of them serious ... .'

'Do you observe he no longer calls her Alee but Alekiri,' one woman whispered to another.

'... First of all, she abandoned our daughter Wibari at the war front ... .'

'No, no, that is false.'

'He is lying; Alee couldn't have done that.'

'*Prrr*. Was this man at the war front at all?'

So many women were having asides that the combined buzz became noticeable. The Kotima's whistle shrilled and enforced silence.

'It was at Omademe,' Ibekwe went on. 'I went to the bush to look for food. Before I came back there was an attack. All the refugees began to run. You all know what it was like. Alekiri was nowhere to be found. A woman who had three of her own children to look after was the person I found clutching my daughter Wibari and wondering what to do with her. I asked, where is Alekiri? She said she had fled. I thanked her and carried the child ... .'

'It was not exactly like that, I am sure.'

97

'He is trying to sweeten his story.'

'He too abandoned his wife and child.'

'... As I ran in the direction in which everyone was going, I saw Alekiri running like a mad woman. I called her several times. She turned round once, saw me, and ran even faster ...'

'I am sure she did not see him.'

'She did not hear him.'

'Who could hear anything with all that shelling?'

'... and disappeared into the bush. That was the last I saw of her until the end of the war. When the war ended and I came back, I asked after her. I was told she was now married to a soldier ... .'

Many turned to stare at Alekiri. Her lips were pursed as her chin rested in her left palm. Her look did not seem to have any focal point. It was the look of someone conjuring up bitter memories of the past.

'... It would be a waste of time to go into any details. You all know this to be true ... .'

'Poor woman, the soldier forced her I am sure.'

'She should have avoided getting pregnant.'

'You can't stop babies when they want to come.'

'Is she really married to the soldier?'

'... In fact she has a baby girl with the man. So, as far as I am concerned, this marriage is ended ... .'

'He is childish. Is Alee the only wife so affected?'

'He should thank the soldier for giving him a free baby, ha! ha! ha!'

'Ibekwe should not be so hard-hearted.'

'... I do not want her father to return the bride price. All I want is for her to leave me alone.'

When Ibekwe had finished, Tia asked:

'Alee, have you any questions to ask him?'

Alekiri shook her head.

'Let's hear your side of the story.'

'What is the need for more words? He has made his position very clear. He does not want me back. I abandoned my baby, took a soldier for a husband and had a baby by him. I admit all. Go on, take a decision and let me go. I am tired.' As she spoke the tears came. One drop from her right eye skirted her nose, drew level with her nostrils, then running along the crease deepened by the civil war, lost itself in her lips. As she felt its salt tang she spat into her handkerchief, drew in a sharp tearful breath, and wiped her eyes.

'Still we want to hear your side of the story,' Tia prodded gently.

'I have admitted everything. There is no story to tell.'

'Do you confirm that you purposefully abandoned your child?' one woman asked. Before Alekiri could reply, Tia added: 'And if that is so, then it is a serious matter indeed and Omirinya will take appropriate action.'

Christie whispered to her sister:

'Don't be dumb. Tell them how you lost your child at the front, otherwise you will create a very bad impression.'

Reluctantly Alekiri began to tell how she lost Wibari at the front. By the time she got to where Major Dansuku rescued her, many women were sobbing.

'Stop, stop', shrieked one woman. 'I can't hear any more. We know that no woman could purposely abandon her child. Stop, I beg you.'

But in fact Alekiri had reached the point at which she intended to stop.

'As for the soldier business, it is true. I have a baby with a soldier, but it is not true I am married to him.'

'Does anyone want to ask any questions?' Tia asked. There were no takers.

'Ibekwe, you and your wife should leave us for a while so that we can take a decision.'

Christie whispered again to Alekiri: 'Tell them about the money he stole from your wardrobe.'

Alekiri refused.

It did not take the women long to arrive at a decision. They recalled Ibekwe and Alekiri and a spokeswoman was asked to deliver the verdict.

'Ibekwe we have heard you. Alekiri we have heard you.

99

This is our decision. Ibekwe, it is not true that your wife abandoned her child. It is cruel to accuse her of that. It is true she has a child by a soldier but she has told us she is not married to the man and we believe her. You are young and proud. You are hurt and you are angry. But you have beaten up your wife harshly. Your anger should go down now. You have flogged her with one hand; take her back with the other. Before that, however, she has to perform a necessary ritual. Alekiri, by sleeping with another man you have desecrated your common hearth. To restore it, you must show remorse and for that you will prepare for your husband a tasty chicken soup and pounded yam to go with it. He will wash it down with a bottle of gin which you will buy. When you have done that, Ibekwe will welcome you back with a piece of high quality george and a blouse to match. These clothes will cover the ugly marks his big stick has made on your smooth body. After that we do not need to tell you both what next to do. If you have no bed, buy one quickly and settle all arrears.'

'We want to hear the bed creak loudly,' one woman added brazenly. There was a roar of laughter.

'As for the child,' continued the spokeswoman, 'she is yours. She is the blessing that has come out of a life-and-death situation. Be a good father to the child. Women, is that the verdict?'

'Yes', came the chorus.

All this time Ibekwe had been studying the floor. He looked up after the spokeswoman had done and said quietly but firmly: 'I thank you Omirinya for attempting to settle the quarrel between Alekiri and me, but I cannot accept your verdict. As far as I am concerned she is no longer my wife.'

Several women spoke at the same time, many of them angrily. All of them condemned Ibekwe's intransigence. He was hard-hearted, childish, foolish and proud for no good reason, they said. Ibekwe retorted, and an uproar ensued. The women got angrier and angrier and one of them said in a loud voice: 'If men could get pregnant, you Ibekwe should have been pregnant several times over. I stayed close to you in

Biafra. Can you swear you did not sleep with women? What of that fat woman whom you were following all over the place, to name only one?'

Ibekwe became extremely angry and shot back.

'I am not like you who were all harlots during the war,' he cried.

'What?' several women shouted. Tia was aghast. The Kotima blew her whistle and there was instant order. Tia was staring at Ibekwe with rage and incredulity.

'Ibekwe', she said, 'repeat what you said last.'

Ibekwe sat still and said nothing.

'Women', Tia said steadily, 'Ibekwe has abused Omirinya in a manner no one has ever done before. He will pay for this.'

The women roared agreement. They asked Ibekwe to leave them while they conferred. Ibekwe rose and began to walk homewards. His mother ran and held him.

'What came over you? Are you mad? Not even an elder could talk to Omirinya like that. Go right back and fall on your knees before them.'

'Never.'

'Can you alone bury me?'

'Yes.'

His mother burst into tears, and clung to him. Presently the Kotima came to where they stood and ordered Ibekwe back to the hall. He stood still. Two relations from among the Omirinya came and with his mother's assistance half-dragged Ibekwe back to the hall. The spokeswoman's announcement was terse and business-like.

'Omirinya has decided that in order to cleanse your mouth of the abominable things you have said, you will feast them with one goat, two jars of palm-wine, a case of beer, a bottle of gin and sixteen plates of *foofoo*. However before they taste your food you will have to kneel before them and beg for pardon. Omirinya, is that your decision?'

'*Oweh*!' came the thunderous response.

Chapter VIII

Although Alekiri had predicted Ibekwe's reaction, she was still shocked when it came. She walked towards her father's place in a daze. As Mama Iyabo had promised, her driver was waiting for them in the compound, ready to take them back to Port Harcourt.

Kinika was not surprised at Ibekwe's reactions. His son-in-law was not one of those cool young men who gave one the impression of early maturity. He was only materially successful.

'Alee, don't worry,' he said, 'you are just a child. You can easily marry again but don't rush. Give yourself plenty of time to think. As for the bride price I shall pay it back as soon as I recover from the war, if you have not remarried by then. But even if I had the money now, I would still want to give Ibekwe a chance to change his mind.'

Christie could no longer restrain herself and said:

'Nana, do you know that Ibekwe stole Alee's money?'

'What?'

Christie told him the story. Kinika sat still thinking.

'Ada, thank you for telling me. Alee why have you kept this from me?'

Alekiri could not answer. Her father studied the profile of her averted face for a while and smiled. He realized Alekiri's heart was still with Ibekwe, and hoped the man would relent.

'Ibekwe cannot get away with that of course, but there is no hurry. We are all here in Ohiamini. Let's wait and see.'

Back in Port Harcourt, Alekiri was taciturn and Christie did not try to draw her into any conversation beyond what was necessary to organize the little household for the night. Alekiri slept very little that night. Did love exist? How could love turn into extreme hatred? Raging hatred. Murderous hatred. Ibekwe's face during that fight formed and loomed large in the utter darkness of the bedroom. It was an angry mask. But is the mind not also open to reason even in moments like this? Ibekwe are you utterly incapable of seeing my predicament during the war? God knows how often I called your name; how often I wished you were close to me. Can't you reach inside my heart and see the truth? I thought you and I were one. Open my heart and know the truth. If I were in your position I would be angry but not for too long. I would forgive you. You too had lovers in Biafra. If you had got a baby with one of them and perhaps got married to her I would still forgive ... now wait ... another woman in your house with a baby ... that would be difficult ... I couldn't cope with that ... I would run back to my father ... but I am not married to Sule, no I am not. That is the difference. If your lover had a baby for you and you brought the baby home, I could care for it. But the baby could not come without its mother. No, I couldn't put up with a co-wife. But you have no co-husband, only a baby, a poor little innocent baby. So there is a difference. You think the baby will remind you of him. So what? Before we married you had a girlfriend. She meant little to me. I came to you as a virgin. Wasn't that something? Have you forgotten all that? Perhaps you love yourself, not me. People only love themselves not their spouses. Love is beyond human beings. They can't reach it. Marriage is a sham, a make-believe. It is not worth it. But ... but ... it is good to love and be loved. Love? Love? Did I love him? Yes, yes, yes. Did he love me? No he didn't. That face, that brutal beating all showed he didn't. Women can love but men can't. Men only love themselves. To them women are mere property. Touch their property and they are mad. And in their madness they destroy the property. Marriage is not worth it. Better to have a lover. Men value lovers more than wives. If I were his lover he would not treat me so badly. He could leave me but there would be no cruel beating or would there be? Some men have murdered their lovers. Some women too. Still it's worse in marriage, much worse. Marriage is a trap, a deadly trap. I am through with it ... .

Alekiri tossed all night and talked in her fitful sleep. In the morning she could not get up. She developed a headache and a fever. Christie ran around for medication.

'Alee, don't let that man kill you.'

'I am through with him, Christie.'

'I doubt it. His name was on your lips all night.'

'What? Did I talk in my sleep?'

'Plenty.'

'Well that's the nearest he will ever get to me – in my dreams.'

'Don't waste your life on the man. He is not worth it. Come with me to Lagos. Rest for a few weeks, then come back and do whatever you want to do.'

'I shall get back into teacher-training.'

'Good.'

'I like teaching.'

'It is a good job but the trouble is teachers are never paid regularly. Why, I can never understand.'

'That was in the civilian days. The military government is doing much better. Teachers are not owed these days.'

'Let's hope the army boys will keep it up. By the way I should like to meet your army friend before I leave and thank him for rescuing you during the war.'

'We can visit him tomorrow. I want to see him too and let him know all that has happened.'

When the next day they called on Major Dansuku, his friend Captain Olaitan was with him. They received them politely and warmly, but Dansuku restrained himself from displaying any emotion. He shook hands with Alekiri and then with Christie as she was introduced to him. In spite of herself, Alekiri was taken aback by the formal handshake. Her world seemed to be falling apart in all directions. She sat down and put up as cheerful a face as she could muster.

Christie's sophistication caught Ola's fancy almost immediately and soon they were both rattling away in Yoruba.

'Alee, I want to speak with you. Let's abandon these Yoruba enthusiasts for a while.'

'I am sorry,' Christie said. 'We didn't mean to be rude.'

'Don't apologize,' Ola said. 'I have heard Sule and Alee chattering away in Hausa and cutting me off.'

'I wish I knew that much Hausa,' Alekiri said as she rose and followed Dansuku to the guest room.

The guest room conjured up very vivid memories and Alekiri's face lit up in a faint involuntary smile. She left the door wide open, determined not to give Dansuku any hints that she wanted to resume the relationship. But Dansuku slowly and calmly closed the door, pulled her to a double chair and embraced her passionately. Alekiri's struggles were shortlived. Soon she returned the embrace and laid her head on his breast. For a while she was still. When he looked at her, he found tears running down her face. He hugged her and kissed her and wiped her eyes with his handkerchief.

'Alee, you seem to have suffered a lot in the past few days.'

She nodded.

'Mama Iyabo told me about the fight you had with your husband and how brutally he beat you up.'

She nodded again.

'And how he has finally said he won't have you back. Is that so?'

'Yes.'

'Well I hope you understand I kept out of the whole show in your own interest.'

'Yes.'

'I am quite capable of giving the man a very rough time.'

'Don't do that.'

'You love him still, I suppose?'

'Sule, love does not exist.'

'What do you mean? Don't you love anybody?'

She shook her head slowly.

'Not even your children?'

'Hey, Sule, listen. My first daughter is alive after all. My husband managed to pick her up.'

As she spoke her eyes lit up suddenly and she bobbed up and down. 'Sule, I was mad with joy. I never dreamt of ever seeing her again.'

'Ah, that is very good news.'

'Yes, it is the only pleasure Ibekwe's return has brought to me. The rest is sadness and confusion.'

She lapsed into a serious mood again.

'Alee.'

'Mm.'

'What are we waiting for?'

'What?'

'Let's get married.'

'No,' she said firmly.

'Why?'

'I have given you all the reasons. I shall not marry again.'

'You don't love me any more?'

'Sule, I don't know what love is.'

'You don't have to know what love is. No one knows. It is enough to feel it.'

'But I feel nothing.'

'You don't have to lie. You feel something, but you are now frightened of men. Listen Alee, don't grow sour and hard, whether you marry me or not.'

'Sule let's leave that. I am confused and I can't think properly. There is something else I want to talk about and that is the house. I shall need about three months to arrange for another house. I am going to Lagos with my sister. I shall be there for a month. I should be able to pack out two months after my return.'

'Why do you want to pack out? Is it not comfortable enough?'

'Well it is your house and now that we are ... we are ... separated, I can't live there.'

'Why not?'

'It is your place.'

'The house is not mine. I merely repaired and furnished that flat for you.'

'The furniture is yours anyway.'

'It is not mine either. I came here with no furniture. I picked up bits and pieces here and there from abandoned houses and fixed up the place. I am not interested in all that. I am only interested in you. The place is yours as long as you want to stay. Remember also you are looking after our child and I should help. The only thing you will have to do is to agree on rents with the landlord whenever he shows up.'

Alekiri embraced him.

'Sule, don't misunderstand me. You have been very good to me and I appreciate all you have done. What is more, you saved my life. I shall be grateful to you as long as I live.'

'Forget that bit. My life has been saved by others several times, so you have nothing to be grateful about. And I don't love you because I saved your life. I saved hundreds of other women like you. Listen, although you say love does not exist, I love you.'

He embraced her passionately and she began to sob again.

'Sule.'

'Yes.'

'Can you wait?'

'For what?'

'For me.'

'I don't understand.'

'You see, my father thinks we should give my husband a chance to cool down. If he does not change his mind then I shall be free to do what I like. I think my father is right. Also, I feel guilty even though the situation was beyond my control.'

'How long would that take?'

'Say one year.'

'You will marry me after that?'

'Yes, if he does not take me back.'

Dansuku laughed aloud but mirthlessly.

'Is it funny?'

'It is. You put me at your husband's mercy. I hate being at

anybody's mercy or picking up what others have rejected.'

'I am sorry you feel that way. I take back what I have said.'

'Alee, I can't wait that long. If you can't marry me now, let's forget it.''

'All right.'

'But I hope we can still be friends.'

'Friends yes, but not lovers. I can hardly expect Ibekwe to change his mind if I continue my affair with you.'

'I see. One last kiss then.'

Alekiri smiled as they kissed and cuddled. Presently he pulled her up and began to move towards the bed.

'No, no. That's not possible any more. Besides, my elder sister is here. That would be an insult to her. No, no.'

'She has her own lovers, hasn't she?'

'Why not? But she would give me the same respect.'

Alekiri opened the door and as they emerged into the sitting room they were greeted by loud laughter.

'You folks are thoroughly enjoying yourself,' Dansuku said.

'Your friend Ola has been telling me stories about your childhood days in Port Harcourt, about egg-knocking and all that.'

'Ah, yes, I gave Ola a very hard time. He did not perfect the technique of testing the strength of an eggshell with his teeth. I was an expert there and he always lost.'

'It was the ring you wore that cracked my eggs.'

'I used to remove it.'

'Not always. Anyway I had my own back in throw-throw. You were not much good there.'

'What was the use of throw-throw? All we had to show for it was a long tiring walk. And you couldn't eat or sell the rubber seeds you won anyway, whereas I could eat or sell my eggs.'

'Well, everything cannot be judged by monetary gain,' Olaitan said, warming up. 'Look at the Olympic games. You train for months or even years and spend a lot of money travelling. All you have in the end is at best a gold medal which may not even be made of gold. Yet the honour you get is great.'

'Agreed, but how many gold medals did you win at the throw-throw?' Sule asked frivolously.

The women laughed. Olaitan was not amused.

'You know, that is what is wrong with us here. We always think in terms of material gain and even when we make a gain we are never satisfied. We go on grabbing for more and more. The gulf between the rich and the poor widens daily, and the estrangement between the two deepens.'

'Christie, you know Ola is a philosopher. If we allow him he will talk politics and philosophy all day. Ola you are in the wrong profession.'

'Which is my right profession?'

'You belong to the classroom. As for me, I am a soldier trained to kill. I have no time for politics or for grabbing money. If I wanted money I should be very rich by now.'

There was a hint of resentment in Dansuku's voice, and it was not lost on Olaitan.

'Of course my remarks were not directed specifically at you,' he said. 'I know you are an honest professional soldier. You are one of those who have borne the brunt of this war, and yet your bank account is in the red more often than not. I know some of your colleagues who are millionaires. But don't copy them. You are the stuff out of which all great nations are built. However you are wrong to think soldiers should not be interested in politics. Where would this country be now without soldiers? We are as deep in politics as the civilians ever were. If I had my way, now that the war is over, all army units should have regular lectures in politics and government. It is a dangerous thing to try to govern people without any training whatsoever on the job.'

'Look,' Christie said, 'all this grammar you are talking here does not mean anything in Lagos. You people here don't know what is happening over there where people talk about nothing but money. There, people grab money when it is within their reach and they don't think of anyone else.'

'What I ask is,' said Alekiri, 'what does anyone do with millions of pounds? How can he spend it usefully?'

'Let me tell you how he spends it,' Olaitan said. 'In this country, when a man holds a public office and is really sitting on money, instead of using it for everybody's good – you know, roads, power, water supply, education, things like that – he steals as much as he can. He cannot spend three-quarters of that money, so he banks it overseas in a secret account. That foreign country uses the money to develop itself. When the man wants to enjoy a holiday he runs to that country where, of course, he owns one or more houses. His children are educated there. He puts up a mansion in the village too, complete with a powerful generator and internal water supply. Then he builds a high wall topped with barbed wire. At the huge iron gate a sign under a skull-and-crossbones reads "beware of trained bulldogs." Outside the walls, his people wallow in grinding poverty. When eventually he dies the obituary reads: "He died in a London teaching hospital after a brief illness. Arrangements are being made to fly his corpse home".'

'I am not a philosopher like Ola,' Dansuku said, 'but sometimes I can't help thinking that part of our problem is that we are new to the job of governing ourselves'.

'That is not true,' Ola said. 'Think of the Benin, Fulani and Oyo empires that existed long before the white men came.'

'That is true, but I am thinking of governing the country as a whole. Some European countries have been governing themselves for over a thousand years and are still making terrible mistakes. We started – when was Independence?'

'1960,' Alekiri said.

'That is ten years ago; so we are raw recruits on the job,' Dansuku concluded.

'But when it comes to stealing,' Christie said, 'we are no recruits. We are … er … what is the highest rank in the army, Ola?'

'Field Marshal.'

'Yes, we are all Field Marshals in stealing public funds: Why?'

After exchanging addresses with Christie, Olaitan left.

'Major Dansuku, I have almost been diverted from my

main purpose of coming to see you.'

'Call me Sule please.'

'Well, then Sule, I have come to know you and to thank you for saving my sister's life and helping her throughout the war.'

'Hm, I am not sure I deserve any thanks. I have caused Alee a lot of problems.'

'It is not your fault. The war situation was confusing.'

'If your sister marries me, things will improve. But she has refused.'

Christie glanced at her sister who was looking out of the window.

'Well, that is something between you two.'

'Help me persuade her. I shall not marry two wives and I shall not put her in purdah. These are her big fears.'

'I shall discuss it with her but I don't promise to influence her.'

'Please drop this topic. I am not a child,' Alekiri said turning round to face them. 'If I want to marry, I shall do so when I am ready.'

'Fair enough, fair enough,' Sule said, his moustache meeting his nose grimly.

Chapter IX

Ibekwe concentrated on restoring his shed in Mile Three market. That helped him to get over the feeling of loneliness and confusion which his quarrel with his wife was generating. Wife? No, he was finished with that woman. Finished! Let the soldier marry her. They were probably married anyway in spite of her denials. She was merely waiting for his reactions before making the marriage public. She knew what to expect and she had got it. Harlot. Ungrateful shameless harlot. Alekiri, once his pride, now his shame. She deserved far more beating than she got. It was the neighbours – and that stranglehold. Next time he laid his hands on her, she would pay for her impudence. How he hated her! He would hurt her, really hurt her. He would get her yet. That soldier would not protect her. They say she had an excuse. She was captured by soldiers and all that. Rubbish. What of the other women caught in the same situation? Why were they not all married to soldiers and nursing soldiers' children? Or that thirty months was too long to expect any woman to abstain from men. Rubbish. Rubbish. Women had been known to abstain for years, or even indefinitely. They did not have the same pressures as men. All right, all right, if the time was too long, a few discreet affairs should have been enough. But no, she quickly got a substitute husband and a baby in the bargain. And now, people would say: a bastard baby for a bastard father! *Cha*, Ibekwe has suffered! She too would suffer. Meanwhile, he had the money. That was some punishment. Strange, she had not complained about it. Even if she complained he would not give it back. He had been injured and he deserved compensation. If he went to court, he could claim damages from the soldier. The money was his damages. But why had she not complained? Surely she had found out by now. Or had she so much money that she did not care about what he had? Perhaps she pitied him and wanted to help him out. What an insult! No, it could not be that. Perhaps she hoped he would take her back. That must be it. A reconciliation. Silly of her to even dream of such a possibility. Anyway, he had to maintain her daughter and the money would be useful. It was not her money really. It was war money, flying all over the place like bullets. This one had flown to him, and he would not let it go. He was not that foolish.

The setting sun lit up a rectangle of light on the floor of Ibekwe's room. As Erinwo approached the door her shadow gradually filled the rectangle like a black menacing reptile creeping in to attack him. Ibekwe looked up. His mother came in.

'Ibekwe.'

'Mm.'

'When will you pay the fine?' He looked at her.

She was set to nag and cry. He had gone through this several times and he was tired.

'Next Sunday,' he said with quiet resignation.

'Should I send a message to Tia?'

'Yes.'

She was taken unawares by Ibekwe's changed attitude and for a moment sat silent. But she had rehearsed a lot of things to say, and some of them still needed to be said in spite of his compromise.

'Thank you my son. In future you must …'

'I shall pay the fine. Now leave me alone.'

Erinwo moistened her lips several times, then rose to go.

'I shall tell Tia.'

'Tell her.'

Ibekwe watched the head of the reptile receding as if it had taken fright.

Alekiri's money was enough to pay the fine a hundred times over. He had no problems with that. The only difficulty was kneeling to beg the women for pardon. He hoped they would not insist.

The most urgent matter was his shed in the market. Fortunately it was largely intact. Part of its wooden partition had been torn off, probably for firewood, but that was a small matter. As he swept out the shed he noticed a faint putrid smell. Perhaps a dead rat, but where? There was nothing in the shed except what looked like an old shoe in one corner. He picked it up and dropped it immediately in extreme disgust. The shoe contained the bony remnant of a human foot. His neighbour had found a whole skeleton in his shed. He wondered if the foot belonged to that skeleton.

Within a few days his shed was in order and looking better than before; the carpenter had done a good job. Only the painting remained. Ibekwe did that himself, choosing bright colours. Then he scouted round the town looking for a 'Merry Christmas' decoration. He found none, but Christmas was two months off and he would certainly get it then. He installed a large mirror and a more comfortable chair. Women liked to sit and haggle for hours; the chair would invite and trap weary customers.

Restocking the shed was easy. He had the money, and ships laden with goods were arriving in Port Harcourt faster than the Ports Authority could clear. Later there was to be an unprecedented congestion in all the harbours of the country. Ibekwe's fellow traders stared with disbelief as his shed filled with expensive goods. While some of them were still sweeping out their sheds Ibekwe was already doing good business. His market smile was on his face and his thin gold chain around his neck. Some of his trader friends suspected that the gold chain was charmed and was the secret of his success. To his amazement, within a month customers were thronging his shed and buying even faster than before the war. Where did these women get the money?

Late one afternoon Ibia came to his shed. She had regained much of her pre-war freshness and beauty. Although there were two other customers watching, she allowed Ibekwe to embrace her lightly.

'I thought you might need this, look,' and she unwrapped a plastic decoration. When she spread it out, it read 'Merry Xmas.' Ibekwe was delighted. So were the two customers who well remembered this sign before the war. Ibekwe hugged Ibia again, this time closely. The two customers looked at each other, then left.

'Thank you Ibia. Where did you find this thing that took me to all corners of the town?'

'In the house next to my sister's. You know the house hit by a bomb.'

'Really?' Ibekwe's enthusiasm lessened somewhat and Ibia noticed.

'Don't worry, the war is over; your shed won't be bombed.'

'That does not bother me. After all, I found a dead man's foot in this shed.'

'Hey!' It was Ibia's turn to be dismayed. 'Christmas, you know the war is not actually ended.'

'What?'

'It won't end until all reminders of the war are removed.'

Ibekwe smiled ruefully and said:

'Then the war will never end for many people. Some reminders cannot be removed.'

Ibia did not reply. She looked at Ibekwe. Their eyes met, and for a while they were silent.

'Christmas I have heard about your quarrel with your wife. I hope you will patch it up. The war has broken many families. Don't let yours be one of them.'

'My marriage with Alekiri is a story of the past.'

'No, no.'

'It is and nothing can patch it up. I don't want to talk about it. How are you?'

'I am all right.'

'You have not told me how you survived the war.'

'There is little to tell. You know my sister was a personal secretary to a high ranking Biafran official. He protected and provided for us. We never starved. Each time the planes brought in supplies he was among the first to receive a share. In fact I gave out food and even clothing to some of my friends.'

'You were very lucky.'

'Yes, we were. It was in the last three months that we had some difficulty. The official was sent overseas and my sister was transferred to another office. Her new boss was not as helpful, but we managed until the end of the war.'

'You were lucky. And how about your job?'

'I am working now. My brother-in-law, my sister's husband, is the new executive engineer of our company. He was in the company before the war but left for a course overseas just before the war. When he came back two months ago, I went back to my job.'

'I thought you had been working for at least six months, from what you told me when we met in January.'

'Not at all. The company started in March but they had more problems than expected. So they employed a skeleton staff until they started to operate fully. I was told to check up at the beginning of every month but they kept dribbling me until my brother-in-law came back, then they took me back.'

'What's his name?'

'Kwaki-Thomas.'

'What?'

'Kwaki-Thomas, it is a double name. Many of his friends call him K.T. He is a nice man.'

It was getting late. Ibekwe began to pack his wares. He needed an assistant. He thought of this only when he was packing and unpacking.

'Ibia, let me offer you a little present.'

'Hey!'

Ibekwe knew that Ibia was a lipstick-mascara-nail-polish girl. He presented her with a vanity packet containing all three. She was delighted but said:

'Christmas, there is no need for this.'

'It is nothing, take it.'

She accepted the gift and embraced him. Ibekwe returned

116

the embrace and pulling her deeper into the shed kissed her. She returned the kiss with enthusiasm. Ibekwe was thrilled and flattered.

Over the next few weeks they met several times, often at the shed, sometimes in town. Once he took her to Ohiamini on his new scooter and immediately the story went round that he had married a new wife. Ibekwe's friend Elei asked him about it. Elei was a wayside mechanic, wresting a living out of the few car owners. He had seen Ibekwe with Ibia several times.

'I am not thinking of marrying yet,' Ibekwe replied.

'You will marry before you know it.'

'Fine. Anything wrong with Ibia?'

'No, but I wish you could take back Alee. I still think she is a fine wife for you. Both of you seem to match very well.'

'That was before the war, not now. And let me tell you, I am not going to marry a woman who has played around with every other soldier in this town. You wouldn't too.'

'Was she so bad? I doubt.'

'I don't doubt. I have all the evidence. You saw those pictures, didn't you?'

'Yes,' Elei grunted thoughtfully.

'And you still think she behaved well?'

'I have not said so.'

'Then what are you saying?'

'That she made a mistake. That if you forgive her, you can both live peacefully together again.'

'If your wife behaved like that would you forgive her?'

'Yes.'

Ibekwe looked at his friend.

'You are not serious,' he said and sped off on his scooter. Elei followed him with his eye until he disappeared in a bend. Elei thought of his own wife. During the war she and other women had to go close to the war front to forage for cassava from abandoned farms. They had to be escorted by Biafran soldiers and he knew what price the soldiers exacted. But there were four children to be fed and he himself was ineffective because he spent much of his time dodging

117

conscription. It had not made any difference to his marriage. Ibekwe was silly casting aside a wife like Alee, he thought.

Ibekwe took Ibia to the village regularly after his chat with his friend. At first he had made up his mind not to rush into marriage. ... He would establish his business firmly first. Ibia was just a companion. It was, strangely enough, Elei who, in his attempt to defend Alekiri, had planted the idea of marriage in his mind. He began to study Ibia closely and thought he liked what he saw.

His mother regarded Ibia as another Alekiri. In fact she thought she was worse, since unlike Alekiri she was not born in Ohiamini. Ibia seemed to belong wholly to Port Harcourt. Her long painted nails disgusted the old woman. Her son was crazy marrying a whore like that. He should marry a village girl who could cope with farming and other chores in the village. When she imagined Ibia trying to uproot cassava with her long painted nails she laughed outright. Ibekwe was stupid, plain stupid.

By Christmas, Ibekwe had made up his mind to marry Ibia whether his mother liked her or not. As their friendship deepened, Ibia established the habit of visiting Ibekwe after work. She soon knew the prices of most of the wares and if Ibekwe was temporarily away for any reason she could sell a few items for him. She also helped in packing and locking up the shed at the end of the day.

Ibia was in her late twenties, about the same age as Ibekwe. She was beginning to worry about marriage. She was a pretty girl but for some mysterious reason she did not inspire men to propose marriage. Only two men had ever proposed marriage to her. She had rejected both. One was too old and the other too rascally and unstable. How could she marry a man who could leave his bicycle at a drinking place and stagger home happily? As the years passed rapidly, Ibia sought advice from her married friends and read books on courtship and marriage. Her sister said she was too free with men: 'That makes them suspicious,' she said. So Ibia had played hard-to-get for a while. That made things worse. Besides, she was not made that way and she felt unhappy. One evening at the market, Ibekwe said:

'Ibia I want to marry you.'

Her heart beat so wildly that she held her chest. Ibekwe did not notice, for a customer was fingering an expensive blouse.

'Twelve pounds,' he said.

'What?'

'Only twelve pounds. This blouse na the latest and na im all ladies want for this Christmas. I manage buy ten for Aba yesterday. Look now, only two remain. Miss, wetin be your size?'

'I no be Miss,' she said with a smile. Ibekwe knew it was safer to call his younger customers 'Miss' instead of 'madam' – the latter implied that the woman was no longer a girl, and some customers reacted strongly to that.

'Madam, I sorry-o. Ah, you be one big man wife. I sure say *oga* give you plenty money for Christmas shopping.'

'Take four pound.'

'Hey, maday, you sef! Four pound no reach half the money wey I take buyam. Okay, if your money no reach, make you buy this one. This na only five pound.'

The customer looked at the suggested alternative and sneered in disapproval.

'I no like that one.'

'Okay, take this one for seven pound.'

Again the woman sneered. Her interest in the first blouse was intensified.

'Take six pound.'

'Madam, you dey try but that price too small. Look, if you see any place wey you fit buy this blouse for eight pound sef, call me, I go buy all.'

The evening breeze wafted the beautiful blouse and it proved irresistible for the woman. Meanwhile, Ibia was cursing her and hoping she would get away quickly. In the end she paid nine pounds. Ibekwe smiled with satisfaction as the woman walked off with the precious blouse tucked away in her shopping bag.

'This blouse is selling well. I have ten more. At this rate they will go before new year.'

Ibia was too confused to reply. Had the man forgotten the important proposal he had just made to her? She waited.

'I think we should begin to pack. Today is Christmas Eve and we should enjoy it.'

'That's true.'

Ibia's patience ran out. She decided to take the initiative.

'Christmas, you asked me a question.'

'Yes. I have been waiting for an answer.'

'But you have been busy selling.'

'I can sell with my eyes closed.'

'But not with your ears closed.'

Ibekwe laughed.

'So what do you say?' Ibia had dreamed of this important occasion over and over and had associated it with many romantic notions. Now that it came, its stark informality was disappointing.

'You know my answer already but I am worried about Alee. You know we were friendly before the war. I won't like her to think I am taking away her husband.'

'I have told you, that marriage is dead.'

'She may not think so.'

'Then she is stupid.'

'Can I find out from her?'

'Find out what?'

'What she thinks about the marriage.'

'That is unnecessary but you may do so if you wish.'

They packed for the day. Ibia was so happy that as she locked the padlock her hand shook. Ibekwe was busy strapping a few things to the carrier of his scooter and did not notice.

Early in the new year Ibia called on Alekiri in Ohaeto Street. She was received warmly but she could see that the warmth was perfunctory. Still, it was better than antagonism.

'Alee.'

120

'Mm.'

'You know we have been friendly for some time.'

'True.'

'And I should not do anything to hurt you.'

'Thank you.'

'How is your marriage with Ibekwe?'

'I don't know.'

'Won't you go back to him?'

'He does not want me; I am a bad wife.'

'Don't say that.'

'That is what he says.'

'I heard the village women tried to settle the quarrel.'

Alekiri's patience and faked good humour were running out.

'Ibia, I don't want to talk about my marriage. Let's discuss something else.'

Ibia cleared her throat twice then said in a low voice.

'Alee, Ibekwe wants me to marry him.'

'Go ahead.'

'I don't want to break your marriage.'

'You won't. Go ahead.'

The two women looked at each other, and Ibia felt very uncomfortable.

'That is what I came to talk about.'

'Tell me, is Ibekwe aware of this visit?'

'Yes.'

'He asked you to come?'

'No. I suggested it and he said it was up to me.'

Alekiri paused to think. She had nothing against Ibia. Her visit showed a certain sensitivity which she appreciated. It also brought to an end a long and painful period of doubts. Ibekwe had opted out of her life. With this conviction came new strength.

'Ibia, you and I have no quarrel. I have nothing against you. Marry Ibekwe if you want to, but ask him to give me back my money.'

'Your money?'

'Yes, the money he took away from this house, from my

121

wardrobe in the bedroom. He says I am a bad wife, he should reject my money too.'

'How much?'

'He knows.'

'Were you there when he took the money?'

'Deliver my message, that's all.'

'I will,' and Ibia rose to go. 'Alee you won't hate me will you?'

'Why? Ibekwe is not the only man in the world,' Alekiri said with a new-found recklessness.

A month later Ibia and Ibekwe were married. Within the next few weeks he repaired and furnished his old apartment in town.

His trade flourished. He said Ibia had brought him luck. As his business expanded he sold his scooter and bought a pick-up truck. On it he inscribed: 'Prince Ibekwe and Co., dealers in fancy goods. Try and see.'

Chapter X

Two years after the civil war, Port Harcourt still bore the marks of the horrors of war. Here and there bombed buildings grinned like huge skulls. Where such buildings still offered some shelter, lunatics and vagrants could be seen, moving inside them like maggots finishing off the last chunks of flesh in the decaying skulls. But feverish attempts at repairs were going on in adjoining buildings, and when these were restored and painted, the neglected ones looked even more cadaverous by contrast. A few restored buildings bore large signs indicating this ministry or that, especially along Ikwerre and Aba roads. Foreign firms were particularly active. The Trans-Amadi industrial layout came alive with the noise, dust and smoke of industrial machines persuaded to function again by expatriate technicians after thirty months of neglect.

Bianco drove furiously along the main road coursing through the industrial complex. On the sides of the new pick-up truck he was driving, the sign 'Texo Construction Company', in flaming red, easily caught the eye. He looked at his watch and pressed the throttle pedal. In a few minutes he stopped in front of his company's main office in a screech of brakes. He paused and looked around. The black shiny Mercedes saloon was not in sight. He took a deep breath and relaxed. The executive engineer normally came in around 9 a.m., but today he had insisted on a meeting at 8 a.m. Bianco shrugged, picked up a rolled plan, got out of the pick-up and banged the door hard. He was a well-built man in his late thirties; the type who would shop for medium-sized clothes. His half-buttoned, checked short-sleeved shirt revealed a broad hairy chest adorned with a gold madonna hanging from a thin gold necklace. His khaki shorts showed off his hairy well-developed legs to advantage. Baked to a freckled deep tan by the tropical sun, his body was already dripping with sweat, though it was only eight o'clock in the morning. His handsome face was framed by a luxuriant growth of jet-black hair so closely curled as to be almost African. Bianco spoke English, French, Italian and two other European languages. From his stories, he seemed to have worked in many parts of the world. When asked where he came from, he would grin boyishly and say 'the world', waving his hands in a semi-circular motion.

He walked into the office with the springy step of an active outdoors man. He smiled roguishly at the receptionist and walked into the office beyond.

'Good morning, Ibia,' he greeted breezily. '*Oga* never come?'

'No, *oga* never come.'

He shrugged and sat on a chair.

'The executive engineer said I should meet him at 8 o'clock.'

'Don't worry, he will soon be here.'

'I should be on the construction site by now. Haa!'

'Don't worry.'

'I worry. Your people don't keep time. They no know how to do business. For my country, business is business. We no waste time. Haa! You here waste time. You lose profits. If no profits, company close.'

Ibia was used to Bianco's impatience and she let him talk.

'This house we dey build, for my country, one month, we finish. Here, six months we no finish.' He raised his right hand and the index finger of his left hand to indicate the number six.

'Bianco, which one be your country, sef?'

'Me? Every country na my country.' Bianco mixed pidgin and English freely.

'Na England or French or Italian? Which one?'

'You want me to take you to my country? Haa! You go like am. My country is fine. Will you come?'

'Yes, take me,' Ibia teased.

124

'Yes?' Bianco got up and moved to Ibia's table and patted her shoulders.

'Sit down, *oga* will soon come.'

He tried to pat her cheeks but she defended them with her hands. A car door slammed outside. Bianco went back to his seat. Moses Kwaki-Thomas came in with a well-polished brief-case. A tall black man of thirty-two or so, he looked elegant in his three-piece suit.

'Ah, Bianco you are here. I am sorry I am late. Come in.' He opened the door and ushered Bianco into his well-furnished office. A powerful air-conditioner chilled the air to near wintry conditions.

'Sit down, Bianco.'

Kwaki-Thomas put his brief-case on a side table and sat down. The metal plate on his table read: 'Chief Moses Kwaki-Thomas, M.Sc., Ph.D., Executive Engineer.' The table was decorated with tourist bric-à-brac. A paper opener bearing the coat of arms of the City of London, a pen-holder in the shape of the Eiffel Tower, a paper-weight in the bust of Abraham Lincoln, they were all there. He extracted an expensive ball pen from the Eiffel tower and joined Bianco at the conference table at the far end of the huge room.

Bianco unrolled a plan and they held consultations for some time.

'We are about to pour concrete on the decking, sir. I remember you said you wanted to examine the reinforcements. That is your specialty.'

'That's right. But er ... let me see ... er. No, I can't make it. I shall come within the week. I trust you, Bianco. Just go right ahead.'

'The site for the other project is being cleared, sir. Do you want to have a look?'

'How far is it?'

'About twenty kilometres.'

'How is the road? I have just spent two hundred pounds to repair my Mercedes; I can't afford another breakdown.'

'The road is okay except the last five kilometres, which is

really bad, but we can do the journey in the pick-up.'

'Bianco, I know you will laugh when I say I can't do without air-conditioning, but that is the truth. One gets used to this damned air-conditioning. When the air-conditioned Land-Rover arrives next month, life will be easier. Bianco I trust you. Get on with the job. Just brief me regularly, okay?'

'Yes, sir.'

Bianco left and Kwaki-Thomas went back to his executive desk. As the air-conditioner purred he breathed deeply and contentedly. Life was good. He was making it. He had joined the company barely two years before the civil war. He had spent the war years abroad acquiring a doctorate degree. His thesis which had to do with reinforced deckings was ranked among the best in his university that year. When he came back, Texo Construction Company, a foreign firm based in London, saw him as a useful symbol of their half-hearted indigenization policy, and he was appointed executive engineer. Whenever any important political figures visited, he took the centre stage. He showed the august visitors round and treated them to tea in his office. Being taciturn, he spoke little, and conveyed an impression of dignity and wisdom. Again, Kwaki-Thomas was indispensable whenever the company had to bribe government officials for the award of contracts. He was their front man and so the expatriates were able to 'keep their noses clean', and on appropriate occasions lament the prevalence of corruption in the country. The company paid over to Kwaki-Thomas whatever bribe he said had been agreed upon, for there was no way of verifying the facts, and he routinely extracted his ten per cent cut before handing over the money.

The expatriates knew what was going on, but business was good and no one bothered. Also the company did not care whether K.T., as they fondly called him, was confined to his office or not. They were well aware that local engineers, no matter how academically brilliant, were reluctant to exercise their skills practically. Bianco and two other expatriates did all the work. They were to be seen on scaffolds in shorts and

126

with bare torso directing operations. They were paid twice as much as K.T. was. The extra remunerations came under the guise of various expatriate allowances. But K.T. did not mind. He enjoyed his position and the prestige it brought him. As an indigenization show-piece he was better known than any other member of staff at Texo. Further, the expatriate engineers had to consult with him and report to him during operations. It was pleasant to wield authority, and he did so calmly and pleasantly. He allowed the expatriate engineers as much initiative as they wanted on the construction sites, if only because he knew that they were better at practical engineering. He did insist on regular reports on projects, but the project engineers had no time or inclination to write up reports. To get round this, he arranged a monthly meeting during which engineers made verbal reports, which were recorded by verbatim reporters. Using these reports he made impressive charts and maps that adorned the end wall of his office. It was not easy to run around project sites, encumbered as he was with administrative duties. There was another inhibiting factor: he had just taken a chieftaincy title, and so running up and down scaffolds, and messing about with mortar, posed serious problems of dignity. This did not undermine his confidence; he was sure he could hold his own academically against anyone in his field, whether he went outdoors or not. Suddenly the air-conditioner ceased purring and K.T. panicked. He knew the stand-by generator had broken down three days before. Had it been repaired? He had begun to unbutton his top coat when, as if in answer, the coolers began to purr again.

The door opened and Ibia poked in her head.

'It's time sir.'

K.T. looked at her, then studied his watch.

'Have you finished typing that interim report?'

'Yes sir.'

'Send it up in a folder.'

Ibia dashed back into her office, and after pulling out and shutting a few drawers noisily, she brought the report.

Although related to her boss by marriage, she took her work seriously and K.T. liked her for that. At first he had retained her in his office as a temporary measure to ensure she was not molested and he was to have sent her to the general office later. But she had worked so hard that he had decided to keep her. Apart from her efficiency, she was discreet and never revealed to her sister the many women who called at K.T.'s office. K.T. always put out that they were sand and gravel subcontractors, but Ibia knew that they were not all contractors, and K.T. knew that she knew. K.T. rewarded her for her loyalty with money and presents. For her part she was convinced she was protecting her sister's marriage by not gossiping about her husband's affairs. As husbands went, she thought K.T. was a good solid husband in spite of a girlfriend here and there, and it would be silly to cause unnecessary conflict in the marriage.

Mrs Kwaki-Thomas was glad that it was her sister who worked with her husband and not another woman. She was saved the torture of wondering what her husband was up to each time he worked late. She herself was a confidential secretary to a senior civil servant, and through her many years on the job she had well understood the emotional hazards of the profession. Although she knew Ibia was by no means a prude, she was sure of her loyalty. K.T. apparently was not interested in Ibia beyond the occasional pat on the back for a piece of typing well and quickly done. Once he patted her rather low on the back, in fact on the bottom, but then he had been studying a typescript closely and had misjudged the position of her back. Ibia had drawn back but such had been his concentration that he had not noticed her gesture of disapproval either. However the incident had not recurred.

K.T. never gave Ibia a ride in his car, ostensibly because she left the house in the morning, and the office in the afternoon, an hour or so before him. But K.T., a man of the world, was in fact protecting himself against the possible jealousy of his wife who had to travel to work at the government secretariat by bus and sometimes taxi.

As Ibia waited at the bus stop that day, Bianco drove up,

horned and beckoned to her.

'Take a lift,' he said, smiling innocently. She could hardly refuse. She climbed into the pick-up and sat beside him on the long front seat.

'Where are you from? I thought you were working in the other part of the town.'

'I went to supervise the clearing of a new site. Big house, you know. Four storeys. Haa, it's hot. I am thirsty.'

'Me too.'

'Come to my place for cold drinks. Fanta. Orange juice. Then I take you back. Won't take time.'

'No, Bianco, thank you.'

'Why?'

'I am married, Bianco.'

'Haa! Married woman cannot drink Fanta?'

Ibia laughed.

'If my husband sees me … .'

'How? He does not come to my house.'

'Or someone who knows me … .'

'Haa! I only say come and drink. I don't want to make love. Haa! Me? No time for that.'

'That's a lie. You are among the white men who run after hotel girls.'

'Not me. I have no girl; true.'

They came to a turning and before Ibia could protest they were heading for Bianco's place. Better to humour the man this one time. It did not matter really.

His house was a bungalow in a walled estate containing five other bungalows, all rented by expatriate technicians. Two of them worked with Bianco at Texo.

A young man, obviously the steward, opened the door and Ibia found herself in a clean living room sparsely but tastefully furnished. There were only four chairs grouped around a small carpet on the polished terrazzo floor. There was a fridge behind a small bamboo bar in a corner. A few local carvings and an Akwete cloth hanging on a wall made up the decoration. What a funny way to use an Akwete cloth, Ibia thought. It was a lovely cloth with intricate patterns and she imagined what it would feel like to wear it as a wrapper.

Bianco deftly mixed Ibia a glass of orange squash and dropped some ice cubes into it. He uncorked a beer and drank from a bronze mug with the face of a bearded old man worked into it.

Ibia studied her watch. It was just as well she had not moved into Ibekwe's house yet.

'So you are married, haa?'

'Yes.'

'How long?'

'Recently. I have not joined my husband yet.'

'Still staying with K.T?'

'Mm.'

'When will you join your husband?'

'Next week.'

'What does he do?'

'He is a trader.'

'What he sell?'

'Cosmetics, women's blouses.'

'He doesn't do contracts?'

'No.'

'Pity.'

'Why?'

'I want contractors to supply sand and gravel for a construction we are doing in the bush for a company. Warehouse, you know. I don't trust the natives there.'

'My husband can do it,' Ibia found herself saying without thinking.

'But, he is a trader. Too busy selling. We don't want people who will waste our time.'

'He won't waste your time,' she said getting excited. 'It is easy to hire a tipper and buy gravel. Very easy.'

'But your husband may not want to do it.'

'Why not? Everybody likes contract work. Contractors are the rich people. Look, Bianco, let me tell my husband about it.'

'All right tell him. If he says okay, then tell K.T. He arranges all contracts.'

Ibia's enthusiasm flagged for a moment.

'Don't you arrange any contracts?'

'I do so only when we are working far in the bush.'

'But you say this is in the bush.'

'Yes.'

'Aha, then you can … .'

'No, no. K.T. knows your husband. Better for him to meet K.T. Easy.'

'All right. Thank you. I must go now.'

'Don't worry, I shall take you.'

That evening Ibia discussed the contract with Ibekwe and he was very enthusiastic. That was the very thing he would like to do to augment his trading. Ibia was to speak to K.T. and later Ibekwe would meet him.

K.T. did not mind, but he wondered how Ibia had found out. She told him exactly what had happened, and he seemed satisfied. He sent for Ibekwe.

'I take it you have never done this kind of contract before.'

'That's true.'

'Well there's nothing to it really except that the materials must be of the right quality and delivered on time.'

'I understand.'

'And don't go round telling your relations that I award contracts.'

'No, no. Trust me. I have no time for gossiping.'

'Fine. Our prices are fixed. That saves us unnecessary haggling. We also pay a fixed rate per mile for the distance you will have to cover from Port Harcourt to the construction site.'

'I understand.'

'Good. Here are the rates. Go to your suppliers and negotiate prices; then let me know by tomorrow if you can supply twenty tippers of gravel.'

When Ibekwe left the office, K.T. sat back in his chair and sighed. He calculated how much he would have gained if he had awarded the contract to himself. Ibekwe was a nuisance. No matter. He was an in-law after all, and this small gesture, which obviously meant so much to the young trader, was worth making.

Usually K.T. bargained with people who posed as contractors and won petty contracts from his company. He executed such contracts through these sham contractors whom he paid a small cut. He usually chose discreet people but everyone knew what was going on. The company did not seem to bother so long as they only paid reasonable prices. Large contracts were awarded by the management board of the company, usually to well-known contractors. Still, from the petty contracts and cuts from bribes paid to government officials, K.T. more than doubled his salary. This was one reason he did not grudge the expatriate engineers their fatter pay-packets. K.T. saved his money carefully, spending only on those things which he thought made him comfortable and gave him the dignity necessary for his job. His black Mercedes was one such thing. He had purchased it through a seaman. As seamen were perpetually broke, he had paid only half the current price for it. He had to find the cash fast, before the man who had actually ordered the car knew what was happening. Thanks to his secret contracts, he had managed all right. He often retold his few friends the exciting story of the clever manoeuvre. The heavy blue tint of the glass made it virtually impossible to identify the occupants of the car no matter how bright the daylight. In this car, with the air-conditioners humming, K.T. was in a different world of imitation leopard-skin upholstery, soft poofs, radio cassettes and white horse-tail fly-whisks. Through the dark glass the outside world with its beggars, garbage and flies looked almost as forbidding as a hostile alien planet.

Ibekwe dashed to the market, sampled prices and calculated his gain. He was amazed. He hardly slept that night. He had been wasting time. He was on the right track to wealth at last. All that money to be earned within a week and for so little work! All he had to do was buy the gravel on credit, hire two tippers and some labourers and show them where to dump the material. Within a week he had made more profit than he would have made in three months of vigorous trading.

His appetite whetted, he went back to K.T. for more contracts, but this time he had a cool reception. K.T. counselled patience. Contracts were not an everyday affair. Also, Ibekwe had to remember that the company had other contractors to look after. Ibekwe fell back on Bianco and had a few more contracts. He befriended him actively and invited him to the village on several festive occasions. Bianco was a playful unassuming man and the villagers liked him. Once he offered to take part in a wrestling match, in spite of Ibekwe's advice to the contrary. A young man took the challenge, but before the contest he demanded and received assurance from the laughing Bianco that there would be no trouble if he threw him. There was much excitement as Bianco pulled off his shirt. Never before had a whiteman wrestled in a local arena. The drums beat wildly. As Bianco's challenger danced, Bianco imitated him comically and the crowd wept with laughter. The wrestlers came to grips, and in a matter of seconds Bianco was flat on his back. But Bianco would not let the young man go. He twisted and turned until he was on top. Then he began to press his opponent's shoulders to the ground for a 'submission'. It took the referees quite some time to separate the two wrestlers. When they told Bianco he had lost the contest as soon as his back touched the ground he was surprised. Then he laughed loudly and shook hands with his equally astonished opponent who was still nursing an arm Bianco had been twisting.

Chapter XI

Three years after the civil war ... Alekiri had passed her grade two teachers' examination with merit. She had been a good student, attentive, mature and confident. Her classmates called her class-mother because of her calmness and willingness to help them. Getting back to school had not been difficult, in spite of Ibekwe's letter to the school authorities urging them not to readmit her. The Ministry of Education had made it clear that they had no business with him, nor were they interested in his domestic problems. If Alekiri was willing to learn, they were willing to teach her. Because of the rapid expansion of schools there was an acute shortage of teachers and the school authorities had no patience for any stumbling blocks in their teacher-training programme.

Alekiri was not surprised at Ibekwe's letter to the Ministry of Education. She had half expected it, considering his obvious desire to punish her. She also knew that Ibekwe was disappointed because so far he had not succeeded in punishing her as much as he would have liked. Although he had taken her money, she did not lack much, thanks to Christie who sent her money regularly. When she resumed her teacher-training course, Ibekwe was even more frustrated. After his letter to the Ministry of Education failed to have the desired effect, there was not much more he could do. Another unprovoked fight with her would not only be unwise but could invite retaliation from her soldier lover. He had heard rumours that Dansuku was planning to marry her and he did not want any confrontation with the military boys. Let the stupid woman go, he advised himself. Ibekwe's attempt to stop her training gave Alekiri further indication, if she still had doubts, of the strength of his hatred. Her marriage was dead. It was time now, she thought, to cut herself loose from her emotional attachment to him. But it was not easy to overcome her feeling of guilt. She ought to have avoided pregnancy, she thought. Although she had made some effort, it had not been enough. True, Sule was an impossible man and difficult to turn down, but perhaps a little more determination, a few more wrestling matches with him, might have saved the situation. But how could she have resisted for thirty months a sex-hungry soldier sharing the same house, sometimes the same room, with her? No, there was really nothing she could have done. It was a pity Ibekwe did not give her a chance to apologize, what with his childish fight. She could have cooked him a good meal and asked for forgiveness even before the abortive settlement by Omirinya. When things want to go bad they will. Events had run out of control. She should not kill herself. It was time to reorder her life.

First, a job. That was easy enough. Every trained teacher got a job automatically. She had been on in-service training and she had even been paid a small monthly allowance as a student. She was posted to a school in Port Harcourt as she had hoped. The one place she did not want to be posted to was Ohiamini. The thought of seeing Ibekwe every other day unnerved her. The comfortable anonymity of a city was what she needed.

She threw herself into her job with a will. She prepared her notes of lessons carefully, delivered them effectively and with enthusiasm, marked the children's assignments and took part in games and other extra-curricular activities. Her headmaster said she was a model teacher and loaded her with even more responsibilities. She did not mind. She even desired it. She strove to work off her frustrations and confusion, but it was not easy.

Now and again the question of how to relate to Dansuku arose. It seemed to have acquired a permanent place in her mind, like a stray cat that had found a home for itself and would not leave no matter how often the house owner drove it away. Her little daughter Binta – the name Sule gave her had stuck – did not help matters, for she constantly reminded her of Sule, whom she closely resembled. Alekiri thought she did not have a fair deal in the matter of resemblance, for Wibari also resembled her father Ibekwe as closely as if she were a boy. What was to be done about Sule? She told herself frankly that going to the North frightened her. There would be no relatives near her. She would have to make new friends, learn a new language, acquire a new culture and perhaps be initiated into a strange religion. She had seen Moslems praying and counting beads at prayer grounds on Fridays. The transition from the Christian Sunday service to the Moslem Friday devotion was daunting. She liked Sule, but to follow him to a strange distant place was something else. Where and to whom would she run if Sule became violent? Sule had been very kind and gentle with her but that was no guarantee he would not get angry and possibly violent when they got married. Look at Ibekwe! She had thought she had the most considerate of husbands, yet did he not turn into a mad man? Would a soldier not be worse? Who would protect her from a mad soldier? The kind of quarrel she had with Ibekwe would of course not arise. She would be faithful, but would that be enough? What about groundless suspicions? Husbands had been known to murder their innocent wives out of unfounded jealousy.

But there was Binta. Yes, Binta. She loved to play with her father and was very fond of him. It would be unfair to deprive her of the benefits of a loving father. It would be a cruel trick if fate deprived her first daughter of her mother and her second daughter of her father. God! At night in her dark lonely bedroom Alekiri wept. She wished she were like her sister Christie – bold, independent, confident, holding her own with men. But she was not like that. Her nature and upbringing were different. Her orientation was home, marriage and children. Perhaps she should accept Dansuku after all. They would have to live in Kano permanently only after he retired.

Before that, he would be transferred from place to place – Port Harcourt, Enugu, Lagos, Ibadan and so on. Perhaps he would not retire until another twenty years. That was a long time. By then she should be more mature and stronger. With luck she would have grown-up children who would cushion the harassment of a cruel husband. All right then. If Dansuku asked her again, she would accept him. Nature had been cruel. A marriage she thought was pleasant and secure had turned into an evil dream. Perhaps in her vagaries, nature might turn a marriage fraught with fears and uncertainties into a happy one. Perhaps. Perhaps.

Although she had by now virtually written off Ibekwe, she could not forget her daughter Wibari. She longed to see her as often as possible. She was now attending the elementary school at Ohiamini. As Ibekwe had forbidden her to visit Wibari in his compound, she realized she had only one alternative, which was to visit her at school. She studied her own timetable to work out when she would be free to visit her. The last period on Wednesday was for singing, in which only the music teacher and his assistant were involved. But forty minutes was too short to dash to Ohiamini and meet Wibari at school. Better were the last two periods on Friday, which were for gardening, supervised by the rural science master. It would be easy to obtain permission from the headmaster and go home. Most of the teachers usually broke off during gardening without formal permission, anyway.

One Friday afternoon, she made it to Ohiamini elementary school. The children were out playing. A quick inquiry took her to her daughter. Wibari was concentrating intensely on *oga*, the clapping and dancing game popular with girls, the essence of which lies in determining who will end up on the wrong leg. The more rapidly it is played the more difficult. Alekiri arrived just as the game ended with Wibari winning and laughing and displaying the loss of two milk teeth. On seeing her mother she cut short her laughter somewhat, and went to her.

Alekiri looked her over. Her school uniform was dirty. The top button was missing and revealed a thin chest covered with craw-craw. Her legs were thin and the knees stuck out. Alekiri fought back her tears. Her own daughter, looking so scruffy and scraggy! She sat on a disused cement block and drew her to her knees. She wiped her dirty face with a corner of her upper wrapper and rummaged in her handbag for biscuits. Just then the bell rang for the children to assemble for the closing song. As Alekiri watched other children running towards the classrooms, she relaxed her hold on Wibari.

'Will you go?'

'Yes.'

'Go, but come back here after closing. I shall be waiting for you.'

Soon the air was rent by the off-key singing of hundreds of young voices, and Alekiri recalled her own school days in this same school. There was her classroom in the final year, and behind it the mango tree that had got her into trouble so often. Beyond it was the school garden, where on many a sunny afternoon she had struggled to make ridges with a hoe much too big for her. Mr Nonji the headmaster, tall, jet black, bony and ugly with two outsize front teeth that looked like the blades of hoes. Mr Anyanwu the rural science master; short, robust, energetic, always wielding a long cane. Mr Koiki, her small, gentle and kind class teacher who made her the class monitor. One day she had carried books to his house as usual. He had praised her for her diligence and had briefly put his left arm around her and had gently caressed her breasts which were then barely noticeable. Koiki's action had meant nothing to her then, but now, through the long misty corridor of years she could see a young gentle teacher fighting to control himself. In those days the missions dealt firmly with teachers who tried to corrupt their female pupils.

The bell rang again.

Graaang … graaang.

'Good afternoon, teacher!'

Graaang … graaang.

'Good afternoon, pupils!'

With those final greetings, the pupils spewed out of the

classrooms in all directions like a colony of soldier ants suddenly disturbed in their nest.

As Wibari ran to her mother on her frail wobbly legs, she looked even thinner. Alekiri made up her mind to take her home and give her some much needed attention.

'Will your father come home today?'

Wibari shook her head.

'I want you to stay with me till tomorrow. Would you like that?'

'Yes.'

'Now look round and call me any of your friends who live near you.'

Wibari ran around and brought two young friends, fretting to run home with the others. Alekiri gave them some biscuits and said:

'Tell Erinwo, you know Erinwo, not so?'

'Yes.'

'Tell her that Wibari will stay with me till tomorrow. Will you?'

'We will, Mama Wibari,' and they disappeared, munching their biscuits.

When Ibekwe came home that afternoon and missed Wibari he was angry and decided to drive straight to Kinika's compound to retrieve his daughter. His mother said nothing to restrain him, but Ibia said:

'Christmas, I see nothing wrong with Wibari staying with her mother overnight.'

'But she has to let me know first.'

'You are not on speaking terms, so how could she let you know?'

'She could have sent a proper message and not through school children.'

'And you would still have said no, I am sure.'

'You women are all the same: you defend one another.'

'Whatever you may say, I don't think it would be a good thing for you to rush to Kinika's compound and ask for Wibari.'

'Well, that is exactly what I am going to do.'

Ibia was getting angry.

'Christmas, let me ask you, is Wibari not Alekiri's daughter too?'

'By custom she is mine, not hers.'

'That custom does not say that a woman may not stay with her child for a day or two. I do not support your ...'

But the rear tyres of Ibekwe's jeep were already raising dust in a violent acceleration. Ibia stared after him open-mouthed and disturbed.

As Ibekwe drew near Kinika's compound, Ibia's advice began to make sense. He had antagonized everybody in that compound and it was not going to be easy to talk to anybody. He parked his car along the broad entrance to the compound and walked in. When Kinika saw him he knew immediately what he had come for, but the old man decided to play-act.

'Ha, Ibekwe my in-law, welcome. I have not seen you for a long time. Come into the reception hall and sit down.'

'My in-law, I greet you,' Ibekwe said, determined not to repeat his childish mistake of three years ago. He was surprised at the transformation in Kinika's compound. All the houses had been renovated. Kinika's reception hall had been rebuilt, iron-roofed, ceiled, dwarf-walled, and painted. Kinika waved him into one of a half-dozen or so metal chairs. Ibekwe was puzzled. Alekiri must have had far more money than he took away. Stupid. Christie of course. This was Christie's rehabilitation effort.

'You have a car now, well done.'

'Thank you.'

Kinika showed no anger and was clearly treating him like a silly little boy. He did not know whether to be abrupt or to play the game. Before he could decide, Kinika had gone off, obviously to fetch cola nut and drinks. He looked around. Alekiri and Wibari were nowhere to be seen. Perhaps she had taken the child to Port Harcourt? Damn the woman. Kinika came back with cola and a bottle of expensive brandy. His hospitality and good manners were remarkable, and this after all that had taken place. It was fake hospitality, Ibekwe knew, but he played along. He accepted the cola and took a tot of brandy.

'I hear Wibari is here.'

'Yes.'

'I have come to take her back.'

'If you want to, yes. She belongs to you by custom.'

'Where is she?'

'I believe Alee took her to a neighbour's for a haircut.'

'Have they been gone for long?'

'Yes. They should be … ah, there they are.'

Ibekwe turned round and saw Wibari and her mother entering the compound. He got up and walked straight towards them. Kinika followed, hot on his heels. Meanwhile Alekiri picked up the eight-year old child and clasped her to her breast. Because of Wibari's size, her legs dangled clumsily.

'Let me have her,' he said coldly.

'I shall bring her tomorrow. Let me clean her up a bit and wash her clothes.'

'Never mind, I shall arrange all that. Hand her over.'

'Ibekwe, can't you wait till tomorrow?' Kinika said.

'No, I can't.'

The neighbours began to gather. They all pleaded with Ibekwe but he remained unmoved. Some elderly women cursed him, but he pretended not to hear. Kinika knew he was on weak ground. According to custom the child belonged to Ibekwe not to her mother, and he knew how strong this patriarchal tradition was.

'Alee, let Wibari go.'

'No, no. Let him kill us both.'

Ibekwe moved towards her, but the crowd restrained him. Kinika took his daughter aside and talked to her for some time. In the end she put Wibari down. Kinika led her to her father and handed her over without a word. As the little crowd watched in silence emphasized by the darkening dusk, Ibekwe drove off with the whimpering child. Alekiri sat in the reception hall and cried.

Alekiri woke up the next morning sad and hollow-eyed. She washed, dressed quickly and returned to Port Harcourt. She could not eat the breakfast her stepmother had painstakingly prepared, but the old woman understood. As the bus sped to Port Harcourt, Alekiri felt that the last link she had with Ibekwe was broken. His behaviour had been more painful than the beating three years before. Ibekwe was out of her life. Out. Out! If Dansuku came again she would say yes, if only to give her daughter Binta the benefit of having two parents. She had read a lot of the possible damage the separation of a married couple could have on their children. Her two children should not both suffer that fate if she could help it. And there was nothing wrong with Sule anyway. Come to think of it, he should make a far better husband than Ibekwe. Even if they settled in Kano, remoteness was not really a problem. In three hours she could fly from Kano to Lagos and from Lagos to Port Harcourt. And when Port Harcourt international airport was completed she would be able to fly direct from Kano to Port Harcourt in two hours or less. Definitely she would marry Dansuku. There was no valid reason she should not. All her objections were childish, even primitive. She was just being stupid, rejecting such a nice man.

When she got to her apartment, she cleaned it thoroughly. Later in the day she went to the hairdresser. When she came back and studied herself in the mirror, she concluded she was not looking bad at all in spite of the ordeal of the night before.

After dinner that night she called on Mama Iyabo. She gave her a big hug, sat her down and plied her with *suya* and drinks. Alekiri noticed that the sitting room was disorganized.

'We are packing away,' Mama Iyabo explained. 'I came to tell you yesterday but you were at the village.'

'Where are you packing to?'

'New Reservation. Doyin has bought a nice house there. It stands alone and there is plenty of space for the children to play in. No noisy neighbours. It is a nice place.'

'Mama Iyabo, I am glad, but I shall miss you very much.'

'I shall miss you too, but I shall visit you as often as possible. You are the best friend I have in Port Harcourt.'

'You must take me to the new place so that I can visit you too.'

'You will know the place tomorrow because you will help me pack.'

'Tomorrow?'

'Yes.'

'But that's Sunday.'

'Sunday is the best day to pack. Little traffic.'

Alekiri had planned to visit Dansuku the next day, but she could not disappoint Mama Iyabo.

'Mama Iyabo, I have come to discuss something important with you, but as your mind is now set on packing, I wonder if ... .'

'Nonsense. Just talk.'

'You know Dansuku has been talking of marriage.'

'I know. That man can never forget your ... .'

'Shut up and listen now.'

Mama Iyabo clamped her lips with her fingers in a comical manner. Alekiri laughed.

'Should I marry him?'

'Why not? That is the most sensible thing to do. That Ibekwe fellow is a very nasty man.'

'Yes he is, and do you know what he did yesterday?'

'Mm-mm.'

'He came to my father's compound and snatched my daughter Wibari from me. I had taken away the child after school to clean her up and give her decent food and to send her back the next day. But Ibekwe came and snatched her away. Mama Iyabo, I am finished with that man, believe me.'

'Marry Dansuku.'

'Yes I will, unless he does not want me any more.'

'Why not?'

'It's over three years now and men are not that patient.'

'But he visits you from time to time.'

'Yes, to see Binta.'

'Only? No shelling?'

'Shut up. You know I have been busy with my studies. Also I wanted to give Ibekwe every chance of changing his mind. But now I am tired.'

'Alee, marry Dansuku. He is a good man.'

'I shall if he asks me again.'

'I am sure he will.'

'He may not.'

'You don't know what you are saying. You are prettier than you were soon after the war. Your body is now more balanced, you know what I mean?'

'I don't.'

'It is women of your age, beauty and build who turn men crazy. One look at you now and Sule will start sweating and ...'

'Shut up.'

The next day, Alekiri helped Mama Iyabo pack to the new place. Neither of them did any heavy work; the brunt of the job fell on servants and hired carriers. Alekiri's chore was mainly to ensure that delicate things like expensive breakable plates and electronic equipment were carefully handled. When they got to the house, Alekiri was impressed. It was a big two-floor apartment with plenty of grounds, gardens and ornamental trees. Birds played boldly as they flew from shrub to shrub or hopped from the half-wall of the front porch to window-sills upstairs. The fearlessness of the birds was an indication of the relative quiet of the new place. In the village hard by, birds were almost always on the wing dodging missiles from hungry and restless children. Even the lizards in the new place appeared to have more dignity than their friends elsewhere. They did not scurry away with the desperate hurry of the slum lizards. They took half a dozen steps, bowed three times and paused to let visitors pass. The ornamental trees with their heavy foliage provided almost perfect shade. Where the sunlight penetrated, a continually shifting mosaic of light and shade formed on the grass as the trees swayed in the wind.

Alekiri walked in the shade, drugged into a momentary feeling of peace by the heavy scent of flowers and the humming of innumerable insects in search of nectar. Trees may lack consciousness, she mused, but they were the most reliable creatures of the earth. The animals were all insane, with man the maddest of them all.

'This is a beautiful place, Mama Iyabo.'

'Alee, we thank God-o.'

'How many bedrooms are there?'

'Doyin says four, excluding a guest room downstairs.'

'Which makes five.'

'Yes.'

'I shall be your first guest.'

They laughed and hugged each other.

Mama Iyabo could not fulfil her promise of frequent visits. She visited Alekiri twice and stopped. Whenever the two friends met accidentally Mama Iyabo complained of lack of time. She had to entertain Doyin's friends, and they were many, and she was usually tired afterwards. Alekiri continued to visit her but gradually she tired of what now looked like a one-way friendship. Also she discovered that Mama Iyabo had acquired many new friends she had not seen before. Where had these large and expensively dressed women been all this time? Alekiri concluded that Mama Iyabo's new residence was the source of attraction when she heard one of the new friends say that she was scared of going to crowded sections of the town. For a start, one would have to pack in the street and so advertise one's presence. Then there were always children rubbing dirty hands on car windows and throwing stones carelessly. These women and their husbands lived either in New Reservation or in similar low density residential areas and it was a case of birds of the same nest flocking together. Alekiri studied the women with some fascination; but in the end she was bored by the endless talk of cars, gold, lace and summer holidays in London. The women on their part found it hard to relate to the taciturn, poorly clad elementary-school teacher. Mama Iyabo remained friendly, but her rich friends took more and more of her attention as they introduced her to the world of the rich. Tucked away in Ohaeto Street she had been earthy and unsophisticated. Her new friends encouraged her to buy more lace and gold and to 'go for summer' in London. Mama Iyabo bothered her husband until he arranged a trip to London. After that trip she thought her education was complete. She sought to pass on what she had learnt to Alekiri but the latter showed very little interest.

'What do you want?' Mama Iyabo asked.

'I am thinking of going to the College of Education.'

'Alee, I praise you. As for me, I am through with reading and all that. But you know, all your reading may end up in Dansuku's kitchen.'

'I shall not let that happen. I shall continue to teach when I am married.'

'And if he refuses?'

'He can't. I shall make that a condition for marrying him.'

'Anyway, Dansuku is not rich. If he grows rich, I do not see why you should continue to work.'

'Mama Iyabo, you know my quarrel with Ibekwe has forced me to think of many things.'

'Like what?'

'Like why men treat women anyhow they like.'

'And what have you found out?'

'They treat us anyhow because we depend on them for everything. Look at my sister Christie; she is independent and no man can treat her the way Ibekwe has treated me.'

'I know rich independent women who have suffered just like you.'

'Such women would have suffered much more if they had been dependent. Perhaps they would have died.'

'Alee, it is too late for me,' Mama Iyabo said with a trace of resentment.

'Don't worry, you are all right. Doyin is a good man. You are lucky.'

As the gulf between the two friends widened, Mama Iyabo, feeling guilty, made half-hearted attempts to maintain contact, but the forces of social stratification were too much for her.

Chapter XII

Mama Iyabo's movement to New Reservation had prevented Alekiri from visiting Dansuku that Sunday as she had planned. Later she changed her mind. She should not go chasing the man around. If he wanted her, he should come. Anyway, he usually called once a week or so to see Binta and she was sure to see him within a few days. But for three weeks Dansuku did not come. Was he sick? Had he travelled? She wished she had a 'phone. Now that Mama Iyabo had moved, she had no neighbour from whose place she could telephone. Mama Iyabo's former place had not yet been re-occupied and through the locked glass door, she could see the telephone lying tantalizingly on the floor. She would have to visit Dansuku after all. That meant another hair-do. The hairdresser performed the same magic on a Saturday morning. Later that evening she chose her dress carefully. There was a particular wrapper which Dansuku admired. She brought it out. The matching blouse was a little crumpled at the hem. It called for a touch of ironing. As she unpacked the iron she heard a knock at the door. It was Dansuku's voice she heard and her heart beat fast, to her annoyance. What was she being excited about? Dansuku was in mufti. His richly embroidered kaftan and hand-made hat became him well.

'Alee.'

'Sule'. She embraced him lightly, then closed the front door. 'I have not seen you for a long time. Did you travel?'

'No.'

'Binta has been asking about you.'

'Where is she?'

'She is asleep.'

'I have brought a dress for her. I hope it fits.'

'Thank you, Sule. Beer?'

'Yes.'

She poured him a beer and an orange drink for herself.

'Cheers, Sule.'

'Cheers.'

If Dansuku noticed her high spirits, he did not show it. Since Alekiri last turned him down he had become more controlled and less playful in her presence. At first it cost him some effort but gradually it had become a habit. Alekiri had found his less ebullient attitude convenient for it meant the end of wrestling sessions. But now, how was she to reverse this attitude? She had to subtly indicate a change in her stand before she could expect any move from him. She realized she had made a tactical error by sitting opposite him instead of by his side on the settee. She could not change seats without giving too much away. No, that would be crude.

'What have you been doing these three weeks?'

'Three weeks?'

'Yes, you were last here three weeks ago.'

'Really? Time is flying these days.'

'You must be working hard or doing something interesting for time to appear to pass quickly.'

'Not really.'

'So what have you been doing?'

'Usual soldier's work.'

The man seemed moody and preoccupied. It was not a good day, but she would keep trying to get him to talk about her.

'Sule I am thinking of going to the College of Education.'

'That's nice. I can see you ending up in a university.'

'I think I am too old and too dull for that.'

'I don't think so.'

Where was the man's humour, his bantering, his infectious laughter? Perhaps she should get him to talk about himself.

'Sule you have been a major for three years now. After all that fighting you should be promoted.'

149

'Actually I was not a substantive major until nearly two years ago. I was what they called a field major.'

'How long does it take to be promoted to colonel?'

'There is no set time. One year, two, three or never. I can retire as a major.'

'God forbid!'

'People in headquarters get much of the promotion, while we see more of the action.'

He laughed. It was a humourless laugh but it was better than nothing. He was opening up. She sipped her drink and paused, hoping he would initiate a line of conversation. But he merely refilled his glass and studied the opposite wall. He probably had not even noticed her expensive hair-do. She was getting exasperated. She tried a bolder line.

'How about your fiancée?'

'I don't know.'

'What?'

'We have not written to each other for nearly a year.'

This was real progress.

'Why?'

'Alee, I don't think the girl is interested in me. She is likely to get into university next September and end up as a professor's wife.'

He chuckled again, this time with what looked like genuine amusement. The leading question, 'What will you do now?' was on her lips, but she could not ask it. Her intentions would be crudely obvious. She paused and caressed her glass, but it appeared to her that even her silence was asking the question. She looked at him and their eyes met. Slowly she lowered her gaze and caressed her glass again. She thought she saw embers of the old flame in those eyes. Her heart thumped. He would either ask her again or come to sit by her as a step towards that. There was a long painful pause. Then she heard the sucking sound of Dansuku draining his glass of beer.

'Alee, I must go now. Tell Binta I came.'

She looked up and with much effort controlled herself.

'I shall.'

'Goodnight, Alee.'

'Goodnight.'

He rose, put on his cap, opened the door, and disappeared into the night.

Later Alekiri reviewed Dansuku's behaviour. Clearly that was not him. He had put on an act. The act of a man determined not to be crushed by unrequited love. She laughed at her inability to play the coquette. She should have gone over to sit by him under the pretext of filling his tumbler or brushing an imaginary insect off his kaftan. Next time she would cast aside her silly shyness and excite the man enough to get him to propose again. And what was she being shy about? He was the father of her child. What was hidden between them? Alee, grow up! She urged herself. She would allow three days and then visit him again. She rehearsed what she would do. As soon as he opened the door she would embrace him and kiss him. That should do it. If all hints failed, she would cast all modesty to the murky creeks of Port Harcourt and say she was ready to marry him. Why not?

Three days later Alekiri dressed carefully and well, called a taxi and made for Dansuku's place. It was dusk and the security light outside had been switched on. She pressed the bell switch, heard it ring clearly, and waited. Nothing happened. She rang again and heard light quick steps approach the door. The lock clicked, and the door opened a chink. A visibly pregnant Arit filled the chink and stared at Alekiri.

'You again?' she said with a sneer, and slammed the door with such violence that Alekiri moved back instinctively. For a moment she stood rooted to the spot, then recovered and turned away. Before she got to the road she heard someone running towards her.

'Madam, madam!'

She turned round and faced Bukar.

'Ah, Bukar, how are you?'

'I dey well. Madam please no vex. I see that wicked woman close door for your face. Don't worry. I go tell Major. Since that woman come back for this house everything don spoil.'

'Never mind, Bukar. Just greet your master for me.'

That night, soon after Alekiri went to bed she heard the door bell ring. It was Dansuku. He came in, took her in his arms and kissed her. But she curtailed the kiss, averted her face and twisted out of his embrace.

'I am sorry for what happened.'

'You don't have to be; it is not your fault.'

'The woman is impossible.'

'Never mind, Sule, just go and leave me alone.'

He sat her down on the settee, held her head in his hands and forced her to look at him.

'Go back to your wife Arit,' she said.

'She is not my wife.'

Alekiri laughed bitterly.

'I suppose that baby she is carrying is not yours.'

'Never mind the baby.'

'Ah, never mind the baby. Arit will become just another Alekiri. I am sure you will visit her once a week with a dress or something for another Binta, and later you will be off for yet another woman.'

'Shut up,' he shouted.

'How many babies have you made with your lovers?'

'Don't be rude,' and he smacked her lightly.

'Sule, go to your Arit and leave me alone.'

'Alee, let's get married.'

'No thank you.'

'Arit is not my wife.'

'She is.'

'She is not.'

'Anyway, she is pregnant by you and you should look after her.'

'That should not prevent our marriage.'

'Sule, leave me alone,' she shouted, nearly hysterical. She fought to control her tears, not wanting to create any impression of helplessness. But it was not easy. If he remained much longer, her tears would overflow. She began to push him towards the door.

'Go. We shall talk some other time,' she coaxed him.

'Shall we?'

'Yes. Goodnight.'

He paused by the door and looked at her but she did not relent.

'Goodnight,' he said at last. As soon as he stepped outside, Alekiri slammed the door and worked the lock noisily. Major Dansuku looked back at the door. It had caught part of the curtain during the violent slam. What was trapped outside seemed to share his rejection and loneliness. With a sigh he walked away.

Chapter XIII

For many days Alekiri's feelings were confused. She kept indoors after school hours and struggled to get a clearer insight into her life in order to plan her next move. Dansuku had called again after two days but she had made it quite clear that the affair was over. To be humiliated by him and Arit in that manner was more than enough, she said. Although Dansuku could understand her feelings, he failed to see where he came in for blame. Over the past four years he had pressed her for marriage without any success, and even now he was ready to marry her. He had known Arit before her and she was well aware of Arit's presence in his life. There was nothing new in all this, except perhaps Arit's pregnancy; but so what? Arit did not want marriage. For years she had been longing for a baby and now that she was about to have one, she was not prepared to hand it over to a man in the name of marriage. All she needed was a man to look after her during pregnancy and lactation. Come to think of it, he was the only one losing in the love drama. He felt annoyed and began to reassess his life. Was it not time to settle down with one woman, good or bad? They were all the same anyway; there was little to choose between them.

He had met quite a few women who looked impressive at first, just the sort he would like to marry. One after the other they had turned petty, jealous, cantankerous, even cruel. Not that Alekiri was all that, but she was certainly unreasonably jealous, Dansuku thought. What did she expect him to do? Wait for her for four years and remain celibate like a priest? And why the bloody hell should she quarrel about Arit's pregnancy when she herself had a child by him? Damn it, women were incomprehensible. Still, he needed a wife. Perhaps Habiba was the answer after all. He had better write to her and re-establish the link. Or should he wait for Alee to cool down and then try again? He really liked that woman. But each time he tried, he received a more hostile reception. In the end his pride was hurt and he let her alone, contenting himself with seeing Binta once in a while.

Christie flew in from Lagos and met Alekiri in her confused and gloomy state.

'Alee, I have told you not to depend on any man for your happiness. Work out your own happiness and be in a position to dictate terms. You are wasting your time with men like Ibekwe and Dansuku. They are all the same. They are interested in you only when you are undressed. Wake up, girl. You have the brain and you are good-looking. I shall give you all the backing I can. You really have no problems once you cut your links with these men.'

'Christie, you are right; men are unreliable.'

'Good talk, Alee. So what are your plans? Do you want to continue this thankless teacher work or will you come with me to Lagos and learn how to do business?'

As a subcontractor Alekiri had made more money in a month than she was paid in a year as a grade-two teacher, but this could not persuade her to take up business as her sister suggested. Deep down she felt she could not cope with all the hustle and pressures of business, especially pressures from men. She had had enough problems from them. Perhaps more important was the fact that she enjoyed reading and teaching in spite of the low and often delayed salaries of teachers. Books took her to other worlds where she could roam and explore at will, where she could enjoy the happiness and freedom which the real world seemed to deny her.

'Christie, someone has to look after our father.'

'Port Harcourt is less than an hour from Lagos by jet.'

'Actually what I want is further training. They have set up a College of Education and I have seen advertisements for the

155

first batch of students. I wish to apply.'

'How long is the course?'

'Three years, I believe.'

'And what do you end up with?'

'NCE.'

'Nigerian ... what?'

'Certificate of Education.'

'It is a good plan. Go ahead. Work out how much you need to equip yourself and let me know. You are on my scholarship.'

Alekiri laughed, comforted by the motherly warmth of her sister. The College of Education was in a hurry to take off, and for the pioneer students there was no entrance examination. Candidates were interviewed and their certificates scrutinized. Alekiri's records were good and she had no difficulty in gaining admission.

Within the first year her mind broadened considerably. Her main subjects were home economics, literature and Bible knowledge, but she read widely. She would have liked to study the sciences, but her educational background made this impossible – science was not taught in grade-two teacher-training institutions then. Still, she enjoyed home economics and literature. As for Bible knowledge, she had tacked it on just to make up her three subjects. As she had been reading and studying the Bible ever since her elementary school days, she could not imagine what more she could learn. She was disillusioned, as it gradually dawned on her that virtually any subject could be studied endlessly. With increasing knowledge came the ability to look at life, especially her life, with a greater measure of objectivity. This new ability did not bring her much peace of mind. Rather, it seemed sometimes to accentuate her feelings of guilt and failure. If there were extenuating circumstances that could lessen her sense of guilt, she found none to lessen her sense of failure. Her marriage had failed through her ineptitude, or so it seemed to her. Worse, she had failed to keep even her seducer. A mere street girl, as she referred to Arit, had snatched him from her grasp, leaving her with yet another child with only one parent. But why should the success of a woman's life be reckoned strictly in terms of marriage? She wondered. Men were not so limited. As she read more and more she became convinced that a high proportion of the famous men in history either could not cope with marriage or did not bother about it. For a start, there was Jesus Christ. This example made her uneasy, as it carried elements of impiety. Christ was supposed to be the Son of God, wasn't he? But the mind can wander out of control sometimes, and before she knew it, she was wondering whether God himself was married.

She shrank from this line of thought, scolded herself, and prayed for forgiveness. Then she came back to earth. Was Aggrey married? What about Bishop Crowther, Usman dan Fodio and others? She brought out her copy of the African Encyclopedia, the pride of her little library, and read through the entries on these names. In no case was marriage mentioned. Then a thought struck her: these famous people were all men. What about famous women? Were they judged by their marriage? She scanned through her knowledge of history. Where were the famous women? Aha, there was Florence Nightingale. Who ever heard of her husband? Her lamp was certainly of more interest to historians than her marital status. How about Joan of Arc? Was she married? Her history books did not say so. Queen Amina of Zaria? She probably was married, but no one bothered about her husband. She looked her up. She was right. There was no mention of her marriage. Psch! Why all the fuss? Marriage was good but it was not everything. She could still make a success of her life in spite of her marital failures. Not that she would ever be a Florence Nightingale or Queen Amina – she chuckled at what seemed a grotesque comparison – but she certainly could make a small contribution to society.

These inner battles gave her a sense of direction, and she worked with so much zeal that by the end of the second year she was near the top of her class. She kept men at arm's length without being prudish. She laughed and joked with her male colleagues but they could sense a wall of reserve. Soon they nicknamed her 'reverend mother'. She took the joke in her stride and laughed with them. She was happy to find Tam Jaja at the College of Education. They resumed their friendship and gradually she told him about her quarrel with her husband. He showed a lot of sympathy and did much to keep her spirits up whenever her problems threatened to overwhelm her.

If she could rationalize her marital failure and put it in its place, she could not forget or ignore her children, especially Wibari who was not staying with her. For two months or so after her confrontation with Ibekwe over the child, she had refrained from seeing her, but thereafter her resolve had broken down. She began to visit her at school again but she did not attempt to take her home. When Erinwo, Ibekwe's mother, died suddenly, Wibari was sent to live with Ibia and attend school in Port Harcourt. Alekiri considered this a better arrangement. Ibia should be able to look after the child far better than old Erinwo had done. Also the child was now within easier reach – a mere fifteen-minute ride by taxi, as compared with the hour-long trip to Ohiamini in a hot and crowded bus on a bumpy road.

One day Alekiri met Ibia at Wibari's school, and was touched by Ibia's concern for her daughter.

'Do you always come to fetch her from school?'

'Not always; only when I am passing this way from the market.'

'She looks healthier and cleaner than she was when she was staying with Erinwo.'

'Why not? Wibari is my child, isn't she?'

Alekiri's eyes moistened and impulsively she embraced Ibia.

'Thank you,' she said huskily, trying to overcome the lump in her throat.

'Alee, you don't have to worry about Wibari. Not all stepmothers are bad. I was brought up by a wicked one but that experience taught me to care for children.'

Alekiri sighed in relief.

'And you can visit the child in our house whenever you want to.'

'Mm-mm. Ibekwe will fight me.'

'He won't. You know, after that incident at the village I was very angry with him, and I told him off.'

'Thank you, but it is enough to see the child at school.'

'I can bring her to your house on weekends.'

'Really?'

'Yes.'

'Won't he be angry?'

'He won't find out.'

'Are you sure?'

'Yes.'

'I don't want you to quarrel with him on my account.'

'We quarrel anyway,' Ibia said smiling.

'Well, that can't be completely avoided, but I should not increase the quarrelling.'

'You won't, don't worry. How about this Saturday?'

'Ibia, I do not want to put you into trouble. If you and Wibari visit me, Ibekwe will eventually find out and make a lot of trouble. I don't want any *wahala* now. I just want to concentrate on my studies.'

'I was only trying to help.'

'I know, and I am grateful. But Ibekwe's hatred for me is such that he will seize the least chance to molest me.'

'Alee, he does not hate you as much as you think. You know, sometimes when we quarrel he says: "Alekiri would not have behaved like that".'

'That is when he is angry and confused. Ibekwe hates me; I know that.'

'Anyway, he has not forgotten the years you spent together.'

As they conversed, Alekiri became convinced of Ibia's good will and with that conviction a heavy load seemed to have been lifted off her mind. Ibia would make a good stepmother for Wibari, she was sure.

Ibia's kindness was a very pleasant surprise. Alekiri had

misjudged her character. In spite of the fact that Ibia had virtually sought her permission to marry Ibekwe, Alekiri could not shake off the belief that she was a coquette and a husband-snatcher. But now that impression was reversed. Ibia studied her watch.

'The school should close in the next twenty minutes. Let's find a place to sit and wait.'

Alekiri looked around and espied a shack with the inscription: 'Paradise Eating House. Try and see.'

'Let's go in there and see if soft drinks are available,' she said. The fat middle-aged woman who ran the eating house was very pleasant. As it was very hot inside, she brought out two chairs and put them under the umbrella tree whose cool shade seemed to form an extension to the shack. The women sat down and the landlady served them two bottles of soft drinks.

'Let me pay,' Alekiri said.

'You have no money; you are a student,' Ibia replied as she fumbled for her purse. They laughed.

'How is the College of Education?'

'Okay.'

'When will you pass out?'

'Next year.'

'Alee, you are doing well. I envy you.'

Alekiri was about to say that she was turning her marital failure to some advantage but that was a touchy line and she did not pursue it.

'But you are doing well too in your job. Have they promoted you yet?'

'I have had only one promotion and that was through the influence of my brother-in-law. You know, these private companies are not interested in promotions. They pay their workers as little as possible so that they can make a lot of profits.'

'Your brother-in-law is a kind man.'

'Yes. Unfortunately he is no longer there.'

'What has happened?'

160

'He has got a high political appointment.'

'Yes, of course. I remember now. That was over six months ago.'

'Yes.'

'Was that wise? Political appointments are not permanent.'

'That's true, but K.T. is a clever man. He got the company to grant him leave without pay. So he can return to the company whenever his political appointment ends.'

'I suppose the government pays him more.'

'I can't say, but as I said, K.T. is not foolish. He is doing more business now. He has a private company which gets a lot of government contracts. Ibekwe runs the company with him.'

'That's good. Your husband must be making a lot of money now.'

'He is doing quite well. Apart from his pick-up, he now has two tipper lorries, one new, the other second-hand. He plans to buy a car next month.'

'That's good,' Alekiri said, wondering why Ibia was revealing all this to her. Did she want her to feel jealous? She studied her as she sipped her drink. Ghost smiles continually played at the corners of her lips. At the least provocation they materialized and spread quickly to the rest of her pleasant face. No, she was not trying to make her jealous. She was just a kind open-minded young woman. For her part, Ibia admired Alekiri's ungrudging nature. Many women in her position would have harrassed and scandalized her, and would have refused to talk to her. But Alekiri remained reasonably amicable in spite of her problems. Ibia thought that the least she could do in return for such generosity was to look after Wibari.

'No wonder Erinwo's funeral was so lavish.'

'Indeed it was. The villagers are still talking about it.'

'How did you get on with her?'

'We did not get on at all. She hated me like poison. I rarely went to the village when she was alive. She expected me to help her with the farming on weekends. Can you imagine that? I told her I needed to rest after working all week at the office.

161

She said I was worse than you.'

Alekiri laughed.

'Then there was the problem of children. Barely six months after we were married she asked Ibekwe to marry another wife who would help her on the farm and produce grandchildren for her. I confess I hated her as much as she hated me.'

'I hope Ibekwe won't do that.'

'He might. I know that he is beginning to worry about the fact that I have still not got a child after nearly three years of marriage.'

'But that's nothing. I know women who did not produce their first child until after seven years of marriage.'

'That's true, but you know how impatient our men are. They expect their wives to fill their houses with children, especially sons, within the first few years of marriage.'

'Have you got medical attention?'

'Yes. And that is what is beginning to annoy him. He thinks he is spending a lot of money without any results.'

Alekiri was amazed at Ibia's candour. She seemed to have no secrets.

'You know I was pregnant in Biafra,' Ibia went on. Alekiri looked at her with undisguised surprise.

'It is true, why should I hide it?'

'And what happened?'

'I suffered a miscarriage, and bled a lot. Since then I have not so much as missed my period.'

Alekiri pondered this revelation. It seemed to her Ibia was trying to establish that she was not sterile. She felt a wave of sympathy.

'Ibia, don't worry. I am sure you will have a child one of these days.'

'Thank you. Ah, the school has closed.'

As they watched, the children ran out of the school.

'That's Wibari there,' Ibia said, rising and walking a few steps. She called twice and the child came running to them. She embraced Ibia, then seeing her mother she embraced her too.

162

Alekiri was happy to notice a considerable improvement in the child. She looked better fed and neater.

'Wibari, I have brought a dress for you. Try it,' Alekiri said, and extracted a beautiful dress with a floral pattern from her handbag. Her eyes twinkling with excitement, the child put on the dress. It was a little tight.

'That's because of the uniform underneath.'

'I think so'.

Later Alekiri saw them off to a point where they hailed a taxi.

Chapter XIV

When Chief Kwaki-Thomas was appointed the chairman of
the State Works Committee, he formally registered his private
company in anticipation of the government contracts he
would win from that Committee. Of course it would be
awkward to manage the company himself, so his first task was
to find a suitable manager. Such a manager had to be reliable,
loyal and if possible related to him; someone who could not steal
his money and vanish. Ibekwe seemed to possess all these qualities. The minor contracts he had done for Texo Construction
Company had shown he was efficient and reliable; he was
K.T.'s in-law; and not the least important, he was a proud,
stable citizen with a family and property. K.T. was sure he
had made a shrewd choice. Ibekwe seized the chance without
hesitation. He employed an assistant to look after his shed in
the market. It would take the young man quite some time to
learn Ibekwe's art, and he would make little profit while he was
learning, but Ibekwe did not bother about that. Big money
was to be made in contracts and that was where to concentrate
his attention. Members of the State Works Committee knew
K.T.'s company. Each time it featured in the list of tenderers
they smiled knowingly at one another. As each had his own
company, no one was resentful. As chairman, K.T. proved a
cool operator. He did not inflate contract prices crudely – just
enough to give him his five per cent cut. The other four
members shared another five per cent. When a member won
a contract the cut was waived. K.T. ensured that members
of the committee did not grab a disproportionate share of the
contracts. He knew that could annoy other contractors who

might then expose him. As it was, K.T.'s rapport with these contractors was good. He was approachable, amiable and suave. Sometimes he would opt out of a contract to give a desperate contractor a chance. They all considered this a wonderful gesture. But it was in the large contracts usually awarded to foreign firms that he made more money. Apart from his five per cent he made separate deals with the firms. Six months after his appointment he had two houses built for him by foreign firms in New Reservation, a low-density residential area.

The working arrangement in K.T.'s company was simple: Ibekwe was to take one-third of profits made from contracts. K.T. did not always show him the contract papers, but Ibekwe did not mind. He was earning relatively large sums of money that had never come his way before, and he was grateful for the chance. After all, K.T. could easily have got someone else to manage his company. Even now, he could sack him if he wished, and he would then have to fall back on minor jobs from Bianco. He shuddered at the thought. No, he would not pry into contract papers. He would accept whatever quotations K.T. disclosed and he would work diligently. He would build himself up gradually, form his own company, and arrive at last at the house of wealth. He would, as his people used to say, slash open the mythical bag of riches and its contents would spill out all around him. And he deserved it. He had suffered for too long. He was tired of wondering where the next meal would come from, tired of merely dreaming of wealth and contentment. What did all the rich people he knew do to deserve their success and wealth? Sometimes he wished he could see God to ask him that question.

He made rapid progress. He bought a second-hand tipper which he hired out to other contractors by the day. The vehicle was a good bargain, for its engine had proved sound. In a few months he had earned enough to enable him to pay a deposit for a new tipper. The new vehicle earned the monthly instalmental payments several times over and paid its way within a short time. But there were several contractors who owned ten or more tippers and Ibekwe's two looked wretched by comparison. But he did not worry. These chaps had started long before him. If he had not lost time fooling around in the market he would have done just as well. There was plenty of time. The important thing was to ensure that his age-mates who had better education than he did not outrun him in the race for money and the good things it can buy. Already it was clear that far from being outrun he was in the lead. His friends who were in the civil service or in private companies had nothing to show except their cars which they bought on hire purchase. After paying the monthly instalments many of them could hardly fuel their vehicles.

Ibekwe's next plan was to buy a car. He was tired of his pick-up which looked increasingly decrepit beside the shining saloons of his friends at village meetings. But then he had no house. He had always been contemptuous of people who bought large expensive cars only to park them in front of dilapidated mud huts in the village. No, he would build a house first. The order would be: a house, a car and then a chieftaincy title. From a prince he would convert to a chief.

Then a problem stared him in the face. After his mother's death, his uncle's compound was empty save for two strangers who, in return for the use of a room, weeded and swept the compound. It was important to have someone in the village to supervise the new building or at least to keep an eye on building materials. Ibia could not live in the village and would be unwilling to do so even if she were not working. A second wife was the answer. This raised many problems. First, what kind of woman could play the role he had in mind – taking care of the village scene, which would include looking after the compound and farming? Clearly an educated woman was out. She would refuse to stay in the village and if she came to town would quarrel with Ibia endlessly. He could marry a young illiterate girl of ten or so and gradually train her to play the role. But such a young girl could not live alone in the village to begin with. Who would look after her? If he brought her to town, Ibia would make trouble. If by a miracle Ibia agreed to such an arrangement and he brought up the girl in town, she would grow to love urban living and would be unwilling to live alone in the village. The only option then was to marry a mature uneducated woman used to village life. Would she too not want to live in town and watch television, at least part of the time? There was a solution to that. He would instal a small generator in the compound to provide light and work a television set. That should keep the woman in the village.

It was not easy to broach the matter with Ibia. One night when he thought she was in a good mood, he said:

'Ibia, you know I should build a house in the village before I buy a car.'

'Yes, if buying a car will make building a house difficult.'

'No,' he said, his pride a little hurt. 'It is not a question of money. It is the odd business of parking a shining car in front of an old mud hut.'

Ibia laughed shortly then said:

'But you have been going to the village in your pick-up.'

'A pick-up is not the same thing as a new saloon.'

'Christmas, there is not much difference. Anyway, there is a way out: we can use the car in town and go to the village in the pick-up.'

'That's funny.'

Ibia laughed. 'Yes it is, but that's how you want it.'

It was not a promising line. He tried again.

'Car or no car, we need a house in the village.'

'That's true. We discussed it and at that time you said you had no money. Are you ready now?'

'No one is ever completely ready to build a house. The important thing is to start. You are bound to finish it.'

'Not always. There are many people in the village living in unfinished, unpainted houses.'

' I have always considered that a shame.'

'Yes.'

'I don't do shameful things.'

'I know, but if your money runs out, you can't kill yourself.'

'That's true. Anyway, I have enough money to build and furnish a decent bungalow.'

'After buying the car?'

That was the trouble with Ibia, she was so logical. Other women wouldn't ask so many questions, he thought. They would jump at the mere mention of a car or a house without bothering about the details. But not Ibia. It must be her job that was affecting her.

'Before or after, it doesn't matter.'

'It's okay, Christmas. You know your own pocket.'

Ibekwe paused and turned to face his wife in bed. The bed creaked. He chose his next words carefully.

'There is a problem.'

'What?'

'Who will supervise the building?'

'You and I. That's no problem.'

'We can't be there always.'

'Must we?'

'Workers can steal building materials.'

Ibia paused then said:

'Some of the labourers can live on the compound and look after our building materials.'

'Who can trust poor and hungry labourers?'

'You have to trust somebody. After all, labourers keep watch over the materials you use for the various contracts you do with K.T.'

'That's different.'

'How?'

'That's a company.'

'But the labourers are the same.'

Ibekwe turned again and lay on his back. The bed creaked yet again.

'We should buy a new bed,' she said.

'Why?'

'This is getting too noisy.'

'And sell this?'

'No, take it to the village.'

'It is too big for the little rooms there.'

'We shall keep it in the new house.'

'A new house should have a new bed,' Ibekwe said, and they laughed.

'We need someone we can trust in the compound.'

'Who?'

Ibekwe cleared his throat. What was he being shy about? he scolded himself.

'Ibia, I am thinking of getting another woman in that compound.'

'Ehe, now you are speaking your mind. All that roundabout talk about car and house was beating about the bush.'

'Ibia, our compound in the village is empty. It is not good. Each time I go home I feel queer.'

'Why?'

'No one to talk to.'

'What of the strangers?'

'They are not always there.'

'We can always go together.'

'And when you are at work?'

'You wait until I am back.'

'And if the matter is urgent?'

'Then you go. There are always villagers to talk to. They enjoy talking anyway.'

'But they don't live in our compound.'

Ibia was becoming irritated.

'Christmas, just say you want to marry another wife and stop giving excuses.'

'Ibia, I am not giving excuses. There is the problem of cooking for instance. I should not be cooking for myself in the village.'

'Why not?'

'What?'

'I said, why not?'

Ibekwe could not decide whether she was serious or not. She had a way of teasing him, unlike Alekiri.

'You are joking of course.'

'I am not joking. Why should women do all the cooking?'

Ibekwe decided she was joking.

169

'Because men earn all the money.'

'But many women earn money too.'

'What kind of money? Money which is never enough for their endless clothes and cosmetics. I deal in women's goods and I know what I am saying. One blouse can clear a woman's pay packet yet she won't think twice about buying it. Working women end up asking their husbands for pocket money.' He cleared his throat mischievously and added: 'There is a twin brother of mine in that position.'

'Christmas, be frank. You are complaining of the pocket money you give me.'

'Did I say so?'

'I am not a child. But even a millionaire woman will like to receive gifts from her husband as a sign of affection.'

'That is different from monthly demands.'

'I don't make monthly demands.'

'Stop dragging yourself into the talk.'

'I am sure you are referring to me indirectly.'

'Do you make monthly demands?'

'Christmas, much depends on how rich a husband is. If you had been a poor clerk, I am sure I won't smell my monthly pay. You will snatch it from me and I shall have to beg you for pocket money. That is what many poor working men do. I know a woman who hands over her entire salary to her husband every month, and the man drinks and womanizes with it. Another has a joint account with her husband, but he holds and signs the cheques.'

'Why can't women earn more money and support their husbands for a change? It is because they are weak. If men do most of the work and earn the money, it is unfair to expect them to cook for themselves – which is where all this argument started.'

'Look, I know a rich woman trader who earns more money than her husband. She supports the whole family and yet she cooks for the husband.'

'Shut up! That's enough.'

Ibekwe reared up and glowered at his wife but the intense

darkness absorbed his angry stare. This was the trouble with Ibia, she was always arguing with him. She was pleasant enough and playful – qualities he liked – but there was a streak of freedom and stubbornness in her. Alekiri was not like that. She was quiet and submissive and would never have dreamt of suggesting that he should cook. What a pity that woman behaved so stupidly and ruined their marriage. In the silence that ensued he thought about his former wife. In many ways she was an admirable woman, he thought. Reserved, hard-working and faithful. Faithful? Yes, before the war she was very faithful to him, hardly glancing at any other man. It was the war that had brutalized her. But then he had not given her a second chance. Perhaps he should have accepted the verdict of Omirinya, at least on a trial basis. By now she would have had two or more children. She was so productive. Ibekwe's prosperity was working a subtle change in him. He was becoming more confident and tolerant. He spoke and acted less impulsively. In those days he would have slapped Ibia for her silly arguments.

'Ibia, listen ... Ibia are you asleep?'

'No.'

'All jokes and arguments aside, I think it is necessary for me to have a woman in the village. It will be to your advantage even. When we go to the village you won't have to run about looking for a broom to sweep out the place and prepare a meal. The woman will do all that.'

'No woman will do that for another woman. Anyway, I won't eat what she cooks.'

'You can cook for yourself then.'

'I won't go home with you when your village queen arrives.'

Ibekwe began to lose his temper.

'If you can't see that I need a woman to stay in our compound in the village then you are stupid.'

'Christmas, just say you want to marry another wife. Otherwise, are you saying that all these men in Port Harcourt who have only one wife each do not have a village?'

'Many are too poor to maintain a second wife.'

'It is not a question of poverty. What of K.T.? He is rich but he has only one wife.'

'K.T. has no village like mine, and you know it.'

It was true. K.T.'s parents died when he was three and a kind Sierra Leonean called Thomas adopted him. Being a Christian, he had likened the child to the abandoned child, Moses, of the Bible, and he had given him that name. Young Moses never visited his village until adolescence, by which time his father's relations had taken over all the land and property. The first time he went to his village, he had felt like a total stranger, a feeling worsened by his inability to speak the language. After some inquiry he was shown his father's compound and only then did his relations know who he was. One or two old people embraced him. Boys of his age stared at him indifferently and he felt alienated and lonely. He decided his best bet was to make good in town and to stay there. The only concession he made to his background was to link his real father's name Kwaki to that of his foster father's. Fortunately he had finished his secondary education before old Thomas died. Working on his own, he had secured a scholarship and studied engineering overseas. But the feeling of alienation had never left him. He kept strictly to himself, and learnt to cope with solitude. At home he was either in his bedroom or study; at work he hardly left the splendid isolation of his chilly office; in between the two he cruised along in his heavily tinted Mercedes, the world flashing by like dream images. Some people thought he was selfish, others that he was a harmless, retiring man with a sombre dignity.

'Many rich men are not like K.T. They have villages to go to.'

'It is not only a question of money. It is a matter of convenience. Even poor villagers have several wives. They need them to help with the farming.'

'You are not really in the village.'

'I am between the town and village, so I need two wives. That's not too many.'

'All right then. I am also between town and village and I

172

need two husbands.'

'Don't be stupid!'

'Give yourself that advice!'

Ibekwe grabbed Ibia's hand but she wriggled out of his grasp. As he fumbled with the bedside switch, Ibia jumped out of bed. When the light came on, he saw her standing by the far wall and holding the door handle in readiness to escape. In spite of his anger Ibekwe was amused.

'Don't force me to handle you roughly.'

'I won't be the first.'

'Don't call Alekiri's name. She is far better than you.'

'True, but where is she now?'

'You want to go where she is gone?'

'Leave Alee out of this. I think you want a second wife because I have no child.'

'It is not.'

'It is.'

'It is not. I have two children already.'

'Two?'

'Yes. Alekiri's two children are mine, are they not?'

'Yes, but they are both girls.'

'It doesn't matter.'

'Christmas, it matters to you, but it is not my fault.'

'Ibia, it is late. Come to bed, I won't touch you.'

He looked up and saw her weeping. He went to her, took her by the hand and led her back to the bed.

'Forget this baby business. That is not my problem.'

'It is.'

As he soothed her, she rested her head on his breast. Suddenly their quarrel, their arguments, their bitterness all melted, and they were lovers again.

In the morning before they rose, Ibia said:

'Ibekwe, I won't be in your way. I don't want people to think I am selfish. Go ahead and marry, but the woman must stay in the village. That is the best I can do.'

Ibekwe was surprised at the concession.

'Of course she will stay in the village. I shall make sure I marry an illiterate woman who will not be interested in coming to bother us here in town.'

It was not easy finding a woman to fit Ibekwe's prescription. The younger women rejected him because they did not want to be second wives. Older ones who liked him made it quite clear they would come to stay with him and Ibia in town. But Oyia, Elei's sister, accepted without any preconditions. Still in her twenties, her husband had been conscripted into the Biafran army and killed. She had not remarried, and some said she was still mourning her husband and two children who died in Biafra. Oyia was quiet. Her beauty was a little roughened by much farm work, but Ibekwe guessed that she would blossom if she enjoyed some comfort and security. He invited Ibia to visit Oyia's people. She refused. Oyia was worried.

'Have you settled with Ibia?' she asked.

'Yes, don't worry,' Ibekwe replied.

Elei was very pleased with the marriage. As a poor roadside mechanic, life was not easy. A rich in-law could make a difference, and he had done much to convince his sister.

Chapter XV

Oyia was born in Ohiamini, so she had no problem settling down in Ibekwe's compound in Kenke village. She knew nearly every woman in her age group and it was a matter of continuing her relationship with them at closer quarters. As Ibekwe's wife, her membership of the young married womens' organization was automatic. There were two such organizations, the other was for older married women, many of whom were the mothers-in-law of the women in the younger group. This separation was necessary since spirited young women could not always control what they said during heated arguments at meetings and mothers-in-law could be very sensitive to insults from their daughters-in-law.

Oyia also joined an *isusu* club to which she contributed two naira every Sunday. At the end of the year when the money box would be 'broken', she calculated that she would have at least 'one bag of naira' with which to buy a lace blouse and george wrappers to celebrate Christmas and the New Year with. She was not going to fold her hands like an urban wife and expect her husband to provide everything. Still, she had to depend on her husband while the first crops she had planted earlier in the year matured.

Young wives in the village breathed a sigh of relief. Here was a Mrs Ibekwe they could relate to. Although Ibia was supposed to be a member of their organization, she scarcely attended meetings, naming ceremonies and funerals. Once in a while she would breeze down with eyes painted like a dibia's, attend a meeting just long enough to display her expensive lace and george, or so the women thought, and disappear without contributing to any debate. In fact she did not know what the discussions were about and she did not care. In contrast, Oyia participated actively in the various activities and spoke her mind with very little inhibition, a quality which the young women admired.

Oyia coped easily with farmwork. She was used to it. She persuaded her husband to grow yams; something he could not do before because there was no one to tend the delicate crop. Erinwo would have found in Oyia the model village wife she had hoped her son would marry.

For all her hard work, Oyia made very few demands. Used to a hard life of privation, she had learnt to make do with little. When she made demands they were so insignificant that Ibekwe was amused. She would ask for a two-naira pair of rubber slippers or a five-naira print blouse. Usually Ibekwe gave her more than she asked but not much more, for fear that she might gradually learn to be extravagant; but he need not have worried for Oyia's simplicity was deeply ingrained. What Ibia spent on cosmetics in a month, Oyia would have spent in years. She used no cosmetics except a cheap powder which she applied generously around her neck during special outings. She and her neighbour plaited each other's hair so she spent nothing on hair-dos. When city girls told her how much they spent on one hair-do alone she concluded they were either outright liars or simply crazy.

Oyia had a plain face but her near perfect teeth seemed to make up for that, especially when she smiled. Black, taller than her husband, and well built, she possessed a dignified presence which men found desirable.

Although she made very little material demands, Oyia expected Ibekwe to conform to the norms of traditional marriage. One day, as her husband was announcing his intention to buy a small generator, she said:

'Ibekwe, there is something we should settle before any other thing.'

'What?'

'Cooking arrangements.'

'But everything is working fine.'

'Because I have not complained so far.'

'But there is nothing to complain about.'

'There is.'

'What?'

'I cook for you at weekends; that's not the tradition.'

'What is the tradition?'

'Ibia and I should each cook for four days at a time alternately.'

Ibekwe pondered awhile.

'You are right, but you know I don't live in the village.'

'You have a car.'

'Yes, but I can't be running to the village every day.'

'Many who have no cars go to work in Port Harcourt from here every morning.'

'Oyia, you are right, but you should not worry about that yet.'

'Are you saying that Ibia should continue to sleep with you six days every week? Am I a wife or a night guard?'

Oyia's forthrightness unnerved Ibekwe. And she was not the type of woman one could cow down easily. She was physically strong, thanks to hard work, and Ibekwe knew it.

'I shall think about it and see what can be arranged.'

After a week, Ibekwe had not rectified the situation. When he came home on Sunday, Tia came to see him.

'Ibe, your wife has lodged a complaint,' she said.

'What is it?'

'You sleep with her only one day in the week. Is that so?'

Ibekwe had not forgotten his clash with Omirinya. He did not want a repetition. This time he would be polite.

'Tia, it is true.'

'Is it right?'

'Of course not. But you know how it is.'

'I know nothing. Oyia is your wife, and a new wife at that, so she must be treated properly. In fact you should spend more time with her, but I am not going to suggest that. Do the right thing.'

'I have already discussed this matter with Oyia. I promised to arrange matters properly but I need time.'

'You don't need any time. You have a car. You can return to the village after work without much trouble. I want to settle this matter personally without involving Omirinya. You don't want another Omirinya problem on your head, do you? They both laughed. In the end Ibekwe promised to do something.

Back in town, he decided not to discuss the new schedule with Ibia. Fortunately he was about to start his new building in the village. That should be enough reason to go to the village frequently. After two weeks Ibia could not stand it.

'Christmas.'

'Mm?'

'You stay in the village far too often these days. I hardly see you.'

'I want to get on with the building.'

'You don't build at night.'

'That's true.'

'So you should at least come back at the end of the day.'

Clearly prevarication would not do. He decided to tackle the question head on.

'Ibia, you know I have to stay with Oyia too.'

'I didn't say you shouldn't. You have been doing so for months.'

'Yes, but one day in the week is not enough.'

'How many does she consider enough?'

'It is not what she thinks, but what tradition demands.'

'Which is?'

'That I should spend four days with you and four with her.'

Ibia was speechless for quite a while.

'So that stupid illiterate woman and I are equal in this house, hm?'

'It is not a matter of equality. It is what tradition says.'

'I don't care what tradition says. This new scheme will not work with me. One night in the village every week is quite enough.'

'It is not so easy. You see, Oyia will complain to Omirinya. I have told you about the clash I had with them last time. They fined me heavily and I had to do everything they

178

demanded before they came to bury my mother. I don't want any more *wahala* with them. I am a busy man.'

'And I am a busy woman!'

'Then get on with your business and leave me alone!'

'I have heard you. We shall see.'

Ibia walked out of the bedroom and slammed the door. She looked back but no irate Ibekwe came charging through the door. She sat in the sitting room which was dimly lit by reflections from the security light in front of the house. Outside, the street was quiet. Even the hawkers of *suya*, cola nuts and cigarettes, who usually waylaid returning cinema fans had gone.

So this was married life, Ibia thought. She remembered how anxious she had been to marry; how suitor after suitor had toyed with her and for no apparent reason disappeared, including the man who had made her pregnant in Biafra; how she had schemed for months to get Ibekwe to propose at last. Was it all for this – to be tossed aside in preference to a dirty, illiterate village woman? Oyia was not even a young girl whose youthful allure could be said to have turned Ibekwe's head. She was certainly more beautiful than Oyia. Ibekwe's excuse was tradition. Rubbish. She knew the real reasons: he wanted to have a different woman every four days. She knew the popular men's joke of *okro* and *egusi* soups. No one wanted to eat one type for days on end. Men simply lacked control. Did they think women did not feel what they felt? And women were more sexually capable for that matter. Children? Yes, he wanted children. That too was a reason, although he refused to admit it. It was not her fault. Every doctor who had examined her had said there was nothing physically wrong with her. Perhaps Ibekwe was to blame? But then he had had a daughter with Alekiri. Yes, Alekiri, he had a daughter with her, but none with me. And he might have a child soon with Oyia … Oyia …

'Oyia, why are you here?'

'This is my husband's house.'

'You should be in the village.'

'Which village?'

'Ohiamini.'

Oyia laughed and drew nearer.

'Get back, go away!'

Oyia drew nearer still, growing bigger in the process.

'Go away! Go! *Go*!'

Oyia held her in a vice-like grip and Ibia could not so much as struggle. She was terror-stricken.

'Oyia, leave me! Oyia! Oyia! Oyiaaaah!'

A sudden flood of light pierced through her eyelids and she woke, sweating. Her husband stood in front of her.

'Stop screaming and come to bed,' he said. It took her some time to recollect where she was.

'Come to bed, the mosquitoes will feast on you here.'

'Let them. I shall sleep here.' To confirm her statement, she stretched herself out on the settee, undid her upper wrapper and covered her head and body with it. Fed up, Ibekwe switched off the light and went back to bed.

For the next few weeks Ibekwe tried to maintain the four-day routine and Ibia sulked. She came back late from work, prepared food carelessly and sometimes not at all, and visited her sister oftener than before. Ibekwe complained to K.T. and his wife, and they spoke to Ibia. She ignored whatever advice they might have given her.

Ibekwe was astonished at the change in her. The fun-loving, playful, smiling woman grew progressively distant and morose. She refused to eat with him and avoided conversation. When they slept together she turned her back to him.

'Ibia, you agreed I should get a second wife, didn't you?' Ibekwe asked desperately one evening.

'You wanted to very much. What was I expected to do?'

'Answer the question. Did we not agree on a second wife?'

'Suppose I had said no?'

'Then your present behaviour would be understandable.'

'What behaviour? Leave me alone *bo*. I don't stop you going to see your village queen. What more do you want?'

'I want good food. I want the house kept clean. I want to

180

find you in the house when I come home.'

'On how many days in the week do I find you at home when I come back from work?'

'But you know where I go to.'

'Oho. You too should know where I go to.'

Ibekwe could not trust himself to speak any longer. For the next few days he pondered the situation. His peace of mind had begun to suffer. He was making money fast, thanks to K.T., and it was important to concentrate his efforts in that direction. It was important that his base in Port Harcourt should be peaceful and comfortable. He could understand Ibia's resentment, it was common enough. Women simply could not tolerate co-wives with grace, no matter how much they pretended to do so. But in spite of everything, Ibia was charming in many ways. It would be a pity to quarrel with her deeply and perhaps lose her. It was no use amassing wealth without a stable home base. The villagers would consider him an *ofogori* incapable of running a family. It was a pity though, Ibia was not producing children. Perhaps Oyia would. He just had to keep both women at all costs. The time had come to consolidate.

Of the two women, he considered that Oyia would be the easier to deal with. She was not half as sophisticated as Ibia and so should be able to tolerate more inequity. He would make a deal with Ibia: five days with her and two days with Oyia every week. Ibia was agreeable, Oyia was indignant, but Ibekwe won over the latter by installing in the village the promised television set and a small electric generator to work it. He bought her expensive clothes and furnished her bedroom. Ibekwe became convinced that polygamy worked if one had money.

Chapter XVI

The demand for teachers was great and as soon as Alekiri passed out of the College of Education she was posted to St. Michael's Girls' Secondary School. The schools had just gone on long vacation and so she had nearly three months in which to rest and, as she told Tam Jaja, 'do those things which she ought not to do'. By the end of her course at the college, she had shed some of her shyness and was even able to tease her male colleagues in spite of her 'reverend mother' image. Tam Jaja knew her much better than any of her other male colleagues. He said: 'Alee you can't change your nature radically just like that.'

'I disagree. People can change their nature radically. A kind person can turn cruel overnight.'

'In that case the person was only pretending to be kind in the first place.'

'How can you tell? You can only judge people by what they say and do.'

'Agreed, but you can sometimes tell when someone is play-acting.'

'Well, if someone is always kind to me in the name of play-acting, I don't mind. I would prefer him to the person who is sincerely cruel!'

Tam Jaja laughed, and said: 'You know, people are cruel because they lack imagination.'

Alekiri waited for him to explain.

'You see the moment you can imagine yourself in someone else's situation, it is difficult to be cruel.'

'I don't think that is always the case,' Alekiri said.

'Sometimes someone's ability to imagine himself in your position gives him a better idea of how to punish you.'

Jaja pondered that awhile.

'You have a point there. You are saying that people may use their knowledge for good or evil.'

'That's it.'

'So you think the humanitarian and the sadist may have an equal insight into human psychology.'

'That's it.'

Jaja's major subject at the college had been educational psychology and he was in his element.

'Still, one should not be forced by other people's bad behaviour to change one's good nature.'

'Tam, I am so confused that I am not sure I know what is good and bad behaviour any more.'

'Don't be silly.'

'I am not joking.'

'Then you should quit teaching.'

'Why?'

'How can you teach and be an example to your students if you can't distinguish between good and bad?'

'I teach them home economics and some literature. These subjects have nothing to do with good and bad behaviour. They are neutral.'

'You must be joking. Surely there is a lot of moral judgement involved in the teaching of literature. How do you appreciate fictional characters for instance?'

'All right. You win. You are pressing too hard. But Tam, what I wanted to say is this: when you do your best to behave well and you end up even worse than someone who behaves badly, then you can get very confused.'

'You shouldn't. People should behave well, not because of what they can gain, but because they know it is good to behave well and they find pleasure in doing so.'

'But how can there be pleasure when you end badly? How can we be sure it is good to behave well if we are hurt in the end?'

'You know why you are confused?'

'I have told you already.'

'That's not it. You are confused because you regard what has happened to you as typical, or as reflecting a universal law. But that is not correct. Occasionally a good person comes to grief or a bad person prospers, but surely those are exceptions. You did your best in your marriage and through circumstances beyond your control it broke up. You cannot now say that all wives and husbands should cease to care for their marriage.'

Alekiri sighed and sipped her soft drink. Tam Jaja, bespectacled and clad in an embroidered print blouse, stared at her intensely as if trying to implant his point of view in her mind. Since that day he had a meal at her place, he had visited her a number of times, but their relationship had remained Platonic and Alekiri liked it that way. Tam Jaja was tall and handsome with piercing deep-set eyes but she was not physically attracted to him. What she admired was his intellect, his honesty and his sensitivity to people. If Jaja was attracted to her, he did not show it.

'Anyway, I am through with marriage.'

'Wrong again.'

'We all don't have to get married. In any case I have had my share of it and the world cannot say I have not tried it out.'

'Every man will not behave like Ibekwe.'

'Ibekwe was a good husband until the war intervened. I won't lie against him. He was a good husband. He was faithful and he looked after me.'

'Why could he not understand what happened to you?'

'He understood but he was not mature enough to bear it. If I had not had a baby he might have forgiven me. The baby made all the difference.'

'But some people adopt other people's children. Why couldn't he at least adopt your child?'

'Well as you would say, he could not put himself in my place.'

'That's true. But there is also the illusion that one owns children.'

'But surely we own our children?'

'You don't. You are a guardian. No one owns any child. Does your father own you?'

'Well, not in the sense that I own, say, this chair.'

'In what sense does he own you then?'

'Em … er … well, I am his daughter.'

They both laughed.

'Answer the question: Does he own you?'

Jaja's intense brown eyes bored into her.

'If I am his daughter then I suppose he owns me.'

'Okay, look at it this way: You can say he is your father, can't you?'

'Yes.'

'Do you own him just because he is your father?'

'I agree I don't own him as I do a piece of furniture, but the relationship is very close.'

'Close relationship does not mean ownership. No one owns any child or anybody, at least, not since slavery was abolished. People take care of other human beings when they are helpless, either because they are closely related to them or because they care.'

'Tam, you are too academic.'

'Perhaps, but you can see what problems the illusion of ownership of children can cause.'

'But Tam, let me ask you, and be honest in your answer: if you were my husband, how would you take it?'

'Knowing the circumstances, I would take you and the child in.'

'And if you didn't know the circumstances?'

'The answer is obvious: I would assume you had fallen in love with someone else, in which case I would let you go.'

Tam Jaja drained his glass of beer, wiped his mouth with a handkerchief and rose to go.

'Alee, in spite of what has happened you should not be bitter. Keep your mind open to life. Don't say you will not do this or that. It is unwise to take firm decisions about future circumstances which are still unknown.'

'Thank you, Tam. And please come again.'

'I seem to do all the coming. You don't even know where I live.'

'That's true, but you've never invited me.'

'That's also true. But Alee, quite frankly I am ashamed of where I live. The yard is terribly congested. When it rains you need a canoe to go to the kitchen. As for the bucket latrine it stinks abominably. I find it difficult to invite anybody to the place.'

'It is not your fault. Landlords are more interested in money than in the welfare of their tenants.'

'I am looking for better quarters; the problem is the money. A flat like yours costs at least a hundred naira a month and the landlord wants a year's rent in advance. By the way, how do you manage?'

'About the rent?'

'Yes.'

'I told you. Binta's father sees to it. I don't know how long this arrangement will last. In fact I expect to be thrown out any day.'

When Tam Jaja left, Alekiri turned her conversation with him over and over in her mind. She concluded he was just being academic. If he were in Ibekwe's position he would in all likelihood chuck her out. Men were the same – cruel and intensely jealous.

Since Mama Iyabo and her husband packed away, she had been relatively lonely and it was good talking to Tam. He did not put on airs and he did not run people down. It was a delight talking to him even when one disagreed with him, she thought.

While at college much of her energy had gone into her studies. It had been possible to suppress her personal problems, and easy to fend off the advances of men. But with her studies over, she told herself she had to look squarely at her problems and work out a formula to live by.

First, marriage. That was out. What had she gained from her marriage but retarded education, beatings and disgrace? What guarantee was there that another marriage would not be worse? And it did not matter how kind and considerate the man was before marriage. Men were highly skilled in the art of pretence during courtship. They could be sugar itself. But once one became a wife, they could turn intensely bitter overnight. The sugar could turn to quinine. Marriage was out, out, out.

And love affairs? Should she avoid that completely? At twenty-nine she was still young and attractive. The confidence which higher education had given her appeared to make her more desirable, especially to men who were more interested in having an affair than in marriage. At the college, three teachers had pursued her, but thanks to a determination born of her experiences, she had been firm and had made it quite clear she was not playing that game. Outside the college walls it was worse. One newly rich politician was so infatuated with her that he plied her with drinks, food and money. It was easy to refuse money but she did not know what to do with the food and drinks he deposited in her house during her absence. She begged him in vain to remove his property. The man said she could have them and more, whether or not she was interested in him. After all, pure Platonic friendship was not completely dead, he said. Finally he offered to take her for a weekend in London with, as he put it, no strings attached. Then she thought of a way out. She told the man Major Dansuku was her lover and the father of her baby, and that he would be extremely angry if he met him in her house. That did it. The man vanished. Marriage had one distinct advantage, she thought afterwards: it protected a woman from harrassment by men. Having discovered this gimmick she applied it, and it worked every time. She wondered how Dansuku would feel if he knew to what use she was putting his past relationship with her.

Still, it was difficult to settle the problem of men once and for all. It was easier to take short-term decisions and review them from time to time in the light of prevailing circumstances. That, in effect, had been Jaja's advice. It was worth taking. Accordingly she decided to say no to all men for a year.

That would give her time to settle down in St. Michael's College and organize her teaching at this higher level. At the end of the year she would review her decision.

Having taken this decision she felt calmer and her chaotic thoughts appeared to come under some control. But there was still the problem of the two men who were the fathers of her children. She could not help coming into contact with them now and then. Her contact with Ibekwe was indirect; not so her contact with Dansuku, who came to see Binta at least once a fortnight. Usually he would have a bottle of beer while playing with Binta. He was formal and avoided any intimacy in word or deed with what looked like military discipline. Alekiri found this cold formality disconcerting at times, but she knew she could not complain. No, that would be the silliest thing to do. She wished Dansuku could behave like Tam Jaja but that was impossible. The two men were completely different.

Binta was another source of confusion. By tradition she was Ibekwe's daughter, but so far he had shown no interest at all in her. Would he try to claim her when she grew up? She would certainly fight against that. After all, she thought, their marriage could be said to have ended when the war separated them, and Dansuku was Binta's biological father. Ibekwe would have no ground to claim her. No? Wait. Ibekwe could claim every child she bore so long as her father did not return the bride price. It was important, indeed urgent, to pay him back the bride price. She would tell her father and give him the money if necessary. But, wait. Ibekwe had stolen her money. Aha, that settled it. The money he stole could pay for the refund fifty times over. Clearly he had no right to Binta. She was Dansuku's child. At least, biologically. But she would bear her own father's name. Binta Kinika. That was the tradition.

Chapter XVII

Ibekwe soon realized that his domestic problems were not solved. When he went to the village one weekend he found Oyia in a bad mood. His experience in three marriages had taught him it was foolhardy to attempt to ask a woman why she was sulking. It was like thrusting one's head into a nest of wasps. The thing to do was to ride the clouds and watch them melt away.

Methodically Oyia did her duties. She served him a warm bath and later a meal of pounded yam with snail-and-*okazi* soup. After the splendid meal Ibekwe yawned contentedly and invited Oyia to bed.

'Let's sit and talk for a moment,' she said with icy firmness. Ibekwe's heart sank. So the clouds would not melt away. His hopes of a peaceful weekend receded somewhat.

'What is it?'

'Sit down first.'

Ibekwe sat down in the tiny living room, determined not to quarrel. He was too tired for that. He had spent the whole day tracking down several bundles of roofing sheets stolen by his workers at a construction site in town and he had looked forward to a quiet weekend in the village.

'Yes, what's the matter?'

'Tell me, have I not been serving you well since you married me?'

'Go on; say what is on your mind. Don't ask me questions.'

'Do I not respect you?'

Ibekwe stared at her.

'Have you found another man in your bed? Is your farm not well looked after?'

'Oyia, what's the matter?'

'You are not treating me well.'

'I am not treating you well?'

'Yes.'

Ibekwe studied the floor. What was she up to? Not treating her well? What ingratitude. Here was a woman who not long ago was living in a leaking mud house, wearing wretched clothes and scarcely able to rub two kobo together. Now she lived in relative comfort, enjoying electricity and television to the envy of her neighbours, and she was talking of being ill used. In spite of his determination to be calm, Ibekwe's temper began to rise. He managed to retain a level voice.

'Explain the bad treatment you suffer.'

'Let me explain first that you are providing for me as a huband should. You buy clothes for me, you give me money for housekeeping, you have installed electricity and television. I thank you for all this.'

'Then what, what is the trouble?'

'I don't want to be married to a television set.'

'What do you mean?' Ibekwe's anger was noticeable.

'I am married to you and not to a television set. Ibia and I should share you four-four days.'

'I thought we had discussed that before. I had explained the nature of my work in town. You have agreed – and I thank you for that – you have agreed I do my duties as a husband. Now where do you expect me to get the money to give you if I spend all my time here?'

'Give me less money but stay with me as you should. You have bought a fast new car. You can drive from Port Harcourt to the village in a shorter time than I can go to the farm and back. I don't see why you can't stay with me four days at a time, unless of course your Mammy-water in town has forbidden you to do so.'

'Say what you like, I can only come here on weekends. Are you telling me what to do in my own compound? Are you marrying me or am I marrying you? Hm?'

'I am not telling you what to do. Who am I? I am only

190

reminding you of our tradition which you seem to have forgotten.'

'That tradition worked for our fathers but it cannot work these days.'

'So you won't agree?'

'We have discussed this matter before and finished with it. I won't listen to anything else.'

'I shall take the matter to Omirinya.'

Ibekwe's anger boiled over.

'Go to Omirinya, you ungrateful woman! Go to Omirinya and see how that will help you. I can decide to come here once a month and no Omirinya can make me change my mind.'

'Ibekwe, you seem to think I am a maidservant brought here to look after your compound and work on your farm. Let me tell you I am not a servant. You should treat Ibia and I equally. If not, then she must come to the village and take her turn at working on your farm.'

'Listen, stupid woman, Ibia earns money and you don't.'

'I earn money too.'

'What money? What money?'

'I earn money and I produce the *garri* and yams which feed you and your Mammy-water in town.'

'You feed me?'

'Yes.'

Ibekwe stood up in anger and as Oyia tried to rise he smacked her on the cheek.

'I have not brought you from your dunghill to come here and insult me, do you hear?'

'Don't slap me again, Ibekwe.'

'And what will you do if I slap you again? What will you do?'

Ibekwe gripped her right wrist but with remarkable ease she freed herself. He tried again, but this time she gripped his left wrist instead. He struggled frantically to free himself, but failed. Surprised and dismayed, sweat broke out on his brow. Gritting his teeth, he took a deep breath and made another attempt, but Oyia's grip still held, thanks to her rough palm, calloused by years of contact with the hoe. Clearly the woman

191

would hold her own in a fight, he thought.

'Don't slap me again,' she said and released him.

Though a little unnerved, Ibekwe was determined to assert his authority.

'Now get out! Go, go to your room.' He pushed her but Oyia hardly moved.

'Ibekwe, all I am saying is that you should not treat me like a housemaid.'

'Get out!' This time he did not push her, but merely pointed at the door. Oyia went out.

The weekend was ruined. What was he to do? Angrily he said: 'Oyia, you can have the compound to yourself since you won't let me rest'. He put on his shirt, shut the door and strode to his car. The tyres screeched as he sped to town.

Back in town, he drove to Port Harcourt Club, of which he was now a proud member, and had a drink. Then, close to midnight, he drove to his residence. Ibia was watching a 'late night movie' on television. When he rang the bell, she peeped through the window first to see who it was. Surprised, she opened the door and went straight back to her chair to watch the film. She did not greet him. Ibekwe opened his mouth to greet her, changed his mind, and walked across to the bedroom. If she did not have the good manners to greet him, he would not greet her either. What was wrong with women anyway?

Just as he was about to lie down the door opened and Ibia came in.

'Ibekwe, where are you from?'

He looked at her and swallowed hard. Should he talk, or just climb into bed and plug his ears? No, it was always better to face these women squarely, otherwise, he thought, they would soon reduce him to a cringing nobody.

'From the village.'

'Which village?'

'Ohiamini.'

'Which village? I ask you. So two wives are no longer enough for you. Is this how you have been spending the weekend with your village queen? I am sorry for the poor woman and for myself.'

He was tired, very tired. The beer made him drowsy.

'Ibia, please let me sleep. I shall explain in the morning. It has been a terrible day. Please.'

Unable to provoke any further response from him, Ibia went back to the living room, switched off the lights and muttered for a while. She was not a great talker. Soon she lay on the settee and slept.

Early in the morning she woke her husband, sat on a chair by the bed and said:

'Are you awake?'

'Yes, what is it?'

'Sit down and let's talk.'

'Speak. I can hear you lying down.'

'Ibekwe.'

'Go on, I said.'

'Where were you from last night?'

'From Ohiamini.'

'That's a lie!'

'It is the truth.'

'It is a lie.'

'You can find out from Oyia.'

'I'll have nothing to do with that woman, do you hear?'

'All right.'

'And who is your third wife?'

'I don't know what you are talking about.'

'Every weekend you pretend you are going to Ohiamini and disappear somewhere else. Ibekwe I am tired of this arrangement.'

'You agreed to the five-two arrangement.'

'Well, it does not work.'

'Look, Ibia, I have no girlfriend if that is what you are worrying about.'

'You can have a thousand girlfriends, that is not my business. What I want to say is that your five-two arrangement can't work.'

'Why not?'

'Because I work from Monday to Friday. The weekend is the only time I can relax. We should be able to go to the cinema on Saturdays and to church on Sundays. I see all my friends with their husbands in the church. I look like a widow. I am fed up.'

'What is your solution?'

'You should visit the village in the middle of the week and spend the weekend here.'

'Do you mean I should spend five days in the village and the weekend here?' he teased.

'You may joke, but I consider this a very serious matter.'

'Just tell me what you want me to do.'

'Okay. You should spend, say, Wednesdays and Thursdays in the village, and the rest of the week here.'

'Why?'

'Why not? Women in the village don't care about weekends. They are busy with their meetings and *isusu* clubs.'

'You forget that I too attend meetings in the village. It is only on Sundays that I can meet people there and discuss village affairs. On other days they are at work on their farms.'

'You can attend meetings when necessary on Sundays and drive back afterwards.'

'I don't see why I should be driving up and down like a crazy fellow.'

'Then you shouldn't have married two wives.'

'Why not? Our fathers married four, five, ten wives.'

'Our fathers needed those women to help on the farms. Times have changed. You are not a farmer.'

'I have a farm and it is run by a woman like you.'

'How dare you say that? Don't I work?'

'And where is the money?'

'Does your village queen give you money?'

'Yes.'

'That's a lie.'

'Who do you think produces the *garri* and the yams I bring from the village? That woman feeds you, if you don't know.'

'Did I beg her for yams and *garri*? And from today onwards don't bring any food from the village. If you do I shall throw it away.'

Ibekwe, at first sleepy-eyed and groggy, was now wide awake and sweating. He sat upright in bed.

'Try it and see.'

'See what?'

'We shall see who is the master here.'

'I am not interested in struggling with you. Have you agreed to my proposal? It is the only way out, since you have already forced me to agree to your taking a second wife.'

'Ibia, we have already agreed that I should spend the weekend in the village and that is the end of the matter.'

'And that is the end of the marriage.'

'You can go to hell!'

'Thank you.'

The following Monday, Ibia asked for two days casual leave. Bianco, who was now her boss, easily granted her request. On Tuesday evening when Ibekwe came back to the house he could not find Ibia. On his bed were two envelopes addressed to him. One was bulky, the other much lighter. He opened the bulky one and a bundle of twenty-naira notes stared at him. His hand shook as he opened the other envelope. It contained a letter in Ibia's neat feminine hand. He read:

Christmas,

After our talk on Monday morning I am now sure our marriage cannot continue. I cannot have a husband on some days of the week and no husband on other days. It is old time idea. All my friends laugh at me. You say you want to copy your father, but was your father a modern businessman living in town? You have no farm. You do not live in the village. How can you copy your father? Imagine. Anyway, I cannot share my husband with another woman. Find out those women who know how to share husband and marry them. I wish you luck.

It is true I agreed you should marry a second wife, but you know I cannot stop you, more so as I have no child. So I am giving you chance to marry twenty wives who will get fifty children for you.

I am not perfect. Nobody is perfect except God. But I did my best. Your food was never late until you started rushing up and down to the village. You did not catch me with another man. I never abused you even one day. Christmas, I did my best.

You will find the bride price you paid enclosed in the other envelope. This is because I do not want any molest. Do not worry my in-law K.T. and his wife. They cannot convince me to come back to you.

I have not removed any of your property. I have no time for other people's things. God must give me my own property one day.

I am sorry for Wibari. You better send her back to her mother Alekiri. Your village queen is illiterate. She cannot look after her.

I wish you luck in your business.

Your former ex-wife
Ibia.

Chapter XVIII

Binta, now seven, had often been invited to her friends' birthday parties. She had never celebrated hers because her mother did not consider it necessary. For Alekiri, birthday parties were a waste of time and money. She herself had never celebrated a birthday and hardly ever thought of it. This led to an incident she could not forget. It was during her first year at the College of Education. She had gone to the registrar's office to submit a form. Among other details she had filled in on the form was her birthday. The administrative officer took the form from her and studied it briefly to check her entries. Then he glanced at a calendar hanging on the wall, smiled at her, and said:

'Congratulations!'

'What for?' Alekiri asked in surprise.

'Today is your birthday, isn't it?'

'Yes, of course. Thank you.'

She had left the office laughing at herself.

Binta was now old enough to demand a celebration of her birthday. Alekiri did not refuse. It was time she returned some of the hospitality she had enjoyed at her friends' parties. Binta's birthday was in July, at the climax of the rainy season. The morning was bright and Alekiri prayed that the weather would hold. She was studying the sky when Tam Jaja arrived with a doll under his arm. She had mentioned Binta's birthday party to Jaja casually during a conversation and she was surprised at his gesture.

'You didn't have to go into all that expense.'

'It is not for you, so you can't complain.'

They laughed.

'Binta, this doll is for you. Happy birthday.'

The child's eyes glowed as she clasped the beautiful doll to her breast.

'Say thank you to uncle,' her mother said.

'Thank you, uncle.'

Jaja drew the child towards him, hugged her and kissed her cheek. Alekiri was moved and said:

'Tam, this is sweet of you. Thanks a lot.'

'Forget it.'

'The party is at 4 p.m. and the edibles are not ready yet.'

'Even if they were, they should be reserved for her little friends.'

'I don't agree that the big friends should starve.'

They laughed. Alekiri extracted a beer from the fridge and served Jaja. She went into the kitchen and brought him a piece of cake on a saucer.

'Manage this?'

'Thanks. Share the beer with me. I don't usually drink during the morning hours.'

Alekiri brought a glass and he filled it.

'Binta, happy birthday!' he said; but the child was in the dining area tilting the doll this way and that to watch its eyes open and shut.

'The cake is good. Did you bake it yourself?'

'No. Major Dansuku brought it for his daughter a few days ago.'

'How is he by the way?'

'He is fine as far as I can see.'

'You can see far, no doubt.'

'Not these days. I told you our affair ended a long time ago. He comes here only to see his daughter.'

'He seems a nice man to me.'

'He is not bad.'

'Why did your affair cease?'

'When my husband – I should say my former husband – when he came back I had to withdraw from Dansuku in the hope that he would take me back.'

'I see,' Jaja said and decided not to pursue the painful subject.

'Did you listen to the radio last week?' he went on.

'Yes, I always do,'

'What do you think of the postponement of civilian rule?'

'That is not new. The Head of State said so in his Independence Anniversary broadcast last year.'

'Well last week the Head of State said it again, I suppose for emphasis this time.'

'Did he give a new date for civilian rule?'

'No. He said the army would take its time to execute its many programmes successfully. Thereafter it would consider the possibility of a change to civilian rule.'

'Tam, quite frankly I don't want any civilian rule in the near future. At least we have some peace and order and freedom from political thugs.'

'That may be so, but the truth is that the army is enjoying political power and does not want to give it up, especially with so much oil money around.'

'Do you think the soldiers are stealing our money?'

'Certainly, but far less than the politicians would steal if they had all that money.'

'I wonder why politicians are so impatient. After all, they are very much in government. All the commissioners and various political appointees at the federal and state levels are politicians.'

'Yes, but they are not controlling political power. It is that control they want. A commissioner under a military governor does exactly as he is told, and he is not in an easy position to take his ten per cent cut from contracts.'

'If I had my way, the army would stay on. After all, soldiers are ordinary Nigerians in uniform. Sometimes I think we are just quarrelling about the kind of dress our rulers should wear – whether khaki or lace.'

Tam Jaja laughed, and rose to go. 'Alee the matter is not as simple as that. It is not a question of who rules; it is the type of government that is important. A military rule is a dictatorship; one man or a few people say what is to be

199

done. In a democracy the people say what they want.'

'Tam, let's be honest. There is no democracy in this country. The leading politicians always do what they like, and care very little for you and me. What our people need is a strong hand, and that is what the army is providing.'

'I hope Dansuku has not influenced you,' Tam said laughing.

'Don't be silly.'

'Bye-bye for now.'

'Bye-bye, Tam, and thanks for the gift.'

In the afternoon Dansuku arrived loaded with gifts. Binta ran to him and settled on his knees.

'Daddy, where is the bicycle?'

'So you haven't forgotten?'

'Where is it?'

Dansuku laughed, peeped out of the door and shouted to his driver to fetch the little bicycle in the Land-Rover. Binta jumped up and down as the driver brought it.

'Sule, thank you,' Alekiri said quietly. 'Do I fetch you a beer?'

'Yes.'

'And some *jollof* rice?'

'No, just the beer.'

There was a crash in the dining area. They turned round and found Binta trying to extricate herself from the bicycle which had fallen on her. Alekiri and Dansuku looked at each other and laughed.

'Binta, you can't learn to ride in the house,' Alekiri said, going to her daughter's aid. 'Let go now. I shall take you to the school playground and teach you to ride.'

A vehicle stopped near the house. Car doors slammed. Presently the front curtains parted and Christie entered the room. Immediately she and her sister went into a long embrace.

'When did you arrive?'

'About an hour ago, Ola and I.'

Captain Olaitan entered. On seeing Major Dansuku he

saluted smartly, and Dansuku acknowledged the salute.

'I went to your house, Major, and Bukar said you were here.'

'That's right. Sit down and have a beer.'

Ola was in uniform. He removed his hat, deposited it along with his cane on an empty chair and sat down.

'Alee how are you?'

'Fine.'

'Long time no see.'

'Na so. Beer?'

'Yes thanks.'

'Christie, beer?'

'Yes. But where is Binta?'

'She is in the bedroom dressing up for her party. It has been a fight restraining her from putting on her new dress before now.'

Christie went into the bedroom with her large handbag. Before long Binta came out to display the dresses and dolls her aunt had given her.

'I didn't know I would find myself in a party,' Ola said. 'What party is this?'

'Binta's birthday party,' Alekiri said.

'I should have brought a present for Binta if I had known. Anyway, Binta, come here.'

The child moved to him. He rummaged stiffly in his well-starched uniform and fished out a ten-naira note.

'Happy birthday,' he said as he gave the child the money.

'Ola, thank you,' Christie said.

'Oh, it's nothing.'

'Thank you, Ola,' Alekiri said.

'You embarrass me.'

Captain Olaitan drank his beer rather quickly, then said:

'Major, I have an important message for you, can we go to your house as soon as you can manage?'

'Certainly. In fact I am about to go.'

201

Dansuku rose, patted Binta on the head and said:

'Alee, you and Christie can organize the party, I am sure. See you later. Ola, you will find me at the house.'

'I shall be right behind you,' Ola said.

Dansuku left. Ola retrieved his hat, put it on, and rose.

'Christie, I expect you in the evening. Why don't you come for dinner with Alee?'

'Not today Ola,' Alekiri said. 'I shall be too tired after this party.'

'You are right. I didn't think of that.'

He walked out and Christie joined him briefly. Alekiri heard the car drive off and Christie re-entered. The two women looked at each other, and Christie detected a faint look of puzzlement on her sister's face.

'Alee, Ola and I have become quite friendly. He visits me each time he comes to Lagos. He has even asked me to marry him.'

'So fast?'

'You know these army boys are a little crazy.'

'Isn't he married already?'

'He was married to an English woman, but they are separated. The woman is back in England with their two daughters. Ola says he visits her and the children once a year. He stays in her house while in UK.'

'So they are not really divorced?'

'I don't know. I didn't bother to find out.'

'And what answer did you give?'

'Alee, you know me too well to ask.'

'But Christie, do you intend to remain single all your life?'

'Yes. From what I have seen of marriage, it is not worth it.'

'Don't judge from mine.'

'The fact is, I do not want any man to boss me and tell me what to do, and bark at me for not preparing his food in time and all that rubbish. I just can't put up with all that shit.'

Alekiri thought for a while.

'Christie, what about children? Don't you want children?'

'I don't need to marry in order to have children. Anyway, even if I marry, I can't have children.'

'Why?'

'The doctors say my tubes are blocked. I have been trying to have a child for the past three years.'

Alekiri stared at her sister with shock, but Christie seemed unmoved.

'But what happened?'

'A doctor said I must have had an infection, but I don't remember ever having such an infection. I have always taken good care of myself. I take it that God does not want me to bear children and leave it at that. After all, our aunt in Lagos has no children of her own but she is happy. She regards me as her child and I do all I can to make her forget she has no child.'

Alekiri listened speechless. Here was her sister's secret sorrow which she had shared with no one until now. She looked at her and Christie returned the stare with a defiant smile, as if assuring her she was more than capable of bearing her misfortune.

'And Alee, if you get more children, you will let one of them live with me, won't you?'

'Yes, of course,' Alekiri replied with a lump in her throat.

Dansuku was waiting for Ola, wondering what message he had for him. As soon as the bell rang, he opened the door and Ola stepped in briskly, saluted and sat down.

Dansuku watched him and observed he was unusually restless. He brought out a packet of cigarettes, lit one and offered Dansuku the packet, one cigarette sticking out of the pack tantalizingly.

'No thanks. Have a beer.'

'No thanks. A soft drink will do.'

Dansuku could not remember ever offering Ola a soft

drink in his house and was surprised.

'What's happening to you?' he asked.

'Nothing. It's just that I have had a beer already and I want to keep a clear head to discuss a very important matter with you.'

'May I have a beer?'

Ola laughed. 'Go ahead, you have my permission.'

'Sule, are you alone?'

'Arit is in the bedroom.'

'Anyone else?'

'No. What's all this?'

'Let's go to your guest room.'

'Why?'

'You will find out soon.'

Dansuku stared at his friend. He collected his beer reluctantly and led the way to his guest room. Once there Ola closed the door. Dansuku watched him warily.

'Sule.'

'Yep.'

'You know the country is stinking with corruption and everyone is fed up.'

'Yep.'

'We want to do something about it.'

'Who?'

'A group of us.'

'I am listening.'

'I want you to join us.'

'What do you want to do?'

'We want to change the leadership.'

'A coup?'

'Well, yes.'

Major Dansuku paused to think.

'I think the Head of State is a good man. It is the men around him who are corrupt.'

'Granting that you are right, where does that get us? Isn't it the job of the head of state to ensure an honest administration?'

204

'Still the man has done a lot for the country.'

'Agreed, but no one is good for all time. Look at Churchill. He saved Britain during the Second World War. But after that they had to throw him out because he was a misfit in post-war Britain. Most leaders are cut out for specific moments in history and few are useful beyond a decade or so.'

'The other point is: will changing the Head of State wipe out corruption? A new Head of State comes into power and for a year or two he tries to keep straight, but sooner or later he and his team slide into the same corruption. Are the coup planners going to change the system so that wealth is more evenly distributed? A country in which millionaires and beggars co-exist is bound to be corrupt, no matter who is Head of State.'

'I didn't know you were such a politician,' Ola said a little sarcastically. 'Join us and bring along your bright ideas.'

'Bright ideas are useless if the Head of State does not share them. Who will be the next Head of State?'

'Join us and find out.'

'I doubt whether there will be any real change. It looks more like a change of guards and that is a waste of time.'

'But you must agree that nothing further can be achieved with the present Head of State.'

'I won't like to see him killed.'

'It's going to be a bloodless coup. At any rate, the Head of State will not be killed.'

'And what would I be expected to do?'

'Hold Port Harcourt.'

'Why me?'

'You are the most capable officer here. You have seen much action at the front and you can take charge of emergency situations.'

'What about my commanding officer?'

'We shall take care of him.'

'Who are the "we"?'

'You and I and other members of the group.'

Major Dansuku lapsed into silence and Ola allowed him to think.

'And if we fail?'

For answer Ola ran his right index finger across his throat.

'Aren't we supposed to hand over to civilians eventually?'

'That's right, but we are very far behind schedule. We have concluded that so long as the present Head of State remains in office we shall never complete the various assignments necessary for handing over power to the civilians.'

Again Major Dansuku lapsed into silence. Then he said:

'Give me a few days to think.'

'That's impossible. Try and make up your mind here and now. We have only a few days to prepare.'

'It seems everything is already set.'

'Not exactly, but you do not want arrangements for a coup to last for more than a few days for obvious reasons of secrecy.'

'And if I say no?'

'Then you must swear to keep your mouth absolutely shut.'

'Ola, you are talking to your superior officer!'

'I am sorry sir,' Ola said with a smile and a salute.

'I say no.'

'Then you must swear to keep what we have discussed secret.'

'And if I refuse?'

'Major, I am afraid you will run into serious difficulties. In fact you will be killed.'

Major Dansuku got up abruptly and rushed out of the room. When he came back, brandishing a revolver, he found Ola still sitting calmly where he had left him.

'You are under arrest,' he said, pointing the gun at him.

'That's no good, Major. I am not as foolish as that.

Members of my group know I am here and are covering your house right now. You have no chance. All I want you to do is to swear to secrecy. I have assured them that you will not squeak when once you promise. If however you can't promise, I am afraid er ...'

'I will be killed?'

'Yes.'

'But you will die first.'

'That does not matter. The success of the coup is more important.'

Dansuku lowered his gun slowly and sat down again.

'Well?' Ola pressed on. 'We have very little time.'

'I shan't take part. It is a waste of time.'

'Swear to secrecy then.'

'I swear.'

'That's enough for me. Remember if you talk, both you and I will die.'

Ola rose and they walked back to the sitting room. He opened the front door and said: 'Okay.'

'Whom are you talking to?'

'My friends.'

Dansuku came to the door just in time to see a Land-Rover full of armed soldiers drive off.

'Ola, listen; someone may squeak and you blame it on me.'

'We have taken care of that possibility. We have a fool-proof checking system.'

'When is this thing coming off?'

Ola laughed. 'Do you expect me to answer that question when you have refused to join us?'

After Ola had left, Dansuku pondered the situation for a long time. He felt extremely uneasy. Clearly there was a lot of danger in the air. The first thing he thought he should do was to ensure that he could move quickly without encumbrance at the shortest possible notice. He got his driver to fill the tank of the Land-Rover and two reserve containers with fuel. The next day he withdrew a large sum of money from the bank, gave some to Arit and asked her to go back to his father's house in Bende Street. He explained he was travelling.

'But I can stay here and keep the house for you.'

'Do as I say.'

She grumbled and packed away.

The Head of State was away visiting another country when the coup occurred three days later. It was bloodless, in the jargon of journalists.

Chapter XIX

The coup which was neatly executed was popular. The new Head of State swung into action without any delay. He began with purges both in the army and the civil service. All the military governors were removed – some retired 'with full benefits', others dismissed with ignominy. Lazy and corrupt civil servants suffered the same fate. For several weeks after the coup, many a civil servant lost weight as he glued his ears and eyes to the radio and television, listening to news of the latest victims of the purge. Students and workers demonstrated in support of the new regime.

Chief Kwaki-Thomas knew what to expect when the new military governor of the state arrived. It was clear to him that no political appointees would be retained. He called the last meeting of the Works Committee and thanked members for their co-operation. There were no drinks, not even tea. It was rumoured that the new regime had abolished all that.

K.T. prepared a detailed report with appendices, one of which showed all the contracts awarded, their cost and stages of completion. Using his engineering knowledge he threw in a few impressive technical terms. Finally he cleared his table of everything except the two new voluminous files which bore the inscription: State Works Committee: Progress Report. One was marked Volume One, the other Volume Two. Every day K.T. went to his office immaculately dressed, and waiting. When finally he was summoned to Government House, he answered the call fully prepared and confident. The Military Governor was so impressed that he promised to retain K.T. there and then. However, a week later, K.T. received a brief letter thanking him for his services and relieving him of his office 'with immediate effect'. From feed-back that filtered to him, it seemed that the military governor had expressed disgust at the fact that K.T. had awarded quite a number of the contracts to his own company. It was said that the military governor had made investigations to ascertain who owned which companies.

K.T. had expected all this and was not very surprised. What unnerved him however was a subsequent announcement which said that outstanding payments to all contractors had been frozen until further notice. That hurt. Still, government would pay eventually. All new regimes started tough: gradually they softened and back-pedalled. He would get his money back yet.

Should he go back to Texo? He decided not to. He would devote full time to his own company and make the best of it. First it would be necessary to engage a qualified engineer as manager. Ibekwe would have to go. He called him and told him so. Ibekwe took it calmly. He thanked K.T. for all his help and hoped that when eventually government paid up, his share of the money, which was quite considerable, would be paid to him. K.T. reassured him.

Ibekwe decided not to go back to trading. There was simply no money to be made in a shed in Mile Three market. He told himself 'his eyes had been opened' to where real money was. He called his young assistant and sold the shed and its contents to him. He was to pay him gradually over two years.

In spite of the car he had bought, and the house under construction in the village, Ibekwe was not in debt. His tippers yielded money daily even though some of them were so old that they had begun to consume in repairs more than they earned. As soon as he could get some more money he would sell off the old tippers and buy new ones. But where was that kind of money to come from? His company was small and unknown. It was kept going only by subcontracts from K.T. The new administration, it was rumoured, had blacklisted K.T.'s company and others and there was no hope of further subcontracts. If only K.T. had gone back to Texo. But then there was Bianco, his good friend, who had taken over from K.T. He should give him contracts.

Bianco was a busy man. It would be futile trying to see him in the office. He would call on him at his residence, preferably in the evening, have a drink or two, and renew acquaintance. He regretted losing touch with Bianco as soon as K.T. was made chairman of the State Works Committee. That was a foolish thing to do. In these days of coups and counter-coups, one should never rely too heavily on the patronage of any government. But Bianco was an easy-going man. He would probably embrace him, slap him on the back and offer him drinks.

When Ibekwe arrived at Bianco's residence he rang the bell and waited. The key clicked, the blind and curtain parted and a feminine voice said 'Come in'. There was an odd familiarity in the voice. Ibekwe looked up and into Ibia's face. He froze at the door as his jaw dropped in utter surprise.

'Come in, Christmas,' she said with a smile.

Like a sleep-walker he walked past her, unable to offer a greeting.

'Sit down. Bianco is in the bath. He is almost through.'

Ibia! Ibekwe's mind reeled. What was happening? He could not look directly at her, but stole side glances instead. She was not dressed like a visitor. That impression was soon confirmed when, coolly and in perfect control of the situation, she said:

'What can I offer you?'

For the first time Ibekwe looked fully at her. She returned the stare still smiling. The staring match went on until Ibekwe gave up and looked down with a sigh. What should he do? Should he accept a drink and wait for Bianco? Could he now ask Bianco for any help? Could he in fact talk to the man? He looked up as Ibia said:

'Sit down while I check something in the oven. I shall be back soon.'

In a split second, Ibekwe made up his mind. It was scarcely a decision. It was more of an impulsive reaction.

'I am sorry I cannot wait. Tell Bianco that I called.'

'But he will soon ...'

Ibekwe had already disappeared through the door. She heard his car door slam and the awful screech of his tyres as he shot off into the night.

Bianco came into the living room in his dressing gown and still combing his hair.

'I thought I heard the bell ring, Ibia.'

'Yes.'

'Who was it?'

'Guess who.'

'Oh I can't guess. Who?'

'My former husband.'

Bianco whistled and Ibia laughed.

'I am glad I didn't come out.'

'Why?'

For answer Bianco punched the air several times and Ibia laughed again.

'No, he can't fight you. I am not his wife now. I paid back the bride price.'

'That's true, but you know man can be angry. In my country men fight for woman's sake. Haa! Serious fight, you know.'

Bianco's relationship with Ibia had taken a deeper turn when Bianco replaced K.T. as executive engineer and Ibia worked directly under him. Each time Ibia came close with typed material he pinched her bottom playfully. At first she resented it, but his mock apologies were so amusing that soon she ceased to bother, regarding bottom-pinching as one of the hazards of working with a crazy man like Bianco. But Bianco proved a helpful boss. He gave her good advice and recommended another promotion for her. Gradually she came to like and trust him. One day when she came to the office looking gloomy, he said:

'Ibia, why you looking sad? Husband box you?'

He boxed the air briskly. Ibia laughed, but said nothing.

'Com'on. Tell me. What's trouble?'

'Bianco, you won't understand.'

When Bianco became Ibia's boss she began to call him 'sir'. But Bianco would have none of that.

'My name is Bianco Piratelli. Call me Bianco, not "Saaar".'

At first she found the informality at the office a little awkward but she adjusted to it.

'What I won't understand? Haa! Com'on, tell me. Sit down.'

Ibia put a file in the in-tray on his table and sat down.

'My husband has married another wife.'

'That makes you sad?'

'Yes.'

'That's your people's custom, not so?'

'Yes, but it is an old custom. It will soon die away.'

'What you want to do? Run away?'

'I can't run. I shall stay.'

'The other wife is worker like you?'

'No. She is an illiterate woman and she lives in the village.'

'You stay in town?'

'Yes.'

'Haa! You should not worry. You enjoy more.'

'My husband goes to the village on weekends.'

'Haa. That's bad. For my country, weekend no joke. Husband and wife they go on picnic, movie and concert. Here, come and type this.' Ibia came to his side and he read out the rough draft of a letter to her. It ended with the inevitable bottom-pinching. Ibia wriggled and giggled. Bianco got up, and without any hestitation, kissed her lips. Surprised, she struggled free and went back to her table to type the letter. She made so many mistakes that she had to retype it.

Bianco was the type of man who would never give up an advantage once gained. Kissing replaced bottom-pinching. At first Ibia struggled, but she came to respond with increasing warmth. Bianco did not go beyond this. He did not invite her to his house and Ibia began to think that kissing in the office was a white man's custom. When Ibia broke with her husband she told Bianco. His response was immediate.

'Come and live with me,' he said. Ibia did not take him seriously at first. But their kissing and cuddling in the office became more prolonged.

'Honest, come live with me. I marry you.'

It was not always easy to determine at first hand Bianco's seriousness but his gestures soon convinced Ibia he meant business. He bought her presents, gave her money and kissed her with a passion that took her breath away. In the end she agreed but not before asking:

'Bianco do you want plenty of children?'

'No, no. No children. Your people, they born too much. One woman ten children, why? Me, no children. No time. You want plenty children?'

'If God gives me one or two I shall take.'

'All right, one, finish.'

When Ibia discussed the matter with K.T. he was very supportive. K.T.'s mind immediately went to business. Through Bianco he would have powerful links in Italy. Why, the marriage was a windfall. Two weeks later the couple were quietly married at the registry. K.T. signed as Ibia's witness. Bianco's witness was another Texo engineer. It was a quiet affair.

214

Chapter XX

The aim of the new regime in carrying out a purge was to get rid of corrupt, inefficient and senile public officers who clogged the bureaucratic wheels of government. It was not always easy to identify such officers. The military high command in Lagos necessarily relied on reports from heads of government agencies and departments and such reports were not always fair and honest. It soon became evident that some people used the chance to eliminate those they considered their enemies or rivals in office.

Major Dansuku wondered what his fate would be. He was convinced he had fought hard and well during the civil war. Surely his promotion to substantive major was an acknowledgement of the fact. He was a keen professional soldier and if he had his way he would stay in the army until retirement age. His commanding officer was not vindictive or unusually selfish and they were on reasonably good terms. He was not likely to recommend him for dismissal or retirement. Or would he? Bloody hell. He had saved his life on one occasion at the front. The CO had once scheduled a visit to his field headquarters. Dansuku had advised him against it since he had just shifted camp and he was not yet sure of his rear. Rebel snipers were still about. The CO in an understandable show of courage had decided to make the visit anyway. He was about to make a report to Lagos, he said, and he wanted to be sure he knew what he was talking about. Dansuku felt apprehensive, so he stationed a search-and-destroy patrol team along the most dangerous part of the route. When the CO arrived at that point he found Dansuku's men holding two rebel soldiers who were about to detonate an *ogbunigwe*. Their hands were tied with the cables which had led from the terminals of a battery some fifty yards away, to the bomb which lay buried along the path very close to where the CO's Land-Rover had stopped. The CO had been so impressed with Dansuku's circumspection and sense of duty that he had included in his report to Lagos a recommendation that Captain Dansuku be promoted to the rank of major. Two weeks later Dansuku sported the eagle of a field major.

Still, the fact that he had refused to take part in the coup hung like a shadow over him as the purge progressed. The new regime could decide to dismiss or retire all those who had refused to take part in the coup. There would be some logic in that, Dansuku thought.

It was time to take a hard look at his life and to decide on just what to do if he found himself out of the army. After fifteen years in the army, what had he achieved? All he had to show was his rank. A major at thirty-two; that was not too bad. He had over twenty more years to serve in the army, and, if his luck held, he could go far yet. If his luck held. That was the vital phrase. A professional soldier's life could end any time, especially during a war. But he was used to that constant element of risk and it did not bother him any more.

What else had he achieved? He had no money. Before the civil war his account had always been in the red. Sometimes he had found it difficult to pay his mess bills. He never could say where the money went. During the war his account had swung back into the black because he had no time for fun, and moreover the army provided free uniform, food, drinks and cigarettes. But his savings were nothing to write home about. Marriage, father's illness, anything of the sort could easily wipe them out.

He had no house, except perhaps his father's old pile in Bende Street. Leaking, dirty and rat-infested, he could not live there without carrying out major repairs which would cost several times his savings.

And there was the problem of marriage. Was it not time he took a wife? Should he copy the British professional soldier who would not think of marrying until he had achieved the rank of colonel at least? He should marry now and begin to settle down. But Habiba had not been encouraging. She had gone to the university and her head seemed to be in the clouds, judging from the fact that she had not replied to his last two letters. Why did university education affect his countrywomen so? He should forget the girl for his own good. Let her marry her professor and pore over books *lai-lai*. Who were the other possibilities? Alekiri was out, thanks to Arit. And Arit. Arit. He should get rid of that girl. Why did he stick to her when she was so devious and unfaithful? As soon as she was out of his sight she would pick up lovers as a matter of routine. He remembered that just before the coup when he had sent her to Bende Street she had done just that. And when he had confronted her she had had the impudence to say: 'After all I am not your wife.'

'Then what are you doing in my house?'

'We are friends, that's all.'

'And why did you bang the door in Alekiri's face?'

'Two captains cannot be in a ship,' she had replied with outrageous calmness. Dansuku had laughed in spite of himself. And that was Arit's ploy, a combination of boldness, helplessness and deviousness which Dansuku found difficult to deal with. Each time he threatened to cut his links with her permanently she had employed one or the other.

Perhaps the most dramatic was her false pregnancy. She had pretended to miss her period and had left Dansuku to infer that she was pregnant. She feigned morning sickness and sometimes Dansuku could hear her vomiting in the toilet. After three months it seemed her belly was filling out. Dansuku could not withold his sympathy and concern. It was only in the fifth month that during a scuffle, her wrapper fell off in the bedroom and Dansuku saw to his amazement and amusement the layers of padding beneath.

217

As Dansuku laughed, Arit had wept – wept so much that Dansuku had stopped laughing and had held her.

'I want a baby, Major. Why can't you make me pregnant as you made Alekiri?'

'I have tried, haven't I?' he said not without some amusement.

'I shall love any man who makes me pregnant. I shall love the ground he walks on. And I shall never look at another man again.'

'Is that why you go from one man to the other?' She nodded and blew her nose. As Dansuku watched her, he thought he had a confused if pitiable woman on his hands. In the past his sympathies for her had always won, but with the conviction that she was neurotic came a new resolution.

She had to go.

'Arit I am sorry I can't make you pregnant. We should part now.'

'Major, I am not blaming you. After all, you made Alekiri pregnant, so I am to blame. Let me stay with you. Forgive my past behaviour. I shall be faithful.'

That was the helplessness ploy, Dansuku thought. But he had had enough.

'My wife will be here next month. I want to get ready for her. You have to pack out of my father's house.'

'Where will I go?'

'I shall find you a room somewhere.'

Dansuku made good his promise. He found Arit a place and hired a truck to move her furniture. He gave her a little money and said bye-bye in a tone in which Arit instinctively recognized a desperate finality.

Whom was he to marry? Dansuku shelved that question. Its answer depended on chance. First he had to bring order to his private life in the same way as he ensured order in his command. Life was war and demanded the same resolution as in the execution of a battle. He had been trained to make intricate analyses and take rational decisions based on them before attacking an enemy. He had to examine his

218

advantages and disadvantages and those of the enemy. He had to take into account courses open to him and to the enemy and on the basis of all this decide on a course of action. Bloody hell, he should not let life toss him this way and that. He would attack it with military efficiency. Now then, down to decisions. On money: he would open a savings account and transfer a definite and unchanging amount to it every month. On woman: Habiba was out, Alekiri was out – he would only maintain Binta – and Arit was out. He would choose his next lady friend carefully and with a view to marrying her. No more nonsense. Bloody hell!

He was pacing up and down in his living room when he heard a car stop outside. The bell rang and when he opened the door Ola came in, beaming. This was their second meeting since the coup. The first had been brief and Ola had been reticent. He was hurrying to the airport and all he could say was that everything had gone according to plan. He did not disclose what role he was playing. This time he did not seem to be in much hurry. He saluted smartly.

'Hello, Major!'

'Hello, Ola. Just back from Lagos?'

'Quite right. Yes.'

Ola was looking well and seemed to have put on weight, Dansuku thought, as he studied him. Then he looked at his shoulder. Instead of three stars, he saw an eagle and a star. Ola was now a lieutenant-colonel. With considerable effort Dansuku overcame his surprise and resentment.

'Congratulations, Ola,' he said and extended his hand for a handshake.

'Oh, this,' Ola said pointing at his shoulders. 'Thank you very much.'

'How long ago?'

'Barely two weeks now.'

The leap from captain to lieutenant-colonel was rare but not impossible. Ola had made it. He must be highly regarded by the new regime, Dansuku thought.

'Have a beer?'

'Yes, thanks.'

As they settled down to drinks, an atmosphere of tension developed. To diffuse it, Ola whipped out a packet of cigarettes. Dansuku thought he ought to accept the offered cigarettes to avoid creating the wrong impression. So they smoked and drank and talked on indifferent matters, but the tension was not diffused. It seemed to build up. Finally Ola could not bear it any more and said:

'I suppose my promotion may seem a little unfair in the eyes of officers like you who bore the brunt of battle.'

Dansuku did not think there was anything to be gained from pretence.

'Quite frankly, I think it is. But I suppose that is your reward for playing an active role in the coup.'

'That is not the whole truth. The fact is, I have some assignments at the headquarters and to carry them out I need a higher rank. It is like giving an officer a field rank so that he can command his men effectively during a war. In any case, my new rank is not substantive yet.'

'Substantive or not, and for whatever reason, you are not going to lose it. You are a lieutenant-colonel and that is that. But don't get me wrong. You are my friend and I am glad you have been promoted, but the principle of the whole thing is wrong.'

'How?'

'You say one should not work only for material gain, but ...'

'Sule, this is for administrative convenience and not ...'

'Will you not receive the pay for the rank?'

'I cannot be expected to refuse.'

'Exactly. So material gain is involved.'

'Well then, material gain is involved in every promotion. It applies to your promotion to the rank of major.'

'My promotion was normal and I worked for it.'

'Are you saying I did not work for mine?'

'You worked at the rear. Was that enough to earn you a

double promotion?'

'I do not belittle the risks of fighting at the front, but you should not be led to think that those of us at the rear were just drinking beer and compiling war reports. Logistics, supplies, propaganda – all these are vital to soldiers doing the actual fighting.'

'Agreed, but does that justify a double promotion? Are you saying that your promotion has nothing to do with the coup?'

'Of course it has. Planning a coup is no picnic. Why did you refuse to take part?'

'I gave my reasons.'

'Which were?'

'I don't want to go into all that.'

'Fine, but if some officers have risked their lives to effect a change of government which everybody supports, such officers must be credited with some achievement, and achievement is the basis of promotion.'

'Ola, let's stop beating about the bush. Tell me, what part did you play in that coup to merit a double promotion?'

'Sule, you can't have it both ways. You refused to take part in the coup. I in turn refuse to disclose to you details of our operation.'

'That is because there is nothing to tell. All you chaps did was sneak into power as soon as the Head of State was away. It was a cowardly coup.'

Ola laughed.

'As a trained combatant, you know the importance of tactics in any operation, and you employ the easiest possible. Besides, you didn't want the Head of State killed, if I remember.'

'Congratulations on your expert planning. But I still maintain that your promotion was made with indecent haste.'

'All right, all right. There is some truth in what you say, but I did not promote myself. If I refused a promotion, it would amount to disobedience and conduct contrary to good order and discipline, wouldn't it?'

'Agreed. But you have also bought a new car.'

'With a loan, yes.'

'What happened to your 'Beetle'?'

'I sold it.'

Dansuku nodded and smiled.

'What are you really driving at?' Ola asked, feeling very uncomfortable.

'Nothing.'

'Don't lie, Sule. Speak your mind.'

'Okay. Look, Ola, a short while ago, you were a captain. You take part in a coup to cure the nation of corruption and so on. Immediately after the coup you receive a double promotion and buy a new and larger car. If you, a junior officer, have enjoyed such advantages, what of those at the top?'

'Nonsense, Sule, nonsense. No matter how honest a regime may be, it must have certain facilities to work with. If, for instance, I have to run up and down between here and Lagos, I must have a new strong car.'

'What of your staff car?'

'There are times when for security reasons it is better to travel in mufti and in a private car. I think you are letting your imagination run a little wild.'

'It is always possible to think of all sorts of excuses to cover actions that are not straightforward.'

'Sule, the new regime is straightforward and time will prove that.'

'You may speak for yourself, but you can't speak for others.'

'Sule, let me warn you, the new regime will not tolerate this kind of scandal.'

'Are you threatening me?'

'I am only giving you a friendly warning.'

'Those who do not want scandal should not give cause for it. If a regime says it is honest, it must be seen to be so.'

'We are honest. The people know it and that is why we have popular support.'

For a while they drank in silence. The tension was heavy. Ola sought to reduce it.

'Sule, give me another beer.'

'Sure, Ola.'

Dansuku uncorked another beer for his friend, but the tension remained. Ola was clever, but Dansuku was not naive.

'I am sorry our conversation has taken this heated turn, but actually I came here for something more pleasant.'

'I am listening.'

'Lagos needs more capable officers at the centre and I have been asked to suggest names of trustworthy and efficient officers I know well. Of course your name came to my mind first.'

'No thanks,' Dansuku said flatly, annoyed that an erstwhile junior officer was now in a position to recommend him for an assignment or promotion.

'It is a bad moment to broach the matter, I know. Think about it. I shall make contact again.'

'My answer is no and that is final.'

'And if Lagos commands it?'

'That's a different matter.'

Ola drained his beer and rose.

'See you again, Sule, but please take care.'

'Thanks for your advice. Bye-bye.'

Dansuku thought Ola looked strange as he hurried away.

223

Chapter XXI

A month after Ibekwe had driven away from Bianco's house he was still to recover from the shock of Ibia's marriage with Bianco. All his friends had picked up the news and he was very disconcerted. When they asked him about it he did not know what to say. Why had he not called them in to arbitrate? they asked. Why had he allowed a white man to snatch his wife from him, or had Bianco 'spoilt her head'? He was too proud to tell them that Ibia had taken a precipitate course of action that had given him no chance to look seriously into their quarrel or even to sue for peace.

Bianco of all people! Ibekwe bit his lips. Bianco. That irresponsible idiot who called himself an engineer, who did nothing except watch native workers do all the dirty work while he received all the fat pay. So, while posing as a friend, the fellow had been carrying on with his wife. When he gave people contracts, he took their wives. So, that was his bribe. He should be taught a lesson, a hard lesson. But how? Waylay him and fight it out? Report him to his employers? Report him to Immigration? The last idea seemed the best. Immigration should take care of the lecherous double-dealer.

When the first surge of anger died, however, he realized there was not much he could do about Ibia and Bianco. Ibia had paid back the bride price and was no longer his wife. He could deny seeing Ibia's money of course but that would be mean; besides, the villagers could ask him to swear before a god, like Amadioha. He would not like to risk that. Ibia was no longer his wife. That was the truth of

224

the matter and Bianco had every right to marry a divorcee. He could make Bianco uncomfortable and perhaps force him out of the country by lying, but what would be the use? Ibia would not come back to him. More important, K.T. was in support of the marriage and he did not want to cross that man's path. He would forget the woman and redirect his life.

Fortunately Wibari had turned eleven and could cook and run the house with a little help from him. So he did not have to send her to the village. In any case she was due to get into a secondary school next September, barely two weeks away, so the problem of looking after her was largely solved. But then who would cook for him? How could he descend to the life of a wretched bachelor, fooling around with gas cookers and making do with bread and sardines half the time? Perhaps a houseboy was the answer; but houseboys were notoriously unreliable. They were more likely to steal his money at the first opportunity and vanish. A housemaid perhaps? Hey, that could not work. Her parents would ask him to negotiate for marriage instead of a monthly pay.

Another wife then? That would take him back to where he started – more quarrels over sleeping arrangements. He could not face that again, at least not immediately. He would just have to be content with Oyia in the meantime. If only she could speak a little English, she could come to town occasionally and even attend government parties with him. After all, she was not bad looking and with a little grooming she could look even better. But Oyia could not speak even pidgin English and most of Ibekwe's friends were not from her clan. What a nuisance.

These days Oyia was very attentive and fussed over him, but every move she made seemed to annoy him. She had virtually chased Ibia away and could not fill the void she had created, he thought. Perhaps he should send her away and choose yet another wife carefully. But what reason would he give? Tradition was firmly on Oyia's side. If he sent her away, he would look irresponsible and wicked and would hardly get another wife from Ohiamini. Moreover breaking with three wives in quick succession would be scandalous. He would be dubbed an *ofogori* who could not manage his own household.

Had he failed? Apart from his misfortunes over marriage he had not done badly. A house, a car, several commercial vehicles – few men in his age group in the village could beat that. Yet he had been very unhappy and unsettled. Did marriage make all that difference? As a poor trader he had been happy before the war. Perhaps Alekiri had made all the difference? Alekiri. She was not really a bad woman, was she? She had been stupid, perhaps unlucky. But she was not a bad woman. The more he thought about their time together, the better she seemed. It was like the memory people had of dead relations and friends. Death washed away much of their imperfections, leaving them purer and more lovable with the purity and loveliness of the unattainable. Alekiri was dead to him and like the dead she had begun to shimmer in the uncertain light of memory with a new radiance.

It was a hot night. His train of thought made him feel hotter still. He decided to go to the Hotel Presidential for a really cold beer. He changed into a lace suit. Then he peeped into Wibari's room. She was sound asleep, surrounded by nearly all that her school prospectus had indicated – broom, bucket, hurricane lamp, plates, cutlery, books, uniform. Each item purchased had made Wibari happy and Ibekwe was glad of this opportunity to please her. He was ready to do anything to help her forget her mother's absence from the house.

At the Hotel Presidential Ibekwe had hardly settled down to the very cold beer he had promised himself, when someone tugged at his sleeve. He turned round. It was Deko, the former railway labourer. Ibekwe was surprised to see him there. Deko shook hands with him and smiled broadly. Ibekwe noticed that he had replaced the three lost teeth and that he was looking rather well.

'Deko, you look well.'

'Ibekwe, we thank God.'

'Are you back to your old job?'

'That dirty job? Not me. I have got a job, a real job, as a clerk at the Wharf. I record the goods as they are taken in and out of the warehouse.'

'That's a nice job.'

'We thank God-o. We thank God.'

'I hope your family is well.'

'Ah, that's a long story.'

'I remember you told me your wife was living with a soldier.'

'Did I tell you?'

'Yes, when we met shortly after the war.'

'You are right. Hm, that soldier man was wicked. Each time I went to talk about Caro, he drove me away. So I said, ah-ah, man only die once. So I wrote a letter to the GOC and the DO. One day some soldiers came to my house. They said the GOC want to see me. Ibekwe I shake-o, I won't tell you lie. I followed them. When I reach there, Ibekwe, I was surprised. I saw Caro and three children. The GOC said: "Is this your wife?" I said, "Yes." "Are these your children?" I was confused. Then I said: "Two are mine." The man asked: "What of this small one?" I said "*Oga*, I don't know; only my wife can say." Caro said she got the baby with the soldier. The GOC said I should go with all the children. My friend Ibekwe, God dey.'

'What did your wife say?'

'What can she say? The soldier forced her to stay with him. Woman has no power. I don't blame her.'

'You were lucky.'

'Yes. Ibekwe, what of your family?'

'All fine.'

'I am sure you have marry again.'

'It is not easy to marry two wives. Women fight and quarrel too much.'

'That is for poor men like me. You rich men can marry many wives. Furnish a flat and buy a car for each one. Every month you give them pocket money. Finish. Money is the thing.'

'So you think money can solve everything.'

'Sure. In this country if you get money you can get anything. You can do anything sef. If police come you take money cover their mouth and eyes. Finish.'

Ibekwe laughed, and said:

'The trouble is to get the money.'

'Ah, for you people who get money, it is easy to make thousands in a day.'

'How?'

Deko lowered his voice: 'Look, at the harbour, business-men like you make thousands every day. The harbour is full of ships with plenty of government cement. The ships cannot offload. Too many. So the whole thing is confuse. The crewmen want to go, so they sell the cement at low-low price and go away.'

'Will the goverment not find out?'

'How? Come to the harbour and you will see what I am telling you.'

As Ibekwe drove home, his conversation with Deko occupied his mind. The man was right. Money was everything. At least it went a long way. If he had bought Ibia a car and sent her every other weekend to shop in London, she might not have run away. With money, real money, even Alekiri might be persuaded to return. He imagined a conversation like this:

'Alee, let's make it up.'

'No. I have had enough.'

'I don't want an answer now. Before that, I want us to travel to UK and get Wibari settled into a boarding school. When we come back you can decide.'

She could not refuse, at least for her child's sake. In London he would overwhelm her with money and presents. Back at Port Harcourt airport, her car would be waiting for her. How could she then refuse? O yes, money could do a lot.

The next day when Ibekwe got to the harbour he was astonished. Although he had heard and read of the harbour congestion he had no idea of its extent. The entire harbour was one solid mass of ships with hardly any room for the small customs boats to manoeuvre. When he finally traced Deko, he was introduced to some seamen who said they were anxious to sell off their cement at a quarter of the price, since the government could not take delivery. Harbour dues were rising so fast that they feared they might soon exceed the worth of the ship itself.

The quantity of cement was large and Ibekwe could only produce about a tenth of the money. He ran to his bankers for help. The branch manager promised to help provided he had fifty per cent of the profits. This help only met a third of the required sum. Ibekwe ran to K.T. He was willing and able. Using one of his houses as a pledge he raised the other two-thirds. As the consignment was huge it was necessary to have traders who would buy up the cement and pay cash on the spot. It was going to be a very quick transaction. It had to be, because the two bank managers wanted their money back in the security of their vaults as soon as possible.

On the appointed evening, as K.T. and Ibekwe drove along Industry Road on their way to the harbour, a taxi overtook them, swerved and blocked their way. K.T. just managed to avoid denting his Mercedes. Before he could react, three armed men jumped out of the taxi and covered them. One of them opened K.T.'s car door and grabbed the brief-case on the back seat. As K.T. gripped the robber's arm, another released a shot that shattered K.T.'s left elbow joint, and he let go with a scream. Meanwhile Ibekwe tried to race off with his own brief-case. A robber tripped him and he fell, but he still held his brief-case firmly. The last thing he remembered was a sharp painful blow on the head.

When Alekiri heard the news, her first thought was Wibari. When she arrived at Ibekwe's place she found her with two of Ibekwe's relatives. They informed her that Oyia was at the hospital. Wibari's eyes were red with weeping. Alekiri cuddled her and whispered some questions. Had she eaten? Were the visitors treating her well? Had she bought everything required for her entry into secondary school? To each question she nodded.

Alekiri announced she was taking Wibari away, but Ibekwe's relatives protested. They needed her, they said, to help them run the house – they were not used to the gas cooker, they did not know how to get to the local market, they could not do this, they could not do that. Alekiri studied their bewildered faces and concluded their needs were genuine.

Alekiri left the house and went straight to the hospital. She thought it would be the right thing to do to visit Ibekwe at the hospital. She might as well get it over with. The nurse in charge said the doctor had forbidden all visitors except his wife. The temptation to say that she was Ibekwe's wife and gain entry was strong, but she resisted it. A tall man with a very worried expression stood by, listening. Apparently he had been making the same plea. Later Alekiri recognized him as the branch manager of Nigerian Business Bank, Ibekwe's bank. He looked extremely nervous and kept biting his lips.

Three days later, Alekiri was able to see Ibekwe. He was surprised and delighted in spite of his pain. Once in a while he would wince, and then quickly put on a smile again. Alekiri was sitting on a visitor's chair close to the bed.

'Thanks Alee,' he said and stretched his left hand to touch her. The hand fell far short of Alekiri and he could not lift his head to judge the distance because of the pain.

'It's nothing. Accept my sympathies.'

'With your visit, I am half recovered already.'

Alekiri managed a perfunctory smile.

'The pain in my head is terrible. The doctor says I may

need an operation.'

'I pray you get well soon.'

'Thank you. Have you seen Wibari?'

'Yes.'

'Will you like to take her away while I am in hospital?'

'Yes, if you let me.'

'Why not? You can take her away.'

'You have to instruct your relatives.'

'No need. They'll allow you.'

'They won't. I have tried.'

A cloud passed over his face briefly and then the smile came back.

'All right, I shall tell them.'

'Thank you.'

'She will enter your school when you re-open.'

'I know. I saw her name.'

'I have bought everything required. I leave the rest to you.'

'Will she be a boarder?'

'It depends on you, Alee.'

'Can she stay with me?'

'Yes, if we can patch up things. Alee, come back and let's settle. I shall give you your money back when I start business again.'

Alekiri looked at him. His head was swathed in wide bloodstained bandages. His right arm was also heavily bandaged just below the elbow. Alekiri remembered the viciousness of that right arm which now lay swollen and weak on the bed. As she looked, he winced with what seemed like a particularly searing jab of pain. It would not do to upset him further.

'Get well first.'

'Shall we talk later?'

'Yes.'

'I beg.'

'We shall talk. Get well first.'

Chapter XXII

Christmas and the New Year passed. The new regime settled down to business. In the public service a new sense of duty was emerging. Indolent public workers afraid of being sacked 'with immediate effect,' bestirred themselves. They went to work on time and idling was greatly reduced.

Teachers, assured of regular pay, worked with a will, Alekiri was now in her second term of secondary school teaching. The principal was quick to notice her devotion to duty and appointed her as house mistress in charge of one of the four boarding houses. This brought her closer to the students and created more work, but she did not mind. She enjoyed the feeling of fulfilment her new assignments brought and for a while she forgot her personal problems.

Wibari lived with her and this further enhanced her peace of mind. Ibekwe had consented at last when he realized that boarding facilities, no matter how good, could never match a loving mother's care. Moreover, Oyia could not stay in Port Harcourt to look after the child.

Wibari was a bait which Ibekwe knew Alekiri could not resist. Through the child he hoped to reach her mother. However when after two months he was discharged from hospital, he found his bank manager waiting at his door, demanding urgent repayment of the money he had borrowed. Preoccupied with these financial problems he could not initiate the delicate process of re-establishing an emotional link with a new and confident Alekiri who had acquired the capacity to look him in the eye.

Then one morning news came of yet another coup. It was

announced that the Head of State had been assassinated but that the coup plotters had been rounded up. There were angry and violent reactions throughout the land. Students and workers held demonstrations all over the country and called for the blood of the assassins. The leader of the abortive coup turned out to be a drunkard who smiled foolishly in press photographs. Under interrogation he maintained the bravado of the damned and named anyone who came to his mind as an accomplice. Scores of officers and other ranks were rounded up and a military tribunal with the power to pass capital punishment was set up.

Three days after the attempted coup Tam Jaja visited Alekiri.

'We did not teach today,' he announced.

'Why?'

'The students were demonstrating in protest against the assassination.'

'I didn't know that man was so popular.'

'His popularity was not surprising.'

'But Tam, apart from the sackings, what really did he achieve?'

'The sackings were only a means to an end. His achievement was his war on corruption. Leaders before him had assumed that corruption was a part of our national life and that nothing could be done about it. But he thought otherwise and I think he was right. Something can and should be done.'

'But will the new Head of State continue like that?'

'Who knows? We can only wait and see.'

'Let's hope we all turn a new leaf, as they say.'

'I believe we will. By the way, Alee, I have got a new place. Nothing big. Two rooms with a decent kitchen and a toilet.'

'Congratulations.'

'Thank you. So when are you coming to know the place?'

'Any time you invite me.'

'Next Saturday?'

'That's fine.'

'Time?'

'10 a.m.'

'Okay.'

'Don't just say okay. I expect to be lavishly entertained.'

'Oh sure. But don't expect the delicious soup I have been enjoying here.'

'I was only teasing. But Tam, I could prepare soup and bring it along. Let me contribute to the opening of the new place.'

Tam Jaja was moved.

'Really?'

'Yes. Why not?'

'Alee, you are a great woman.'

'Not at all, but thanks all the same.'

Tam Jaja looked at her steadily and her face fell.

'Alee, you know I have been thinking.'

'What?'

'That we should get married.'

She laughed lightly.

'I am sure I brought that on myself.'

'Not at all. In fact I have been thinking about it, but I must confess I couldn't summon up the courage to ask you.'

'Tam, don't spoil our relationship.'

'Marriage will improve it, not spoil it. And look, Alee, we should make a good couple. We are in the same profession and we enjoy each other's company.'

'Tam, forget it.'

'What have you against it?'

She thought for a while.

'To begin with I am older than you.'

'That's not true. How old are you?'

'Twenty-seven plus.'

'Well, I am twenty-eight plus.'

Alekiri laughed. 'I was foolish. You should have told me your age first.'

'Honest, I am nearly twenty-nine. I have eaten a lot of yams, you know.'

'Then, I have two daughters from two fathers. You are too young to cope with that. You would develop what you psychologists call ... er ...'

'A complex.'

'Yes, a complex.'

'Not if I am aware of the facts before marriage. Alee, I do not want an answer now. Take some time to consider the matter, and we can talk again later.'

'Tam, the answer is no. We are good friends. Let's leave it at that. Marriage has a way of turning relationships sour sometimes.'

'And sometimes it strengthens relationships.'

Tam Jaja thought it would be easier to make his point if he sat closer to her. All along he had been shy to ask her, but having broached the matter, it seemed to gather momentum in his mind. As he rose, the door bell rang. The curtain parted and Dansuku came in. He was in uniform. Tam Jaja sat down in temporary confusion.

'Sule, welcome. This is Tam Jaja, a fellow teacher. Tam, this is Major Dansuku, Binta's father.'

The two men shook hands. Soon afterwards Jaja rose to go.

'I hope I am not driving you away,' Dansuku said.

'Not at all. I have been here for some time.'

Then he left. Alekiri looked up at Dansuku.

'Beer as usual?'

'Yes, thanks.'

'You are still in uniform at this time.'

'We are on full alert.'

'Because of the attempted coup?'

'Yes.'

'What is the present position?'

'Everything is under control. They are still rounding up the coup plotters.'

'A pity they killed the man. He was very popular.'

'Well, that's a soldier's life. Death can come any time.'

She shuddered as she poured him a glass of beer.

'Alee, you are looking well. What have you been eating?'

'*Garri* as usual.'

'Where is Binta?'

'She is out playing.'

As Dansuku sipped his beer she watched him. Yes, she was sure of it: there was a subtle change in him. She was right. Having made his resolutions, he was sticking to them. Now that he was sure he was not going to marry her, he felt more in control of himself and that made him relax.

'Do you want some cake with your beer?'

'Yep.'

When she came back with a saucer full of cake slices, he said:

'Thanks. Sit down; let's talk.'

Alekiri sat down, watching him all the time.

'There is a lot of movement in the army these days. I have been here since the war and I may be moved any time. So I want you to take charge of your housing arrangement. The owner of this house has appeared at last. He has met me. He says he will not demand any arrears of rent if he regains possession of the house. So I shall ask him to discuss any future arrangements with you.'

'Don't. I don't earn enough to pay for a flat like this. I shall move into the teachers' quarters at St. Michael's. Fortunately, a teacher is about to go on transfer.'

'Excellent. That problem is solved.'

'What happens to the furniture? Do I pack it to your quarters or will you arrange that yourself?'

'Alee, you can have the furniture. I don't need it.'

'Are you sure?'

'Don't be silly.'

'Thank you, Sule, thank you. Hey, that will save me a lot of money.'

'As for Binta, I shall send you a small monthly allowance for her maintenance.'

'You talk as if you have actually been transferred.'

'I am still here, but it is time to get these matters sorted out.'

'I hope you will continue to visit her.'

'Of course, why not?'

'Sule, how can I thank you for all your ...'

The door bell rang insistently. A little annoyed, Dansuku put down his glass of beer and stared at the door. The curtains parted and a Provost-Marshal entered with two soldiers. He saluted smartly and said:

'Sir, you are under arrest.'

For long seconds Dansuku stared at the Provost-Marshal in utter surprise.

'Who ordered my arrest?'

'Orders from Lagos, sir.'

Alekiri looked on in shocked silence.

'May we proceed sir?'

'But what's the matter?' Alekiri asked in an unsteady voice. The Provost-Marshal looked at her but said nothing.

'All right,' Dansuku said and rose. Immediately, the Provost-Marshal removed his pistol.

'Let me have your belt and cap, sir.'

Quietly Major Dansuku undid his belt, picked up his cap from a chair and handed both to the military policeman.

'Can we proceed, sir?'

When Dansuku got to the door he turned round.

'Alee, come to the house quickly.'

As soon as they left the house Alekiri locked the door and went to the military police Land-Rover.

'He says I should come with him,' she explained.

'You are a civilian: you cannot ride in a military vehicle except with special permission.'

'Alee, take a taxi.'

By the time they got to Dansuku's place Alekiri was already there. Once inside the house, the Provost-Marshal began a thorough search of the place.

'Sule, what is the matter?' Alekiri whispered tearfully.

'I don't know.'

'Has it anything to do with the coup?'

'It is possible. But don't panic. Sit down and let me arrange a few things.'

Quickly Major Dansuku brought out a writing pad and began to scribble furiously. He used up two sheets of paper, and put them together with his savings book in an envelope which he addressed to his father. Then he wrote a cheque which he handed to Alekiri.

'That's for you and Binta.'

'Sule, I can't take it.'

'Sssh! You can't argue in a moment like this. There is no time. Take it.'

Alekiri reluctantly took the cheque.

'Ensure that this envelope gets to my father if you don't see me again. Look after Binta.'

The Provost-Marshal and his men emerged from the last room, having finished their search. He gave Major Dansuku a smart salute and said:

'We are ready to move, sir.'

As Dansuku began to walk towards the door Alekiri clung to him weeping. The soldiers tore her from him and marched him to the Land-Rover. She watched with despair as the vehicle sped out of sight. She sat on the dwarf wall in the porch and wept.

'Madam, don't worry. God dey.'

She turned round and saw Bukar. He too was crying.

'Bukar, why they take Major?'

'I no know, but sometime na because of the coup.'

When Alekiri got back to her house, she tried to collect her thoughts. What could she do? Whom could she talk to? Ola came to her mind. She hailed a taxi and made for Ola's place.

'Lt. Col. Olaitan dey for Lagos,' a soldier on guard told her.

'When will he come back?'

'Madam, he go transfer.'

Desperately she ran to the commanding officer's quar-

238

ters. She was told he too had travelled to Lagos.

Back again in her house, her head spun as she cast around restlessly. The next day, she bought an air ticket and flew to Lagos, after scribbling a hasty note to her principal.

Christie was surprised to see her. Her countenance alarmed her.

'Is father all right?'

'Yes,' Alekiri said.

'Is home all right?'

'Yes.'

'What's the matter? You look terrible.'

'Dansuku has been arrested.'

'When?'

'Yesterday, in my house.'

'What for?'

'I don't know but it may be in connection with the coup.'

'*Chei*!' Christie shouted, then lowering her voice asked: 'Did he take part?'

'I don't know. I don't think so. Christie, can you speak to Ola? Can you speak to anyone with influence?'

'I can speak to Ola. Let me try the 'phone.'

After several minutes of fruitless dialling, she gave up. Let's use the car.'

They jumped into the car and sped off. Alekiri was surprised at her sister's driving ability. She wove in and out of the traffic and exchanged curse for curse with the taxi drivers. When they got to their destination, the guard on duty said Colonel Olaitan was not available, and he did not know when he would come back.

'Can we wait?'

'No,' the guard snapped.

They drove back to Christie's house and Christie tried 'phoning again. When eventually she got Ola's number, a feminine voice said Ola was out of town. For the next three days they made frantic efforts to contact some influential army officers but failed. They gave up finally when a friend

239

of Christie's warned her that she and her sister could be arrested if they showed unusual interest in anyone arrested in connection with the coup. She revealed that some civilians had been arrested already. In despair Alekiri flew back to Port Harcourt.

During the following days, the newspapers were filled with news of the trial of the coup plotters. Within a few days several officers and other ranks were executed by a firing squad. The trial, judgement and execution had been extremely swift. Alekiri listened with a thumping heart to the radio as an announcer read out the names of those executed. She did not hear Dansuku's name. But then the announcement had begun with the phrase 'among those executed were ...' Did that mean the list was not exhaustive? The next day, she bought all the Sunday newspapers she could find and scanned them. She did not find Dansuku's name. But then two newspapers said that the trials had not ended and that further executions were expected. Also two suspects were said to be still at large and a price had been put on their heads. On the whole, about thirty-two soldiers had been executed, the papers said.

On Monday, Alekiri dragged herself to school but such was her headache that she could not teach. She obtained permission and went home and straight to bed.

Olaitan entered the house. Alekiri rushed to meet him.

'Ola, I have been looking for you.'

'Why?'

'To see what you can do for Dansuku.'

'Dansuku is a foolish man. He does not know how to look after himself.'

'You must try to save him.'

'I can't save him. Everyone has to save himself.'

'How can he save himself?'

'Easy. Let him wear a white arm band. Look at mine. It shows I was not involved in the coup.'

For the first time Alekiri noticed that Ola's right arm was

bandaged.

'Where can one get it?'

'Outside. Come and see.'

Alekiri looked outside and saw a huge crowd in front of her house.

'Go and join the queue. When your turn comes they will give you a white arm band.'

'But what of Dansuku?'

'He is there.'

Alekiri looked and saw Dansuku in the milling crowd. She saw Mama Iyabo near the head of the queue. Her husband was behind her. She saw Ibekwe and his wife Oyia. Bianco and Ibia were there, but not in the queue, and they did not seem to care. Christie was there too and she was carrying a baby. There were children playing around, buying groundnuts and ice cream from vendors. Alekiri saw her daughters Binta and Wibari playing with other children. She went after them and tried to drag them to the queue. Someone told her children did not need arm bands. She went back to the queue and found Dansuku right behind her. Two army officers appeared to be in charge of distributing the arm bands. A third had a bell. Each time he rang the bell someone moved to a table before the soldiers, signed some papers and received an arm band. The signing process seemed very long and presently the soldiers, looking tired, announced that only thirty-two arm bands were available. Immediately there was a stampede but Alekiri held her place in the queue. The bell rang and Mama Iyabo went to the table to sign. She kept talking in a loud voice declaring her innocence. 'I know nothing of the coup,' she said repeatedly. Somehow Alekiri found herself behind Mama Iyabo. The bell rang and she moved forward only to find K.T. in front of her. 'No, it's not your turn,' she cried. K.T. turned round to stare at her. 'Yes, it is not your turn,' a soldier said, and pushed K.T. out of the line. As he walked away Alekiri noticed he had an arm band. She was wondering how he did it when the bell rang again. She got to the table. They gave her a pen to sign the papers. It was a huge pen, so large that she barely managed to hold it with one hand. But she found it easy to write with. It was as if it moved of its own accord. After signing, they gave her an arm band. The bell rang again and she made way for Dansuku but he was no longer there. He had moved to the tail of the queue, where she saw him talking with Arit who was laughing and pulling him further away. Dismayed, she rushed towards him but the surging crowd made movement impossible. The bell rang again. 'Sule it is your turn,' she shouted, but he had disappeared. She wept as, with agonizing slowness, she clawed her way through the crowd in search of him.

Suddenly Alekiri woke and found herself crying and her pillow wet with tears. But the bell continued to ring. It turned out to be the door bell. With considerable effort she dragged herself to the door and as she opened it Dansuku stepped into the room. With a loud cry she leaped high into his arms and sobbed. Dansuku, staggering under her weight, managed at last to sit down, and carried her like a baby. She buried her face in his chest and huge sobs shook her. It took her a long time to calm down. She looked up into his face to make sure it was not a continuation of the dream.

'Sule!'

'Alee.'

'So you escaped!'

'Yes. My commanding officer testified strongly in my favour, and his statements agreed with the contents of my diary which the military police took away when they searched my house.'

A spasm of joy shook her and she grabbed him in another long embrace.

'Alee, I have decided to retire from the army,' he said sadly and reluctantly.

'I think you should.'

'Can we share this flat when I retire?'

'My mother would be angry.'

'I thought you said she died in Biafra.'

'True.'

'Idiot.'

She laughed that childlike laugh which always reinforced his image of her as an unspoilt village woman. His woman.

'Alee, marry me.'

She paused as if his words had stung her. There was something desperate in his voice.

'Marry me.'

'You have me already, don't you? What more do you want?'

'Marriage, marriage.'

'But we are happy. Marriage might spoil everything.'

'You mean I should remain a bachelor *lailai*?'

'Not necessarily.'

'So?'

She paused and fumbled with her necklace of glass beads, which Sule had brought her from Bida.

'Sule, I don't know. I am ... afraid.'

'Of me?'

'Yes, of you, of men.'

'Why?'

'See how Ibekwe treated me.'

'But you said he was a good husband before the war.'

'Yes.'

'Blame the war, not men.'

'I suppose so, but ...'

'But what?'

She looked Dansuku in the face. It was the face of an impatient commander anxious to get on with life's battles.

'Don't spoil things by rushing. I have not recovered from the war. Give me time.'

'I haven't recovered either, but I can't wait any more.'

'If you cared for me, you would wait.'

'And if you cared for me, you wouldn't wait.'

243

Spontaneously they uncoiled from each other's arm. Alekiri slipped from his lap onto the settee. Dansuku's well-developed lips thinned out as he compressed them in restrained resentment … Women were all the same, so silly, forever vacillating, never knowing what they wanted, never using their heads, those small silly heads with fingers of plaited hair. What a pity men couldn't do without them …

He looked at her expectantly. She fumbled with her beads again. The silence solidified.

'That means no. Fair enough. Better to be honest. You don't like me enough to marry me. We've had a wartime romance. You needed my protection. I needed your companionship. The war is over. You go your way. I go mine. Take care of the baby. Make sure …'

All through the staccato speech, Alekiri's eyes were closed in pain. As the words tumbled out they seemed shorn of love, like maize bereft of sweetness after the harvest day. Men were all the same. Impatient. Incapable of real love.

Suddenly her eyes brimmed over with tears and she gripped his shirt fiercely.

'Are you sure you will let me finish my education? Are you sure you won't marry Habiba? Are you sure you won't beat me up and maim me when no-one is around to defend me? Are you sure, are you sure?'

'Yes Alee, I am sure, I am,' he said, pressing her to him once more.

She did not believe him. He would marry four wives; he would put her in purdah; he would sit on her belly and unleash painful jabs to her face in moments of insane hatred; but as in the act of love itself, she knew she had reached that point of no return.

'All right,' she whimpered as she lay limp in his arms, benumbed by a strange mixture of desire and despair.